THE SOWER'S HARVEST

Paula Adamson

LifeRich
PUBLISHING

LifeRich Publishing books may be ordered through booksellers or by contacting:

LifeRich Publishing
1663 Liberty Drive
Bloomington, IN 47403
www.liferichpublishing.com
844-686-9607

ISBN: 978-1-4897-4375-6 (sc)
ISBN: 978-1-4897-4374-9 (hc)
ISBN: 978-1-4897-4376-3 (e)

Library of Congress Control Number: 2022916175

Print information available on the last page.

LifeRich Publishing rev. date: 03/13/2023

This book is dedicated to the memory of Barnetta Boyd –
thank you, Mom, for bringing me up as a child of God.

Prologue

"As newborn babes, desire the sincere milk of the word that ye may grow thereby:"

1 Peter 2:2

Zoe Todvue had a special hunger, but not the way most people would think. She felt the need to have her appetite satisfied even if she had to miss out on daily entertainment to remain nourished. She went through extremes almost every day to satisfy this yearning.

Her desire left her feeling shunned by the world. People called her narrow-minded and sanctimonious. Her craving encouraged potential dates into calling her snobbish. Former friends told her she created a prison for herself that no one could endure, including herself. Her ignorance of the latest TV shows, music, and fashions rendered her speechless during most gatherings, making her an object of ridicule and judgment.

Her parents had instilled this hunger into her spirit at an early age. Though she and her family attended church regularly and had family devotions, none of her sisters exemplified their importance as she did.

During her freshman year in college tragedy struck. A drunk driver took both of her parents' lives when he misjudged a curve on a two-lane highway. He turned too wide, and his pickup hit their car head-on.

Zoe reached out to her grandparents to make sure they took care of her and her younger sister. However, she realized they didn't exemplify the same zeal and hunger that her parents instilled in her causing her to feel out of place and alone.

Her two older sisters ostracized her and excluded her like an outcast. Her oldest sister, Brenna, hadn't spoken to her in years and treated her with contempt. Her sister Sophia had a shallow outlook on life and was in love with getting rich which made having a relationship with her challenging. She had a closer relationship with Onia than the other two. However, her younger sister had a tendency to get rapt by the cares and worries of the world. Not only did any of her sisters have the special yearning she had, they didn't want it.

Zoe was a misfit trying to relate in a world plagued with depravity.

Chapter 1

Brood of Beelzebub

"And when he sowed, some seeds fell by the way side, and the fowls came and devoured them."

Matthew 13:4

Sirens clamored as emergency vehicles rushed to the apocalypse. A blaze had consumed a brand new furniture store near Atlanta. Bodies lay on the ground like lifeless mannequins, some suffering from smoke inhalation. Paramedics wondered whether life remained as many lay on the ground, blood-stained and unconscious.

The contents inside the building crackled like crumpling paper as embers sparked from windows like fireworks. The building creaked and moaned as flames spewed from it like a fire-breathing dragon. The windows, two in the middle especially, had a demonic glow about them as if they were eyeing their next morsel. Firefighters labored to squelch the conflagration to no avail.

Cars careened out of control. People heard tires screeching and metal crunching as vehicles collided. The maniacs behind the wheels gawked at the scene, causing them to hit poles, each other, and pedestrians. Tires hissed as life drained from them due to the impact.

Paparazzi-like bystanders scrambled to the commotion and dripped with sweat as they gazed in the sweltering August heat.

They raised their cell phones in anticipation of posting the chaos on social media. Others waved at TV cameras in attempts to grasp their five minutes of fame.

News reporters from three major networks swarmed the area like bees and jockeyed for position, eager to be the first to share their version of the catastrophe.

Brenna Staithe sprang up from her pillow as the mayhem jolted her from her stupor in her Druid Hills home. Her head throbbed like a pulsating heart from last night's overindulgence.

She was the oldest of her siblings in her late forties; however, plastic surgery and her contributions to the cosmetic industry masked her aging appearance. Her eyes were green emeralds. Her physique remained intact and could turn heads, thanks to her dedication to her treadmill and weights.

Despite her efforts to stay young, Brenna felt like an aging crone abandoned in a nursing home and left to rot. Her cad of a husband put her on display when he entertained guests on rare occasions, if he decided to come home at all. He would have his way with her both physically (nothing she ever did or said was appropriate in front of company), and sexually, to satisfy his drunken appetite, once the guests had left. Since he acquired her as one of his conquests, he had pretty much done away with her.

Her husband, Chad Staithe, worked as a biotechnology engineer. He had swept her off her feet in college and charmed her into marrying him. He tended to her long enough to consummate and propagate, but left her to rear three spoiled imps who had since grown up to become ungrateful ogres.

The Staithes' home flaunted wealth with pretentiousness. The custom-built mansion had a built-in swimming pool and Jacuzzi. Each occupant had his own bedroom suite with all of the accommodations of a small apartment unit.

A long, curved, oak wood staircase, embellished by a wrought-iron banister, separated the upstairs from the first floor. A decorative chandelier descended from the top of the house to the center, crying for attention. The living room, a den, and an open kitchen beautified the home with red oak hardwood floors.

The kitchen was a surgical suite made of stainless steel designed to create a pristine ambience. Except for the arched brick wall that hung over the stove, the canary yellow walls with white trim emanated brightness as they shrouded the gloominess hidden within. Every room was an immaculate veil trying to mask the stains and obscenities that plagued this household.

The high ceilings in each room displayed custom-made chandelier-fans for circulating the much needed air conditioning on hot Atlanta days. Their guest house, near the pool area, was a den of debauchery.

"CJ, come here!" Brenna sat up and yelled. "There are sirens everywhere! Go turn on the TV downstairs!"

"Turn it on your own dumb self! I'm in my bedroom!" he said as he scowled, his eyes glued to his computer screen.

Twenty-four-year-old Chad Junior, the oldest of the brood, had brown eyes which had become cold and dark like a lost soul. A scar on his forehead tainted his handsome looks. Every time he looked in the mirror he wished he could turn back the clock. He had accidentally scratched his father's Beamer while riding his bike when he was nine. His father hurled a shoe at him in a fit of rage. The injury left permanent scars that went beyond the surface. Afterwards his bike collected dust and rusted away much like his relationship with his dad.

Despite his scar-tainted forehead, girls drooled over him. However, he preferred girls in his world of virtual reality. He relied on his fetish as a form of escapism, however, it spiraled into an addiction. Since his pubescence, he mainly stayed in his room like a hermit. His obsession created erotic arousals which led to his premature impotence.

He barely finished high school, yet his father compelled him to go to college. He dropped out after a semester as his father cared about his grades more than he did.

He tore himself away from his computer to grab some binoculars he had bought to make admiring the woman across the street worthwhile. He noticed billowing clouds of black smoke as the inferno, which looked like a small forest fire by now, could be seen for blocks.

"Get outta that bedroom, Chad, and get a life!" Brenna screamed. "I'm tired of you staring at that dumb computer all day!" She began to place her feet on the floor until his words stopped her in her tracks.

"You get a life and quit drinking like a fish!" he yelled back. "What's wrong with the TV in your room anyway?"

She didn't answer. Her TV laid shattered and lifeless much like her marriage. In her drunkenness she neglected to turn on the light as she attempted to reach her bed. She lost balance as she groped in the dark. She grabbed onto the closest thing to break her fall. The TV supported her before it didn't.

Crash!

Brenna jumped up and scrambled for her gun. She staggered down the stairs with gnarly, mussed hair wearing yesterday's clothes. She limped to the kitchen.

"It's just me, Mother," her daughter Charlotte said as she giggled. "Put that thing away." A male playmate accompanied her. He was mauling her and drooling over her like a bear, kissing her neck.

"What happened?" Brenna said, eyes wide open, gun ready to fire.

"Whoa!" her friend said as he jumped back and held his hands up.

"We knocked over the fruit bowl on the counter that's all." Charlotte said.

"How? Never mind. I don't think I want to know." She relaxed and set the gun down.

"This is Doug." Charlotte explained between kisses. "We had a private party last night." She gazed at her lover and giggled again. They pecked each other on the lips making short smacking noises as they moaned.

"That's the third time this week! Didn't the guy the other night go by a different name?" Brenna used her fingers as a comb and brushed her hands over her dress.

"Oh, Mom, who keeps track? Doug doesn't mind, do you?" Charlotte asked as she eyed her blonde-haired, blue-eyed admirer while still in his embrace.

He pressed her body against his as he said, "Of course not. You can invite him, and maybe I can bring someone too next time." He ogled her as he swayed her back and forth, arms around her waist. He tore his eyes away from his tramp and looked around for a moment before returning his gaze. "You've got a nice place here, Mrs. Stiathe."

"Thank you." She breathed a sigh of relief. Then she rolled her eyes and walked away.

Charlotte squealed and giggled like a school girl in the arms of her muscle-bound lover. She had brunette hair and emerald eyes like her mother. She inherited her father's height and charm. Her long flowing hair, curvaceous build, and smooth olive skin indicated she could have been a model. Her appetite for appeasing the opposite sex took precedence over her studies which hindered her chances of attending college.

She longed for the right man to pamper her and take care of her at any cost. Some of the brutes had forced themselves on her without much resistance; however, their pushiness with her flirtations disqualified them from future engagements. Though she didn't usually object to their advances, she preferred a gentler approach. She enjoyed flirting with most of her prospects with whom she consented to rendezvous. Their performance and level of romance kept them in the competition. She kept a list of candidates whom she rated in a special book. Her present lover was at the top.

"Late breaking news: A five alarm fire broke out in a furniture store in Druid Hills this morning. Casualties spatter the ground like a triage scene from a war zone. Pandemonium is everywhere as people run and scream in panic. Let's take you to a reporter just outside the building."

"Thank you, Mike," the reporter said. "As you can see, people are in a frenzy out here as firefighters scramble to put out the blaze. Folks are scattering everywhere, afraid they'll get burned as flames shoot from windows. People are crying over loved ones and victims. There's mass hysteria behind me!"

The reporter flinched as an explosion from the building startled him.

"Reports indicate arson to be the cause," he said as he looked back at the building.

"Do they have a lead on who's responsible?" the anchorman asked.

"Some people who escaped said a disgruntled employee had made threats. Investigators are pursuing him as a person of interest."

"Okay, Thank you, Stu."

"You're welcome. This is Stu Blancher reporting to you live from Channel 17 news."

"Wow!" Brenna said as she turned up the volume.

"What's all the commotion?" Craig asked. He meandered down the staircase rubbing his eyes.

Seventeen-year-old Craig, Brenna's youngest, inherited his father's height, however, his wiry build, stringy blonde hair, and brown eyes made Chad question if he was his. He had an androgynous look, and most of the time he appeared bewildered, both of which turned most girls away. He waited in anticipation for his eighteenth birthday to reveal a secret.

Trauma, unknown to Brenna, repressed his development. He took longer to potty train than his siblings. He bore the brunt of ridicule among his peers because he stuttered and kept wetting himself.

The changes in his speech and behavior baffled his mother, so she took him to therapy. When she informed Chad of their son's struggles and possible causes, he began taking business trips instead of offering support.

"Sh-h-h," Brenna whispered as she waved her hand and looked away.

"Excuse *me*," he said as he turned his head and strolled into the kitchen. He fixed himself a bowl of cereal.

He heard noises and looked in the den to find Charlotte and Doug rolling around like two wrestlers, groping and caressing each other. "Do you have to do that in here? That's what the guest house is for." He shook his head in repulsion at the carnal escapade.

"Mom?" Craig said.

Brenna remained glued to the built-in TV. It hung above an ornate granite mantel shelf like a shrine. "What?"

"Can I talk to you?" He looked like a timid school boy approaching a taskmaster.

"About what?" she said, still eyeing the news.

"Um, it's about Aunt Zoe."

Her head snapped toward Craig, eyes glaring at him. "What about her?" she sneered. "I thought I told you not to mention that name around here anymore."

"Well, I told her about some things I've been going through lately. She called me the other day and offered to let me stay with her."

"She *what*? She has some nerve trying to take my son away from me." Her eyebrows furrowed. "You tell her 'no'!"

He cowered and took a step back. "But..."

"Why don't you come to me?"

"Sh-she understands me."

"Humph. That's out of the question," she said and turned away as if he wasn't there.

He turned away with his head down and took his food to his bedroom.

Chapter 2

Sibling Relationships

"Some fell upon stony places, where they had not much earth: and forthwith they sprung up, because they had no deepness of earth:"

Matthew 13:5-6

Craig's request to stay with Zoe riled Brenna into turning off the TV. She felt a bubble in the pit of her stomach. She decided to rant to her sister Sophia.

Forty-six-year-old Sophia had been Brenna's closest sister. She had emulated her older sister throughout their childhood. They both had brunette hair, but Sophia had hazel eyes, bedazzled with gold flecks. She knew Brenna wished she had her eyes which gave her a sense of pride. She had aged prematurely because her propensity for food had taken its toll on her physique.

The two sisters remained close until they attended Georgia Tech. Their bond had slowly turned rancid like milk left out to spoil. Brenna had already become love-stricken by Chad whom she had met at a frat party, leaving Sophia feeling abandoned. Chad persuaded Brenna to marry him before she could graduate. His proposal disappointed Sophia and perpetuated her resentment for him.

Sophia caused more friction in their relationship when she served as Brenna's maid of honor. She dragged her feet on buying her dress and almost missed the wedding. Though she rarely attended church herself at that time, she suggested that Brenna have her wedding in one. Her sister shunned her for a while after that. They had since reconciled, but having a relationship with Brenna compelled her to tread lightly.

During her last year in college Sophia met her husband, Dave Altimoone, at a grocery store. He had already graduated, so she made him wait until she finished school before they married. They settled in Atlanta to start a family because jobs as a product designer were scarce where she grew up making uprooting from his hometown futile. They had two sons, Josh and Steve, who had finished college and moved away.

"Hey, Sophia, how are you?" Her eyes looked cold and lifeless as she spoke.

"Brenna, is that you? You sound angry." Sophia was watching her favorite televangelist. "Yes, preacher, preach. Amen!"

"Who are you talking to?" Brenna asked, turning up her nose.

"I'm watching Pastor Whitaker. He's talking about being successful. He said we should think our bad thoughts away and speak the good into existence. I even watched him heal somebody today!"

"Can you turn that thing off? I've got something to tell you."

"I'll call you back later then. I have to see this."

"Yeah, right," Brenna said as she rolled her eyes. "Why do you watch that junk?"

"I guess because that's the way we grew up, except my preacher is on TV! I'm so on fire for the Lord!" she said wide-eyed. "Our preacher told us to give a hundred dollars, and God will turn it into a thousand! We sure could use the money." She wolfed down some donuts, filling her mouth like a chipmunk.

"So I see you're trying to be like Zoe now," Brenna said with sharpness to her tone.

"Bite your tongue!" Sophia said, her speech muffled.

"Just kidding. Who would want to be like her? As far as I'm concerned she's adopted."

"Maybe Mom and Dad were given the wrong baby at the hospital," Sophia said.

They both laughed.

"Anyway, they brought us up to believe in that stuff, but I never really did. I just went to church, because they made us," Brenna admitted. "Besides, I noticed when we got older they just dropped us off and never came in."

"That's not true. They dropped us off and went to park the car. They sat somewhere else and let us sit by ourselves. You never noticed them in church when it was over?"

"How can you be so stupid? Of course we saw them after church. They came back to pick us up."

"I don't believe you."

"You don't have to, but it's true."

"Well, Dave and I have a better church anyway. You should come and visit sometime." She washed her donuts down with a soda.

"Um, not in this lifetime."

"What made you bring up Zoe anyway? You know I don't talk to her."

"That's what I called you for. You know what she had the nerve to do?" Brenna said in a huff.

"What?" Sophia said as she grabbed another donut.

"She offered to let Craig come live with her."

Chunks of donuts fell from Sophia's mouth as it dropped open. "Did I hear you right?"

"She keeps trying to push that Jesus mess on my family. I don't care if she wants to believe that junk, but she better leave us alone, if she knows what's good for her."

"Our church is different. We give a lot of money, but our pastor told us we can get rich from giving."

"So you said. Look, I told you I don't want to have anything to do with that garbage. Brenna was ready to hang up. "Anyway, it's all a lie. He's just conning you!"

"No he isn't. Dave said this could bring in a little extra income for our family. You know I haven't worked since my baby girl died while I was at work." She began to choke up.

"What family? Your boys left home as soon as they finished school to get away from you and your bingeing." Brenna snarled. "Your daughter's death is not an excuse for bingeing or you choosing not to get a job. You're able to work instead of eating food all day!"

"You can be so cruel sometimes." Sophia's eyes began to water.

"I'm just telling you what you need to do."

"What about *you*? You're such a lush," Sophia said, her voice quivering. "Why don't you get help?"

"You're the one who needs help. I can stop drinking anytime I want."

"That's what they all say. Can you say, Alcoholics Anonymous?" Though she grinned, tears streamed down her face.

"At least my kids didn't run away from me. If they want to live with me for the rest of their lives, I'll let them."

"That's because you haven't taught them independence. They don't have to do anything. You just give them everything they want."

"At least I have something to give them," Brenna said with bitterness in her voice.

"Listen, my boys are hard-working and independent. All your kids do is live at home and mooch like freeloaders."

"Your boys have to be independent. You don't have anything to give them. You have nothing to show for finishing college."

"There you go bringing that up as usual. That's going to change anyway. My preacher is teaching me how to get rich. You'll see. All I have to do is give a little money and call on the name of Jesus. It's like an investment."

"Well, you keep on believing that. While your TV preacher is giving you idle promises, I'm already rich. I have a beautiful home, a fancy car, all the dressy clothes I want, lots of fine jewelry, and anything else I want. You should have married a man with money. I have it all."

"You have everything but happiness. You're just a trophy collecting dust on Chad's shelf, and you know it."

"You take that back!"

"No! Every time you call you brag about how rich you are, and that's all we do is argue. By the way, how *is* that wonderful husband of yours?"

"Look, I didn't call you to argue. I just wanted to tell you about Zoe always butting in trying to be somebody's savior with her "holier than thou" attitude."

"Well, at least we agree on that. That's why I don't talk to her. She's always trying to tell me that Jesus is the only way as if her way is the right way."

"I know. She always acts like everything should be done her way," Brenna said. "That's why I'm sick of her."

That evening Brenna watched the news again. She sat in awe as she eyed charred remains where a building used to exist. An anchorwoman reported that the blaze had taken almost six hours to extinguish.

"And some fell among thorns; and the thorns sprung up, and choked them:"

Matthew 13:7

Onia Fairweather had curly blonde hair and blue eyes. Her flawless skin revealed that she had aged gracefully in her mid thirties. One would never know she bore five children, two of which were twins.

Being coddled during her childhood delayed Onia's independence. She enjoyed letting her husband take care of her. She welcomed it like a party guest. She moved from home to become his wife shortly after graduating from high school against her family's wishes. They thought she could do better than to marry some divorcee much older than she.

Ryan, her husband, had tremendous regard for his family life. He took great pride in being the provider. He had no children of his own until they married. He also adopted her love child, Brett, whose real father had nothing to do with him. Ryan's first wife abandoned him within the first few months of their marriage.

He had a lucrative career as an accountant in the marketing department of a local company. He had a distinguished look about him. Except for the touch of gray near his temples, his tall and slender build didn't disclose the thirteen-year age disparity between him and Onia.

The Fairweather home had a modern look made of colonial brownstone with gables. They lived in a suburb of Milwaukee. Though they didn't have as much as her sister Brenna, they had modern conveniences and luxuries to flaunt. They used their furnished basement for entertainment. It contained a large, flat screen TV which was mainly used for playing video games. The yard had a small swimming pool and a half basketball court which existed as sources of envy for the neighbors.

Bret moved away after he had graduated from high school, yet he managed to make his way back into their lives when he needed financial help. He had no desire to go to college because he earned a decent living as a manager of a clothing store. However, he squandered his earnings with his gambling obsession.

Twelve-year-old Rachel, their oldest, was a hybrid. She had straight hair like her dad and blonde hair and blue eyes like her mom. Her dimples complemented her appearance like a permanent beauty mark. She had already reached the age where boys started noticing her, and she wore clothes to demonstrate her reciprocity.

Onia and Ryan brought Nathan, a spitting image of his dad, into the world a few years after Rachel. The basement was his hideout. He would play video games like a recluse if he had been allowed.

Their twins, Aaron and Amber, age five, were unforeseen. Aaron struggled with being entranced in his own world. Onia noticed something was unusual about him when he was a toddler.

"Mom, I can't find my shoes!" Rachel yelled.

"Which ones are you looking for?"

"My black ones!"

"Then wear your brown ones."

"They don't look right with my outfit."

"We have to get going! We're already late for church, and your dad is waiting out in the car!"

Amber started giggling as she came into the room. She was playing tug-of-war with a snarling, drooling German shepherd and a pair of mangled shoes.

"Are these the ones you're looking for?" she asked as she snatched the shoes from the dog's jowls.

"Dumb dog!" Rachel yelled as she smacked the enormous canine on the rear end. "Mom, this dumb mutt chewed up my shoes!"

"Well, I guess you have no choice but to wear the brown ones after all. Now let's go."

"Aren't you going to thank George for helping you decide which shoes to wear?" Amber asked.

"Shut up!"

"But other fell into good ground, and brought forth fruit, some an hundredfold, some sixtyfold, some thirtyfold."

Matthew 13:8

Zoe Todvue looked so unique that her appearance was inimitable much like her morals. She had silky, auburn red hair, fair skin, and blue eyes. Her tall slender figure and extraordinary character accentuated both her inner and outer beauty.

Though her comprehensive beauty attracted many young beaus, unlike her sisters, she never found an ideal significant other. She had hoped to be married with children at this point in her life, but the values of her potential companions paled in comparison to hers. Her prospective mates couldn't measure up to the exemplary lifestyle she lived for her Lord and Savior.

At this point in her life she had relinquished all hope of finding a God-fearing husband.

Zoe always woke up half an hour earlier to mellow tunes from her cell phone. She needed extra time to go through her morning ritual. As she entered a special room in her apartment she smiled and reminisced about the times when she and her sisters raced to the bathroom to be the first to get ready for church. She never reached the bathroom first, but she wished life could be the way it was back then.

Her extra room was her sanctuary. She called it her battlefield. It had a makeshift altar made of a small rectangular table draped with a tablecloth. A votive candle sat on each end with a Bible, a prayer journal, and a pen in the center. A little cross hung above it which she cherished from her confirmation. A little bulletin board was mounted on the wall beneath the cross. Names and prayers of friends, family, and especially children decorated it. A pillow-laden stool where she knelt to pray sat underneath the front of the table. The other walls were decorated with framed Bible passages.

She remembered her pastor telling her the best way to fight her battles was on her knees. She went to this special room for Bible study and to spend time alone with God. Every now and then she would listen to Christian music.

Later that morning Zoe approached the home of some children who were frolicking on their yard. She waved and motioned to them. Four children rushed to her car to greet her before she could get out. She introduced herself to them.

The littlest one named Little John-John ran with a limp. He squeezed her like a bear cub when he reached her. Then he hopped in the front seat. Ten-year-old Marvin slid in the back first, so he wouldn't get trapped in the middle. Phillip, his eight-year-old brother, refused to get in until seven-year-old Tamika had gotten in. The kids shared the same mother, however; illegitimacy was tantamount to each of them.

As soon as he sat down Marvin asked, "What kind of music is *this*?" He turned up his nose.

"Christian music," she replied.

"What kind of music is that?"

"It's music about Jesus, what He did, and what He still does in my life. It makes me happy."

"I listen to rap music. My older brother plays it. It makes me happy 'cuz I like the beat. The beat be lit!"

An uproar of laughter ensued from the back seat. Then Phillip and Tamika nodded. Little John-John sat in the front and rocked forward and back to the music.

"When in Rome, do as the Romans do." Zoe said. "Your little brother doesn't seem to mind."

"Huh? We not in Rome," Marvin said as he and the others eyed each other.

"It's just a saying which means you do what someone else does when you're with them. You're in my car, so you listen to my kind of music," she continued.

She began singing a gospel song.

"Wha's that mean?" Little John-John asked.

Zoe turned the music down. "What?"

"What they singin' about?"

"We're winners no matter what people or the devil tries to do to us. We win even when bad people attack us."

"Wha's a devil?"

"Not what, but who? He's God's enemy, and that makes him our enemy too. He's a bad guy."

"I think I know who he is," Marvin answered. "He wears a red suit with horns and a tail, and he carries a pitchfork. I saw him on TV. How is he our enemy? He was funny to me."

She chuckled. "He wants you to think he's harmless. He tried to overpower God, who's our friend, and he tries to get us to sin."

"Wha's sin?" Little John-John asked.

"Sin is doing things that are wrong or not doing things that are right. It's when your mother tells you to do something, and you don't do it, or you do something that you know you're not supposed to do."

"Marvin sins all the time," Tamika said. "He never listens when mama tells him to leave me alone," she said.

Marvin elbowed her.

"Oww! Stop!" she yelled.

"We all sin. That's why we all need Jesus. God's word says that everybody sins."

"God's word? What's that?" Phillip asked.

"That's the Bible. It tells us all about Jesus and how he took our sins away, so we can go to heaven. You'll learn more about him in Sunday school."

The only sound heard for the rest of the trip was the soft singing voices on the CD.

"Hi, Onia," Zoe said. "What time did you get here? I didn't see you at the beginning of the service. Were you late?"

"Yes. Rachel couldn't find her shoes. It turns out the dog had chewed them up. I tell you I should get rid of him. He costs us more money than anything."

"No!" Amber screamed, turning heads and drawing attention to herself.

"Maybe Rachel could spend the night with me some Saturdays, and I could bring her to church."

Rachel turned her head and rolled her eyes.

"Who are these kids? Do we have a family that I don't know about?" Onia asked.

"Don't you remember the outreach program called Bible Buddies that pastor encouraged us to get involved in? When I had alone time with God he called me to sign up for it. These are the children I'm assigned to pick up."

"You and your alone time with God. Do you still have that shrine set up in your apartment?"

"It's not a shrine. It's my prayer room. I go there to pray, and I listen to God talk to me."

"Wee-ooo, Wee-ooo, Wee-ooo. Whatever...I don't know about this Bible Buddies thing. It smells like a liability to me. Aren't you worried you might get sued if something happens?"

"Onia, you worry too much about money. We don't need to worry about that or anything else. We're in God's hands, and so are these children. Besides, He called me to do this. I'm sure he'll equip me to handle it regardless of what the devil might try to do to ruin it."

"All right, *suit* yourself. No pun intended," she said as she laughed. "Get it? Suit yourself? Lawsuit?"

"I get it," Zoe responded as she smirked. "Bye, Onia. I'll see you next week on time, right?"

"Okay, Zoe. Call me before then."

"Okay."

"So, how was Sunday School? Did you like it?"

"Gray!" Little John-John said. "We learn Jesus love us!"

"Why is that 'gray'?"

"He means *great*," Marvin explained.

"Wonderful!" She replied with a smile on her face.

"I thought we were going to get something to eat," Marvin said.

"What made you think that?"

"The last time we went to a church they fed us."

Her smile turned to a frown.

Chapter 3

College Sweethearts

"…and the contentions of a wife are a continual dropping."

Proverbs 19:13b

"Husbands, love your wives, and be not bitter against them."

Colossians 3:19

Zoe decided to call her estranged sister. Anytime they kept in touch she initiated the encounter. Her love for God compelled her to fight the urge to write her sister off.

"Hi Brenna, how are you doing?"

"Who is this?" Brenna said.

"It's Zoe, your sister."

"I don't have a sister by that name."

Zoe gasped.

"I'm just kidding. What do you want?"

"I just called to see how you're doing. I haven't heard from you for a long time."

"I'm doing just fine. I'll do even better if you keep your nose out of my business."

"What do you mean?"

"Don't pretend like you don't know. You always make yourself seem so innocent."

"Honestly, I don't know what you're talking about."

"I don't appreciate you telling my son he could come and live with you."

"What? He misunderstood me. I invited him to stay for the summer, that's all."

"Well that's not what he said."

"That's what I told him."

"I don't care what you said! You have some nerve asking him behind my back! I'm his mother! Come talk to me, if you have anything to say!"

"You don't have to yell."

"Don't tell me what to do! You better stay away from my son, and stop trying to push that Jesus junk on him!"

"I'm sorry. I didn't mean to..."

Click.

Zoe stared at her phone and hoped her call had dropped as her mouth did. Her cheeks felt flush and tears filled her eyes. She just knew her own sister didn't hang up without at least saying goodbye. However, she couldn't risk the heartache by calling again.

She tried to figure out what went wrong. She felt out of place in her own family. Was her 'craving' the cause? She hardly knew who Brenna was anymore and didn't know how to mend the rift in their relationship. Why did Brenna push her away?

"What now?" Brenna said as the doorbell rang, still agitated by her sister's intrusion. Brenna's face dropped as she opened the door and saw who it was. There Chad stood, impatient, as he glared at her, alcohol on his breath. He had been away for almost two weeks.

Chad was tall and usually clean cut. This morning, however, he was scruffy and unshaven, shirt tail wrinkled and hanging out like a mini skirt. His olive skin, brown eyes, and designer clothes were sources of attraction like a white-washed tomb.

"What took you so long to come to the door?"

"Where's your key?"

"I don't know," he mumbled as he brushed past her.

"It's about time you finally decided to come home."

"Is that all you do is nag? I get anything but a hello around here, and why don't you fix yourself up sometime?"

"I don't have anyone to look good for. You're never around anymore."

"How about having a little self respect?"

She sneered at him behind his back as he staggered into the kitchen.

"Brenna, there's no food in the refrigerator! Why haven't you gone shopping?" He scowled.

"I just went shopping a few days ago. Now who's nagging?" she said under her breath.

"What did you say?" He turned towards her and snarled like an angry dog.

She flinched and said, "Nothing. I didn't say anything."

"Uh huh. I don't see anything in here for me."

"I never know when you're coming home. Then you come home after being gone for God knows how long, and I'm supposed to know what you like to eat. All you do is complain."

"It's my house. I'll do what I want."

"Why didn't you grab something to eat on your way back home? Better yet, why didn't your lover cook something for you?" she said as she backed away.

He turned around and snapped at her. "Look! I make the money for this family, and I expect food to be in this house for me at all times." He walked toward her. She could feel his breath in her face. "It's the least you can do, since you don't do much else around here! Now go to the store and get me something to eat, woman!" He grabbed her by her hair.

"Ouch! All right!" She slapped his wrist to make him let go.

He let go of her hair in exchange for a shove. Brenna fell to the floor. She picked herself up and stumbled into the other room.

Tears rolled down her cheeks as she tried to collect herself. She rubbed her head. Then she slammed the front door behind her.

"Hey, Brenna!"

She looked up and eyed an attractive man. He looked familiar, around her age. Except for the crow's feet when he smiled, he maintained his good looks. Since his younger years he had gained a few extra pounds giving him a more manly appearance. He was taller than her husband by a few inches. He had wavy, dark brown hair which curled up at the bangs and at the nape of his neck.

As she inched closer she recognized the cleft in his chin. She couldn't mistake his furrowed eyebrows which brought attention to his blue eyes for anyone other than... "Devon? Devon Botticelli? From computer science class?"

"The one and only. You remembered," he said as he grabbed his bag of groceries and approached her. "How've you been? It's been a long time."

He set his bag down, wrapped his arms around her, and pressed his body against hers. She felt a tingling and warmth in his embrace that rekindled former passions between them. Part of her wanted to hold on longer before they broke apart.

"I could be better," she said. "How are *you*? Last time I saw you, you were with..." She snapped her fingers. "What's her name?"

"Gabriella. I'm so much better now that I got rid of that old ball and chain."

"Really? I thought you two were going to be together forever after you and I broke up."

"I never should have broken up with you."

"Excuse me? I broke up with you," she said with a smile.

"Whoever did the breaking up doesn't matter anyway. We should have stayed together. We were good for each other. I had strong feelings for you, Brenna. Why did you break up with me anyway?"

"You accused me of cheating on you."

He snapped his fingers, "Oh yeah, that's right. One of your friends told me you were seeing some guy named Chad."

"I found out he had bribed her into telling you that so he could date me. Unfortunately, I was charmed into it."

"You fell for that?" He cleared his throat. "I'm sorry. That didn't come out right. One thing I admired about you was how smart you were. You answered and asked a lot of questions in class all the time."

"That was book smarts. Apparently I was stupid and naive."

"So what ever happened to you and that Chad dude?"

"I married him," she said, her voice trailing off.

"You don't sound too thrilled."

"I'm not," she said as she curled her upper lip.

"Oh," he responded. "Umm, are you still married? Do you have any children?"

"Yes, you can say we're still married. We have three kids - two boys and one girl."

"So how are you and your lucky husband doing?"

"What's with the twenty questions? Don't you think that's kind of personal?"

"I just want to know how you're doing. It's been a long time. I didn't mean anything by it, okay?"

"Okay." She looked down at the floor.

"C'mon, now. Tell me the truth. I can tell you're hiding something. Where's the effervescence you used to have?"

"You always could read me. Maybe we can talk about it later. I have to get some groceries for my...'loving husband'," she said as she cleared her throat and turned up her nose. She felt sick to her stomach.

"I would like that," he said as he smiled.

"Why don't you give me your phone number? We can talk over coffee sometime."

"I'd like that," he answered, eyes twinkling. He pulled out his cell phone. "Hey, why don't you meet me in...say... an hour at the coffee shop on the corner?"

"Okay. I'll drop off the groceries, but let's meet at the coffee shop on Druid Hills Rd. It's closer to my house."

"You live in Druid Hills?"

"Yes."

"Wow, your old man has some money, huh?"

"You can say that."

"I'll be waiting with bated breath," he said.

"That's kind of corny, Devon. I see you haven't changed." She touched his shoulder. "I seem to have a weakness for charm," she said as she giggled with a wink.

He studied her and smiled until she disappeared down one of the aisles.

The coffee shop was packed, and it buzzed with life. People chattered as they indulged in tasty treats and relished each other's company on the sultry afternoon. The smell of fresh brewed coffee and freshly baked pastries greeted Devon as he entered the quaint little shop. The warmth and coziness reminded him of holiday gatherings at his grandma's. He found a small table near a window. He sat there for almost half an hour before he began tapping his fingers and shaking his legs. He wondered whether he had been stood up.

The aroma overwhelmed his senses and invited him to partake, so he decided to order a cappuccino and a cinnamon roll.

He peered out the window and finally saw Brenna approaching. He almost didn't recognize her, wearing sunglasses and a substantial amount of make-up. It glistened in the sunlight as if her face had been thawing like a corpse in the heat.

"Hi. I didn't think you were coming," he said as he stood up from the table. He smiled and pulled out a chair. He motioned for her to sit down.

"Thank you," she said under her breath.

He didn't know much about make-up, but he noticed discoloration and tear stains on her face. "So tell me about your kids," he said, trying to ignore her dispirited look.

"They're hardly kids anymore," she answered in a sharp tone.

"You sure have changed. You used to be so jovial. Why are you so glum?"

She sat in silence and looked away.

"I know you didn't meet me here to ignore me. What's going on, and why are you wearing sunglasses in here, Brenna? Take them off, so I can see your pretty eyes."

"I don't know what to do," she finally said as she began to sob.

"About what?"

"About my clumsiness." She pulled off her sunglasses and revealed a shiner as big as a boxer in a lost battle. "I keep running into things, and I don't know what to do about it."

"Oh, I see. How did this happen? Have you gone to the doctor about this 'problem'?" he asked.

She looked down towards the floor.

The waitress came over. "Can I get something for your friend?"

"What would you like to order?" Devon asked.

"I'll have an espresso."

"Brenna, tell me what you're talking about."

"I don't know if I should."

"So you're just going to leave me hanging after you brought it up?"

She shrugged her shoulders.

"You can't possibly expect me to believe you have a problem running into things. You're hiding something. Besides, I know you better than that."

"All right. As I told you, I have a weakness for charming men. I married a charmer who only cares about himself with a serious right hook."

"Really?"

"We've drifted apart a long time ago. Every time he comes home he's more distant and angrier than the time before. He pretends to be nice to me around other people, but when we're alone he reveals his iron fist and makes me his punching bag."

"Oh, one of those types. I'm sorry for doubting you and I'm sorry that this happened to you. You need someone who will love you and take care of you. Why don't you get a divorce?"

"I can't right now. I don't have any money or anyone else to go to. When all of my kids become grownups, he won't even have to support us anymore. I have no job skills because he talked me into marrying him before I could graduate and get a job. I think that was his plan all along, so he could control me. He has me where he wants me." Her voice was parched. She gasped for air between sips of coffee, streaks of mascara streaming down her face.

He took her hands into his, nearly knocking her cup from her grip. He stared directly into her swollen, watery eyes.

"That's not all. I also suspect he's cheating on me."

"What makes you think that?"

"He's gone for weeks at a time. He's never around to help with the kids. Everything is all about him when he does come home."

"Really."

"One day his boss called the house to contact him."

"So, what's that supposed to mean?"

She hesitated. "He wa-wa-wasn't h-home," she stuttered as she choked on her words.

"That doesn't mean he was cheating."

"Are you trying to stick up for him? Shouldn't his boss know where he is?"

"Not necessarily."

"You men are all alike. This has been going on for years. Every time I confront him about it he tells me he's away on business."

"I apologize. I'm sorry this happened to you too. No one should have to put up with this, especially you. You deserve better. I can help."

"How?"

"I'll get you a job at my business. Save your money, and then you can leave him. How are your computer skills?"

"I know some things from three years of studying computer science. I had to quit when I got married though."

"Don't remind me."

"Huh?"

"Never mind. I'll train you."

"I don't know. I don't remember everything I learned," she said.

"It's pretty easy."

"That's a lot to think about."

"Take your time, but don't take too long. I don't want to hear your name on the news. I still care about you, and I want to help. I'm here for you and I always will be." He smiled and caressed her hands.

His touch sent another tingling sensation coursing through her body. She met his stare with a receptive smile.

"All right, I'll do it. When do I start?"

"You can start right away on Monday."

They talked about old times as they consumed scrumptious pastries and drank coffee. Brenna felt alive again.

Chapter 4

Benighted Souls

"Thus saith the LORD of hosts, hearken not unto the words of the prophets that prophesy unto you: they make you vain: they speak a vision of their own heart, and not out of the mouth of the LORD."

Jeremiah 23:16

"Hi honey, I'm home." Dave Altimoone waddled over to Sophia.

He had an oversized physique due to his taste for beer and food. She stared at the TV while he gave her a kiss on the top of her head.

"Hi, honey."

Their single-family cape cod was a modest cracker box in downtown Atlanta. It had two small bedrooms hardly big enough for a family of four, let alone two oversized adults. Sophia sat in the den where she idolized her televangelists. The two front rooms sandwiched the front entrance. A little foyer alongside the upstairs led to a kitchen hardly big enough for dining.

"How ya doin'?"

"I'm fine, sweetie," she replied, smiling, eyes still glued to the TV.

"Who ya watchin' today?"

"Reverend Whitaker, our preacher. Your dinner is ready."

"It smells good," he said as he lumbered into the kitchen. "Leftovers again?"

"We can't afford much else right now. We gave a thousand dollars to the church this month remember? We have to cut back."

"Oh, yeah, I forgot. It's a gamble, but it's worth it I guess. Any day we might get a windfall so we can move from this shack," he said. He joined Sophia in their televangelist haven with his plate of food.

"That's right, sweetheart. Speak it into existence." She smiled.

"The more money you give, the less you have to fight with the devil (pause), because money is the root of all kinds of evil! Can I get an 'amen'? I'm here to help you part with that unnecessary evil and keep the devil off your back!" the preacher shouted as they watched him deliver his message. Beads of sweat dripped down his face. He dabbed himself with a silk handkerchief to prevent his lavish suit and fine jewelry from getting wet.

Pastor Whitaker spoke with an entrancing roll to his voice like the steady beat of a metronome. The organ sang with vibrato like a vocalist, stirring up emotions in the audience. The emotional intensity increased as the crowd clapped, cheered, and danced. The drummer thumped on the kick drum like a pulsating heart in rhythm with the organ. Some people fanned themselves while others "fell out".

"He's so good!" Dave said as he munched on a piece of stale bread.

"And charismatic," Sophia added. "I wish we were there right now. By the way, he's planning a week long Bible cruise to the Bahamas! Can we go?"

"How much does it cost, honey bun?"

"It'll cost six thousand dollars for both of us."

"*Hwee*! That's steep. We can't afford that."

"It'll make a nice getaway."

"It's out of the question."

"Please, honey. I can go back to work."

"When is it?"

"It's late next summer. I think we should go."

"That's more than most cruises, and it's certainly more than we have in our savings, honey."

"The kids are grown now, and I attended college to get a decent job not to be a housewife all my life."

"You chose to stop working."

"I know, but I want to go back now. Besides, I would do almost anything to go on that trip."

"I don't know. Remember, we still have to tithe."

"We have up to three months before the trip to send in a down payment."

"When exactly is the trip?" he asked again.

"I don't know the exact date, sweetie. I just know it's sometime in August next year. We can ask the reverend for more details when we see him in church. We could use our credit card to pay for part of it, if we don't have enough saved up by then."

"I guess I can give up my beer drinking for a while too," he said as he cracked open a can.

"I suppose I could cut back on eating so many donuts. Going to the Bahamas is worth the sacrifice."

They chuckled.

After much discussion, they wrote about their dream trip in a special diary filled with other goals and aspirations. They prayed and closed with their usual mantra: "Speak it into existence and it will happen." Then they went back into the den to watch other televangelists.

"Hey, Shirley! How are you doing this morning?" Sophia asked. She gave her a hug.

"I'm okay, I guess," she said with watery eyes.

"What's wrong?"

"I had to file for bankruptcy."

"You what?!" Rita Mathis said as she slithered over to their conversation like a snake near a river. "I thought nurses got paid a fortune."

"What on earth for?" Sophia asked ignoring her comment.

"All of my money got wiped out giving to this church. The bank had to foreclose on my home as well. My retirement money...*gone*."

"Oh wow!" Sophia said with her mouth agape.

"How could that happen? You must have lacked faith. That's why it happened," Rita answered.

"Don't listen to her, Shirley," Sophia said. "Have you tried speaking the mantra the reverend suggests?"

"No."

"That doesn't work," Rita said.

"We've noticed a little change, but these things take time," Sophia said.

"Time?" I've given this church everything...my time...my dedication. Everyone who knows me knows I'm a devout member. I don't know what else to do."

"It'll get better. Try the mantra. What have you got to lose?"

"Nothing. I don't have anything left to lose. It certainly can't hurt."

"I'm confident it'll work. Dave and I are praying to go on the Bible cruise to the Bahamas."

"Be careful what you pray for you just might get it," Rita answered. "Some people don't come back alive."

"What are you talking about? That's nonsense."

"Deacon Tom told me they have some water activity. I forgot the name of it. What happens is, the reverend volunteers people to be lowered to the top of the water to test their faith. They test to see whether the people can walk on water like...Who was that guy who walked on water with Jesus?"

"Peter," Shirley said.

"So, what happens?"

"The people come back in a body bag," Rita whispered. "Tom said they cover up what happened by saying the people fell overboard."

"You're lying."

"I've known the reverend for too long to believe that," Shirley said.

"Why would a deacon tell you something like that anyway?" Sophia asked.

"I used to date him. Reverend Whitaker pays him a little money under the table to keep quiet."

Sophia rolled her eyes. "That doesn't make any sense. Why would he tell you then? You're the last person he should trust to keep a secret."

"I resent that remark. Anyway, we were seriously involved. I mean *seriously*. My lovin' is like a truth serum."

"Oh for goodness sakes! I've heard enough. Goodbye, Sophia."

"Goodbye." They both laughed. Sophia rolled her eyes.

"Thank you for your help," Shirley said. She walked away shaking her head.

"Remember the mantra!"

"What's all the drama?" Dave asked as he approached them.

"Shirley's having money problems, and Rita claims people have been dying on the cruise."

"What? That's ridiculous," Dave said. "Everybody would know about it."

"Don't believe me then. You'll find out for yourself," Rita said as she strutted away.

"We're planning on it," Sophia said.

"Alright, suit yourself. You might come home in a body bag," Rita yelled. She laughed.

Dave looked puzzled.

"Ignore her. She said Deacon Tom told her people on the cruise try to walk on water to test their faith and drown."

"Well, they must have lacked faith," he answered. "Don't believe that."

"I don't. I consider the source. Rita could make a gossip columnist sound believable."

They both laughed.

Zoe called later that evening to check up on Sophia. She hadn't spoken to her in a while. However, less time had passed than with her sister Brenna.

"Zoe, how've you been?"

"I'm hangin' in there."

"What's the matter?"

"Oh, nothing really. At least you're okay with hearing from me."

"What do you mean?" She chuckled.

"Brenna hung up on me."

"You know she has issues."

"I don't really know her anymore."

"I think she prefers it that way. She told me she doesn't like you."

Zoe hesitated. "Anyway, I called to see what you've been up to."

"Nothing much. Dave and I are going on a Bible cruise with our minister. We just need to scrape up enough money, and we're there."

"You're not still giving all your money to that church are you?"

"No. We just give more than a tithe sometimes. It's like an investment."

"How so?"

"Our pastor tells us to give so we can get more."

"He sounds like one of those prosperity gospel preachers."

"I don't know about that, but we love his messages. They're exciting and uplifting."

"I suppose, as long as he preaches about Jesus. He's the only way, you know."

"Reverend Whitaker says there's more than one way to get to heaven."

"Name another way besides Jesus."

"He says giving is another way, and I like the way he preaches. He must be right."

"Remember what we learned in church when we were little?"

"Not really. I didn't understand most of it. I feel so much better about my faith now."

"Read God's word and you'll see who the only way is."

"Zoe, you have your way, and I have mine."

"I'll keep you in my prayers."

"That won't be necessary," Sophia said and turned up her nose. "That's why I don't talk to you much. You think you have to be everyone's savior. You think you're always right."

"I'm only trying to tell you what God's word says because I care about your eternal wellbeing."

"I don't see things the way you do, so I'm fine with my wellbeing. Now we can talk about something else or end this conversation."

Zoe changed the subject. She struggled as usual with any conversation other than talking about Jesus. Lately every discussion she had with her two older sisters has been a struggle.

Zoe felt like she's outside in the bitter cold looking into the window of a warm cabin watching her two sisters socialize. She knocks on the door, but neither one of them let her in as they watch her shiver.

Chapter 5

Better Days

"...Let not your heart be troubled, neither let it be afraid."

John 14:27b

"Why do we have to eat this disgusting food?" Rachel said.

"It's veal parmigiana, and it's not for you. There's pizza baking in the oven for you."

"What a relief."

"Today is our anniversary, and I decided to surprise your dad by cooking his favorite meal. Is that okay with you?"

Rachel shrugged her shoulders and walked away.

Onia created an ambience for romance. She dolled herself up in her best dress, fine jewelry, high heels, and lipstick as if she was going out on the town. She set the table like that of a fine restaurant. She placed two tapers in the center waiting to be lit. She set out neatly folded cloth napkins next to her grandma's fine china.

"Where have you been?" Onia asked in a sharp tone. She had been waiting for what seemed like hours with a cell phone next to her plate, a box of Kleenex, and food that had turned to ice.

"Don't bother me right now, Onia."

"I was worried about you." She smelled the strong reek of alcohol. "You've been drinking!" she said.

"Really? Whatever gave you that impression?" He stumbled past her.

"I fixed your favorite meal, and now it's cold!"

"*Veal*? That's too expensive. What's the occasion?"

"You forgot? It's our anniversary," she said, her puffy eyes welling up with tears.

"Well, Happy Anniversary, dear! For your anniversary gift you receive one unemployed husband!"

She gasped. Then she walked him over to a chair as he teetered and sat him down.

"What happened, honey?"

"The company is restructuring my department, so they offered me a buyout, and I took it."

Her heart sank. "After all the years you put into that company. How could they do this to you?"

"They can do anything they want with people's lives."

He started blubbering.

She placed his head on her chest and caressed his back as his body trembled, tears drenching her dress. When he calmed down she escorted him to bed.

The next morning Onia went into the dining room to clear the table from last night's untouched meal. She found the table pillaged by a ravenous mutt with an insatiable appetite. Everything on the table was in disarray as if she had walked into a war zone.

After she cleaned up the remnants she prepared a meager breakfast.

Rachel raced down the stairs. She imagined herself sinking her teeth into some fluffy pancakes, one of her favorites. She plopped her books on the floor. "What's this?"

"It's oatmeal."

"I hate oatmeal. What happened to pancakes or scrambled eggs and bacon?"

"Do you wake up complaining, Rachel?"

"That's what I ask myself all the time," Nathan chimed in. He came to the kitchen wearing his backpack before he set it down.

"Why don't you shut up and stay out of it?"

"Why don't you make me?" he said and stuck out his tongue.

"That's enough!" Onia said.

"I like oatmeal," Amber said as she came down the stairs.

"Me too," Andrew agreed.

They both sat down next to each other like two peas in a pod.

"It's Friday," Rachel said.

"I know what day it is."

"You always make a big breakfast on Fridays."

"We're going to have to cut back. Dad lost his job yesterday."

"What?" Rachel said.

"They cut his whole department out. We need to help out around here and be supportive. We may even have to get rid of George."

"No!" Amber said.

"That dog costs us too much money. Last night he was the only one who enjoyed the veal your dad and I were supposed to have. He has his own food, yet he eats everything in sight. Who left him in the house anyway?"

"I guess I did," Rachel said. "I must have forgotten to take him out when I got off the phone."

"Your forgetfulness cost us a lot of money. Veal is not cheap."

"I'm sorry, okay."

"You should be," Nathan said as he grabbed his backpack and ran to the door.

"You didn't finish your..." Onia yelled.

"You *better* run!" Rachel yelled. She picked up a few pencils and hurled them at him. He turned around and said, "You missed me!" He stuck out his tongue and slammed the door.

Rachel forced her oatmeal down before she left to catch her bus.

"Bye, Mom."

"Have a good day."

"It's going to be great. Ellen and I are going to hang out at the high school football game." Rachel and her friend liked to masquerade as high school students hoping to get noticed.

"Alright, but come home right after."

"Can we go somewhere to eat afterwards?"

"I said come right home. We have food here."

"Okay. Okay."

"Better yet, be home by six-thirty whether the game is over or not. It gets dark earlier, and there are some crazy people out there these days."

"But, Mom!"

"Do you want me to come pick you up without going to see any of the game?"

"No. I'll be home," Rachel said as she rolled her eyes and sighed. She hoped her eyes got stuck. Maybe her mother would have pity on her and let her stay out longer.

"All right you two munchkins get your books, so I can take you to school," Onia said.

"I didn't finish eating," Amber said.

"Well hurry up, so you won't be late."

Amber wolfed down what was left of a tepid bowl of oatmeal.

Ryan was still sleeping when Onia returned. She fixed herself a cup of coffee as she pondered whether she should wake him up. She decided to just let him sleep. As she sipped her coffee she worried what would happen to their lives without his income. Her stomach knotted up. She trudged to the bathroom and purged what she had for breakfast. She lay down on the couch and forced herself to sleep.

When she woke up she cleaned the house to stop her mind from racing. She wanted to call Zoe, but she was at work. The morning turned to afternoon when she realized Ryan still hadn't gotten out of bed. She paced and moped around the house wondering what she could scrape together for dinner.

"Mom, I'm home!" Rachel announced. She thought making a grand entrance would appease her tardiness.

"Quiet, your dad is still asleep."

"Since last night?" Rachel asked, surprised.

"Yes he is, so don't disturb him. I'll wake him up when I'm finished cooking dinner."

"What are we having?"

"Hamburgers and french fries."

"Where are Nathan and the twins?"

"What's with all the questions? They're all upstairs in their rooms. They've been home for a while. Where have you been?"

"Ellen and I hung out with some friends after the game. I won't get to see them again until Monday."

"The only time you'll get to see them after school will be after a week. Rachel, I told you to be home by six-thirty. It's now seven forty-five. You're coming straight home for the next week. I'll be taking you to school and bringing you back to make sure that happens."

"That's not fair! It's Friday night. Other kids can stay out late."

"Don't raise your voice at me. You were late, and I gave you clear directions on what time I expected you to be home. Do you want more than a week?"

"No, ma'am."

Rachel walked away mumbling as she stormed upstairs.

When dinner was ready Onia went to wake Ryan up. She crept into the room afraid of what she might find.

"Ryan, honey, are you okay?"

He lay motionless.

Onia reached her hand out, reluctant to touch him. She nudged him anyway. "Wake up. Dinner's ready."

He moaned.

She shook him again before his eyes finally opened.

"Huh?"

"It's time for dinner."

"Dinner?" He sat up. "I'm late for work! Why didn't you wake me sooner?" Like a blow to his head he slumped back down as he remembered what happened. He wished it was a bad dream.

"You lost your job, remember?"

"Don't remind me. What time is it?" He asked, rubbing his eyes.

"It's almost eight o'clock."

"I can't believe I slept this long. I need to get dressed."

"Don't worry about that. We've seen you in your pajamas before. Besides, dinner is getting cold."

"Don't tell me what to do. I'm getting dressed."

He put on his robe and stumbled to the bathroom to get into the shower. Onia went downstairs to set the table for the kids. He came down half an hour later after everyone else had eaten.

"Why didn't you wait for me before you ate?"

"I told you the food was getting cold. You chose to change clothes, and we chose to eat."

Onia reheated his food in the microwave.

He bit into his burger. "This tastes like rubber!"

"What's gotten into you? There was nothing wrong with this meal. Why didn't you come down when it was ready?"

"Oh, so now it's my fault?"

"I didn't say that, honey. It's just you never complained about my cooking before. Maybe all that sleep tainted your taste buds." she said under her breath.

"There's nothing wrong with my taste buds!" he shouted.

"Will the sweet and thoughtful Ryan I know and love please come back?"

He arose from the dinner table and stormed from the kitchen.

"Zoe, it's me, Onia."

"What's up? Why are you crying?"

"Ryan lost his job. He seems depressed. I'm scared. What if we don't have enough money to eat? What if we lose our house?"

"What do you need?"

"I'm worried. He's cranky, and I don't know how much of it I can take."

"I'll pray for you. Better yet, we can pray together right now."

Zoe stopped to pray at that moment with Onia. However, she knew comforting Onia would be short-lived. They never had enough money to her even when Ryan was working.

Chapter 6

Blind Date and Narrow Gate

"Because strait is the gate, and narrow is the way, which leadeth unto life, and few there be that find it."

Matthew 7:14

The bell rang to end the day at Living Word Elementary School. All of the students filed into the hallways pushing and shoving each other anticipating the freedom the weekend brought.

An older lady hobbled into Zoe's classroom. "Zoe, what are your plans this weekend?"

"Hi, Resa, I'm going on a blind date," she said, excited. Dorothy is setting me up with her brother," she continued. She smiled.

"Dorothy Banks? I've known her for years. She's certainly changed."

"How?"

"She's not the Christian she used to be. Her walk has turned a little to the left lately."

"What do you mean?"

"She's fallen into the pattern of the world. You know...backslid."

"How do you know?"

"I've been trying not to gossip. Just keep her in your prayers."

"How will I know what to pray about?"

"Nice try, Zoe. The Holy Spirit knows. Let's just say she needs lots of prayer."

"What are your plans for the weekend?" Zoe asked.

"Well, for starters, my husband and I were hoping to have you over this evening. He makes a mean batch of catfish, and I have a secret recipe for coleslaw."

"If you'd have only asked me earlier in the week, I would've taken you up on the offer. I'll take a rain check though. Can you bring me some leftovers for lunch on Monday?"

"I could do that. I still would like to have you over sometime. Now, about this blind date; you be careful. What do you know about this guy other than he's Dorothy's brother?"

"Dorothy told me he's a Christian. She said he's an active member in their church. He's the drummer in their praise band."

"He sounds harmless enough, but be careful, okay."

"Yes, Mother. Don't you know me by now?"

"It's not you I'm worried about."

"I don't go anywhere without Jesus. I'm in good hands."

Zoe looked up and imagined him as the one she could establish a lasting and compatible relationship with. After all, he played for Jesus, and she sang in the choir. *'I'll bet he and I would make a great worship team'* she thought. Her eyes glazed over as she pictured him proposing to her in front of the church.

"Zoe! What are you looking at? Snap out of it," Resa said as she waved her hand across Zoe's face.

"Oh! I was just dreaming."

"I see. Don't get too hopeful. Do you know what they say about musicians?"

"He's a *church* musician. He plays for the Lord."

"All right, if you say so. I won't say I told you so, if he's no different from any of the rest of them."

"*Rest of them*? You're stereotyping. All musicians aren't that way."

"That's true, but most are. Just be careful, okay."

"You keep telling me that. I'll be fine."

"Hi, Mrs. Williams. Hi, Miss T."

The two women looked at each other.

"Victor Daniels, what are you still doing here?" Zoe asked.

"I came back to say goodbye and have a nice weekend. Miss T, don't date him. He's no good for you."

"Were you eavesdropping?"

"I was just being polite."

"Really?"

"Yeah, I was waitin' for you to get done talkin'. Please don't go on that date."

"You have to stop following me around."

"But he might be mean to you."

"As I told Mrs. Williams, Jesus will be with me."

"I'll see you Monday," Resa said. "Have a great weekend, and remember what I said."

"Okay. I'll be fine. Don't worry."

Resa limped away on her cane.

"I don't believe Jesus will be with you. I can't believe in someone I can't see, and he took my mother away."

"Honey, God didn't take your mother away. An asthma attack did."

"He let it happen."

"We live in a fallen world filled with sin and disease. That's all the more reason why we need Jesus."

"I'm just not sure God is real," Victor said as he shook his head.

"You see evidence of his existence everywhere you go. His creation is fascinating, and it proves he exists. He's our Intelligent Designer."

"Designer? He makes clothes? Maybe He can hook me up."

"No, silly...he made everything out of nothing and he made it well. What he does for us proves he's real."

"Then why did he let my mother die?"

"You remember when I prayed for him to give you comfort? You won't completely get over your loss, but you have to admit he helped you through the tougher times. He put great people in your life to support you like your uncle and me."

"I guess so."

"You *guess* so? I've been praying for you all year, and I see how God has answered. You're staying with a supportive uncle who loves you. He allowed you to stay in a great school where you learn about Jesus every day. You've maintained good grades lately, and you have *me*. I'm here for you whenever you need someone to talk to."

"Thanks for prayin', but I still don't know."

"I'll keep praying," she said as she packed up. "As much as I love you and want to continue this conversation, I have a date to get ready for. You have a great weekend, and I'll see you Monday." She hugged him and walked away.

He lagged behind. "I love you too, Miss Todvue," he said under his breath.

As soon as Zoe had gotten home she freshened up and primped herself. She buzzed her mystery date into her apartment around six forty-five. A tall, handsome man around her age greeted her with flowers. He had dark brown, wavy hair and brown eyes. His skin was smooth and dark like chocolate pudding.

"Hi, I'm Brandon," he said in a rich voice as he handed her the bouquet. "Dorothy didn't tell me you were beautiful."

"Thank you. C'mon in while I put these flowers in a vase. Would you like something to drink?"

"No thank you. My sister told me you're a teacher."

"We teach at the same school."

"I notice a lot of crosses and Jesus pictures hanging on your walls," he said as he surveyed her apartment. "You take your religion seriously, don't you?"

"I take my faith in Jesus very seriously. My religion just determines where I go to church regularly."

"I stand corrected. Here, let me help you with that," he said. He held her coat up for her. "Are you ready for a good time?" he said as she slipped her arms in.

"I'm ready as I'll ever be."

"After you, my princess," he said with a smile. He held the door open for her. "My chariot awaits."

"Thank you," she responded. She rolled her eyes and thought "*How cliche*".

Brandon took her to a fancy Bistro by the lake.

"You didn't have to bring me here," she said, "I would have been fine with a simple American family restaurant."

"Erdman, table for two," the maitre d said.

"That's us."

He escorted them to their table.

"Nothing but the best for you," he replied as he placed his hand on her lower back.

His hand slid lower than what she felt comfortable, so she walked a little faster.

"Your sister tells me you're a musician at your church."

"She's partly right. I'm a musician there, but that's *her* church. I've been a drummer there for almost seven years just for a little extra money. She told me about the gig, so I took her up on it. It helps put gas in my car. I'm a musician by trade though," he said as he sipped a glass of merlot. "I play at nightclubs three times a week. I also DJ a few nights, and do parties," he continued. He pulled out a business card and handed it to her, "You should come support me sometime."

"No thank you. Does Dorothy know you're not interested in her church?"

"What she doesn't know won't hurt her."

"That seems a bit pretentious," Zoe said as her face dropped. She looked away.

"That's the way it is."

"Have you ever been with a woman?" Zoe asked.

"Whoa! What kind of question is that?"

"I was just curious."

"I'm a musician. It comes with the territory. Girls flock to me wherever I perform. I perform at hotels sometimes which make the perks very easy, if you know what I mean. I wouldn't be a man if I turned down offers like that. What about you?"

"What *about* me?"

"Have you ever been with a man?" He took another sip of wine. He eyed her as if he was savoring her.

"No. I'm saving myself for my future husband."

He coughed and cleared his throat. "Sorry, my drink went down the wrong pipe." He cleared his throat again. "Why is a beautiful woman like you celibate? That's a waste," he said.

She shrugged her shoulders. "Life isn't about looks," she replied.

"So what made you want to be a teacher?"

"It's a long story, and you probably wouldn't understand."

"Try me. We've got time."

"My parents couldn't afford to send me to college after they put me through a Christian boarding school. The principal knew I wanted to become a Christian teacher, and he also knew we had financial problems. We still owed money at the school after I graduated. Every day that summer I prayed 'Lord, if you really want me to become a teacher, please let me be able to go to that Christian teacher college'. I knew there was no chance for me to go to college if I didn't go right away."

"What made you think that?"

"It's just harder. Especially if I would have found a job that I liked. To make matters worse, both of my parents died in a car crash my senior year in high school."

"Oh. I'm sorry to hear that."

"Anyway, one day...out of the blue...the principal called our house to tell me he had gotten a grant for me to use to either pay off the tuition debt, or use it as a down payment for college. By that time I lived with my grandparents. They could have easily chosen to pay off the tuition instead of incurring my parents' debt. Instead they told him to let me use the money to get started in college. God answered my prayer."

"I'd love to meet your grandparents. They seem like wonderful people like you."

"You'll have to wait until you get to eternal life. I made a vow to pursue my dream to honor them for their sacrifice and to honor God for answering my prayer."

"That's beautiful. Personally I don't know how you can do it. I can't stand kids."

Zoe froze and didn't have much else to say except to answer a barrage of superficial queries from her companion.

After a date that seemed like it wouldn't end to Zoe, they finally arrived back at her apartment. He escorted her to her door and tried to put his arms around her. She nudged him aside, but he blocked the doorway.

"Excuse me," she said.

"What? Don't I get a goodnight kiss?"

"I hardly know you."

"After all the money I spent on you? I thought we could have breakfast in bed together."

"I'll give you money for my share of the meal. Will that make you feel better?"

"That won't be necessary. At least I deserve a kiss."

She turned towards him and kissed him on the cheek. "Don't bother to call me anymore. We won't work out."

"What? So it's like that. You think you're too good for me?"

"We have different values. My body is God's temple, and I plan on saving it for my future husband I told you."

"That's what a lot of church women say, but they don't mean it. They usually give in."

"Well, I'm not one of those women," she said as she stepped into her apartment.

"Aw, c'mon. A beautiful woman like you shouldn't waste her good looks."

"I'm not wasting them. I'm *saving* them."

"I know...I know...for your future husband. Can't I be a future prospect?"

"You can't handle what I have."

"Whoa! What's that supposed to mean?"

"What I have is Jesus, and you can't handle that. You also should be open with your sister."

"Going to church doesn't mean you have Jesus."

"True. You're living proof of that. However, believing in Jesus as my personal Savior and walking the talk does. Goodnight, Brandon. Thank you for the meal."

She shut her apartment door before he could try to come in, but not before she heard him sputter vulgar expletives directed at her.

Zoe sulked to her special room. She cried out to God before she wrote in her prayer journal.

> *Lord, I feel so alone and disappointed. Is there anyone out there who loves you like I do? I'm sure in your time you'll bring the right guy into my life, if you have someone in mind for me. Help me to be patient.*

Then she wrote:

> *Thank you for providing food for me this evening through this dinner date. Please help Brandon to get to know you someday. You are awesome and I love you! In Jesus' name I pray. Amen.*

"Hi, Dorothy," Zoe said Monday morning.

Dorothy ignored her as she walked down the hallway with another teacher.

"She's another one of those snobs who works here," she overheard Dorothy say.

Zoe asked for God's strength to persevere as she collected herself.

"How did your date go?" Resa asked.

"Terrible."

"Here, maybe my catfish sandwich and coleslaw will cheer you up."

"You don't have to say I told you so because I will," Zoe said. She sank her teeth into the sandwich. "This is delicious. Anyway, you were right. Just because my date went to church doesn't mean he loves the Lord. And now Dorothy won't speak to me. Why can't I seem to relate to other Christians?"

"You're a rare gem. There aren't many people who are as serious about their relationship with the Lord like you are. You're special, because you don't compromise. I admire you for that. Most people can't, I should say *won't*, live up to that level of obedience. I did some terrible things before I was saved."

"Like what?"

"For one, I slept with my boyfriend before he became my husband."

"That's why it's so hard. Guys expect you to do that on dates nowadays and I refuse."

"Of course it is. Don't feel like you're alone though. You always have the Lord. You have a friend in me too."

"Thank you."

"No problem." She gave Zoe a hug.

"Thank you for the sandwich too. You're a good cook."

"So is my husband." Resa smiled and gave her a wink. "There's plenty more where that came from."

Chapter 7

The Wide Road to Destruction

"Enter ye in at the strait gate: for wide is the gate, and broad is the way, that leadeth to destruction, and many there be which go in there at:."

Matthew 7:13

"And likewise also the men, leaving the natural use of the woman, burned in their lust one toward another; men with men working that which is unseemly, and receiving in themselves that recompense of their error which was meet."

Romans 1:27

"Craig, my sister Gina likes you," a voice whispered.

The voice came from a boy named Ritchie Matthews whose locker was next to his.

"Oh, really," His cheeks felt flush.

"Yeah, she thinks you're hot."

"Umm...I'm really not interested," Craig said.

"Why not? My sister is gorgeous! What's wrong with you? Are you gay or something?"

A boy named Ian Rivera snickered.

"Boys line up to ask her out," Ritchie said.

"That's nice," Craig said with a quiver in his voice. "I have to get to class."

"Look, nobody turns my sister down. You must be one of those freaks! Hey everybody, Craig is a freak!" Ritchie said. "He turned down *my* sister for a date."

"Really?" Some of the guys said. They raised their eyebrows.

"I'll date her. Ask her if she'll go out with me," a boy named Jeremy Wendell said.

"I'll see," he answered before he slammed Craig's head into his locker. "Weirdo! Nobody turns my sister down unless something's wrong with them!"

Craig tried to walk away, but Jeremy tripped him. Both boys laughed. He scrambled to his feet. Tears welled up in his eyes as he picked up his books.

"Aww, look, he's going to cry," Jeremy said.

"Forget him," said Ritchie. "I'll see if my sister will date you. She'll show you a good time. C'mon, let's go."

Craig swaggered out of school that Friday afternoon, anxious for the weekend. Despite the ridicule and abuse he endured from his peers he anticipated consummating his one year relationship with his lover. He intended to reveal the truth about his obscure romance as he celebrated his eighteenth birthday with his family.

He spotted a BMW. A man with dark, wavy hair who was in his early thirties sat behind the wheel. A pair of designer glasses and a pristinely trimmed van dyke decorated the man's face. He motioned for Craig to come. Craig raced over to the driver's side and looked around before he gave his special friend a kiss. Then he pranced over to the passenger side. Though he toiled over the right words to break the news of this anomaly to his family, he considered the obscurity to be a greater emotional burden.

"How was your day?" the mysterious man asked. His name was Evan Devareaux.

"It could have been better. Kids kept picking on me about our relationship. I told a few so-called friends who practically told the whole school. Then some boy tried to get me to date his sister as a joke. My day just got better, though. I'm kinda nervous and excited about tonight."

"That's good, I'm excited too. I thought people would be more accepting of this by now."

"Most of them are. My friends think our age difference is weird. They keep calling you my dad. They say stuff like, 'Is your dad coming to pick you up today?'"

Evan chuckled.

"Age is just a number. I love you, Craig. That's all that matters. I can't wait to show you tonight."

The scent of garlic bread and lasagna overwhelmed Craig when he entered his home.

"It smells like my mother made my favorite meal," he said with a smile. He led Evan into the dining room.

"The birthday boy, or should I say, man is here!" Brenna announced.

"Happy birthday!" everyone shouted.

They all rushed to their chairs including Chad who managed to show up for the occasion.

"Thank you for making my favorite meal, Mom."

"Uh-mmm," Brenna said, clearing her throat. "I had the meal catered."

"Oh."

"Your mother cook? That'll be the day."

"I used to cook all the time when everyone was at home together, or have you forgotten? Charlotte is always out with some guy. Craig says he isn't hungry most of the time. CJ lives in his room, and you haven't been home regularly in years for it to matter."

"Excuses, excuses, we're all here now," Chad said. "When was the last time you cooked?"

"When was the last time you were home to know?" She answered as she took the lasagna from the oven and began to cut it.

"Can you two please give it a rest?" CJ asked.

"He's just trying to ruin a happy occasion as usual," Brenna said.

"It won't be me who ruins it," Chad answered.

"What's that supposed to mean?" Brenna stopped putting the food on plates to glare at him.

"Who's this guy with you?" Charlotte asked. She eyed Evan as if she wanted to eat him.

"He's my friend," Craig said.

"He's handsome. Does your friend have a name?"

"My name is Evan."

"Evan, that's my sister Charlotte."

"What do you do for a living, Evan?" Chad asked.

"Quit badgering him!" Brenna said.

"It's okay, Mrs. Staithe. I work at a bank," he answered.

"Now there's a man after my own heart," Chad said. "Where did you two meet? You seem too old to be hanging around my son."

"We met online," Evan said.

Charlotte looked at CJ with a wry smile as she snickered. CJ coughed and leered back at her.

Chad's mouth dropped open. "Son, you're not..."

"Gay," Craig finished. "I'm gay, and Evan is my lover. We've been together for about a year now."

Brenna gasped. Silence pierced the room like a knife for the next few minutes.

Craig turned red and put his head down.

"It's okay, son. It's accepted now more than it used to be," his dad said.

Brenna mumbled under her breath as she trudged to the kitchen to bring out the birthday cake.

"What did you say?" Chad said.

"I'm okay with it, but it's all your fault," she said.

"What do you mean *my fault*?"

"Everyone knows a boy needs his father's love, acceptance, and guidance. You have *never* spent quality time with him let alone the rest of them," Brenna continued. "I dare not mention what you did to him."

"You better watch how you talk to me!"

Craig's head snapped up. "Would you both just stop it? It's neither one of your faults. This is just the way I am," Craig said.

His words mitigated the hostility for the moment just enough for everyone to sing a labored version of "Happy Birthday". Then they grabbed a piece of cake and went their separate ways to their rooms. Craig noticed a text from Aunt Zoe, as he munched on his cake. He didn't want to text her back. He called her instead, but there was no answer.

He and Evan snuck away to the guest house after they finished their cake. As soon as he opened the door, he pinched his nose. The stale air smacked him in the face. It reeked of rotten food and a faint scent of skunk. He and Evan cringed as they stepped over used condoms and dirty clothes on their way to the couch. Half-eaten food speckled with mold plastered the table.

"Would you like a drink, Craig? I brought some wine and a movie."

"I never drank before." He looked like a lost puppy.

"It's okay. You're with me."

"I just don't know if I'll like it."

"You will. It tastes smooth," Evan said and smiled.

"All right, just a little."

"Good. Do you have any glasses?"

"Let me check."

He found some glasses with lipstick stains and grease marks. Some still had liquid in them. He picked one up and smelled it. He drew back from the stench. He washed and dried them.

Craig called his aunt again as Evan went to the bathroom. "Hi, Aunt Zoe. Thank you for the text."

"Hi. Happy eighteenth birthday! Did you celebrate?"

"Sort of."

"Sort of?"

"Mom and Dad did more fighting than celebrating."

"I wish I could do more than text you, but your mother wouldn't let me."

"Thank you for being here for me."

"Of course. How are you holding up?"

"I'm okay. I still struggle with girls and stuff. You remember what I talked to you about. Kids pick on me because of it."

"Struggling is good. If you didn't struggle, you would give in."

"I guess so. But it's hard."

"A Christian's life is hard. We're constantly under attack by the world. The devil puts thoughts and emotions in our heads to try to destroy us and to steal our joy and sometimes the people in our lives push us away."

"Yeah, like my mom. Why does she hate you anyway?"

"All of us sisters grew up knowing God. Your mother drifted away, and she hates that I didn't. In fact, she hates any mention of Jesus and the Bible."

"I noticed. She yelled at me for asking her if I could live with you."

"You're eighteen now. You can live anywhere you want."

"I'm scared to live by myself, Aunt Zoe. I never had a job either. Can I live with you?"

"I'm sorry, Craig, if I gave you the impression that you could live with me. My place is too small. I invited you to stay for a while in the summer, that's all. You would have had to sleep on the couch all the while. That wouldn't be very comfortable."

"I could live with you until I find a job and save up enough money."

"That could take a while. Let me pray about it. Better yet, we should pray together."

"Okay."

"Dear heavenly Father, you are bigger than any struggles that we face in life. Please lift the burden of temptation, guilt, and depression from Craig's spirit. Help him to continue to look to you and your word for answers and for strength. If it is your will, please allow him to get a job and move away from home. Please give me the wisdom as to how I can help him. In Jesus' name I pray. Amen."

"Thank you, Aunt Zoe."

"I'll keep in touch. We can face time. I'll let you know what God leads me to do. In the meantime, you can call me anytime to let me know what's going on and when you need someone to pray with, okay?"

"Okay. I love you."

"I love you too, sweetie."

"I gotta go," he said as Evan came back into the room.

"Bye bye."

"Who was that?" Evan asked.

"My aunt." Craig looked up at Evan. "Hey, I'm not so sure this is a good idea."

"What do you mean? We've been waiting a long time for this. Don't back out now."

"I'm just not sure this is what I want."

"You'll be fine. I'll take good care of you."

Evan put a movie in the VCR.

"What are we watching?" Craig asked.

"You'll see. It's just a little something to set the mood."

"Is that a man dressed like a woman?"

"Yes it is," Evan said as he poured the wine. He handed one glass to Craig and raised his glass up for a toast. They clanged their glasses together before they took a sip. Evan placed his hand behind Craig's neck and pulled him towards him to kiss him.

Craig hesitated.

"Come sit closer," Evan said as he patted the couch.

They sat down and watched the movie while they caressed each other. Craig felt a wave of emotions come over him. Though he felt euphoria, he wasn't sure whether the source was from being with Evan or from the wine. Confusion surfaced like an ocean wave crashing in his face. All he could keep his mind on was Zoe and their conversation. He thought about the book she gave him. He blinked and shook his head.

"Is something wrong?" Evan asked.

"No...I guess not." He drank more wine to numb his inhibitions.

He and Evan lay asleep entwined in each others' arms after a night of passion. Guilt came over Craig. He tossed and turned. Suddenly Evan's cell phone vibrated. He sat up. Evan remained asleep, so he reached over to turn the phone off, but not before he noticed a text message which read: "*Hey, Evan. This is Steve. I'm back in town. I can't wait to see you. I look forward to our time together. I love you.*"

Craig's heart sank. He was too despondent to sleep, so he sat up and lay motionless for the rest of the night.

Though the sun shone through the window the next morning, he felt dark inside. He woke Evan up after wondering what he should say. "I thought you loved me," he finally said.

"What?" Evan asked half asleep.

"I thought you *loved* me," Craig repeated. "I loved you."

"I do. What's this all about?"

"Who is Steve?"

"What? How do you know about him? Have you been spying on me?"

"Last night your phone vibrated, and the noise woke me up. I turned it off because I didn't want to wake you. I read a text from some guy named Steve." He choked up. His throat felt dry, his eyes bloodshot with dark circles under them.

"What did you go and do that for? That's none of your business."

"Who is he, Evan?"

"I have a business on the side. He's one of my clients."

"Since when does a client tell you he loves you? Tell me the truth."

"All right! He's a lover of mine."

"I trusted you. How could you do this to me?" Craig's voice quivered.

"What do you want me to say? I didn't want you to find out like this, but that's how it is. It's something you get used to."

"I loved you."

"Craig, you're making more of this than there is. Don't be so serious. I care about you more than the others."

"Others?!" he said between sobs. "There are more guys than Steve?"

"Sure. I can fix you up with some of them."

"I don't want any of them. I wanted you, and I wanted to be the only one for you. I thought I could trust you. I mean, I told you things...stuff I never told anyone else but my aunt. You talked me into this just to leave me. All of this is so overwhelming."

"I'm sorry, Craig. I love you, but I love other men too."

"How could you do this to me? Can you just leave?" He started sobbing.

"You ruined a good thing, Craig," Evan said as he snatched his belongings.

"Good for whom? Why do I feel so confused then?"

Evan slammed the door behind him.

Craig had brought a diary from Aunt Zoe with him. He wrote a prayer asking for the Lord's forgiveness. However, the previous night was Craig's last birthday celebration, and that morning was the last time he saw Evan or anyone else.

That Saturday evening Charlotte planned a "private party" in the guest house with one of her companions. She noticed a peculiar silhouette hanging from the chandelier which could be seen through the partitioned panes of glass. She opened the door. She gasped and screamed and slammed it shut. She ran to the house in a state of panic and left her friend trailing behind.

"Charlotte, wait up! What's going on?" he yelled as he tried to keep up.

"Mom, Dad, CJ...it's Craig!" She cried.

"What's going on?" Brenna asked with swollen lips as she turned away from the dishes.

"It's Craig...It's Craig..."

"What about him?"

"He's *dead!*"

One of the dishes slipped from her hands and crashed to the floor.

"What?"

"He's hanging from the chandelier in the guest house."

"*Dead?* No! He can't be!"

"If that friend of his did it, I'll kill him," Chad shouted as he ran to the guest house. They all followed him.

"Oh my God!" Chad yelled. "Call 911!"

Brenna yowled and let out an ear-piercing screech when she reached the guest house. "My son! My baby!" she screamed when she saw Craig hanging like a piece of fruit from a tree. "How could you do this to me?" She wailed as her body froze. She felt her head spin. Then she fell to the ground.

"My little brother. I can't believe it," CJ said.

The Staithes stood paralyzed by the scene from a horror movie. Charlotte clung on to her playmate and whimpered like a little kid. Chad looked pale and frozen as if he had just seen a ghost. Brenna and CJ stood motionless as sirens lit up the night.

Two men put Craig in a body bag and carried him away.

Chapter 8

Preacher or False Prophet

"Beware of false prophets, which come to you in sheep's clothing, but inwardly they are ravening wolves. Ye shall know them by their fruits...?"

Matthew 7:15-16a

Sophia lifted her head from her tear-stained pillow as she sat up in bed. Had she been dreaming? As her mind cleared she realized the tragedy was real. Her nephew was dead. The thought kept haunting her.

"Let's go, honey," Dave said. "We have to get to church."

"I don't feel like going today."

"C'mon. It'll cheer you up and get your mind off what happened. Besides, don't you want to find out more about the cruise?"

"Oh yeah, that."

The cruise seemed like a trivial endeavor to Sophia. Everything seemed meaningless. She managed to get dressed and drag herself to church.

Though they arrived late, Dave anticipated hearing more about their excursion. Reverend Whitaker was preaching his usual mantra.

"*God wants you to give from your first fruits, because you will know them by their fruits he says in his word. That means you can tell a true believer by how much he gives. Can I get an 'amen'? How many of you are believers today? I challenge you to prove it this morning by what you give. The Lord says your vats will be filled when you give. You can't out give God. I want you to repeat that with me. You can't out give God.*"

"You can't out give God!" Dave said as he and Sophia sat down.

The reverend's words renewed Sophia with vigor. His delivery mesmerized her and helped her forget about her grief.

"Reverend Whitaker!" Dave bellowed after the service.

The reverend looked at the two of them with a pretentious smile. He had a certain mystique about him like a magician. His effervescence masked a hidden truth.

"What can I do for you?" he asked.

"I'm Dave Altimoone, and this is my wife Sophia."

"Oh-h-h. I was meaning to talk with you. Step into my office."

They followed him down a dark hallway which led to the back of the church. He guided them to a room that was elaborately furnished with a cherry wood desk and plush matching chairs.

A portentous aura permeated the office which was dimly lit with candles everywhere like an impending séance. A lenticular picture hung over a cluster of candles as if it was a kind of idol. It looked like a landscape from one angle. Another angle revealed a man's face which had a menacing stare to anyone who dared to look at it.

"Have a seat."

As they sat down Dave asked him to tell them more about the cruise.

"That's what I'd like to talk to you about."

The reverend opened a file cabinet and pulled out a manila folder with their name on it.

"My records indicate you two have been quite charitable with your giving."

"Yes, reverend, we have," Dave replied.

"We thought that would increase our blessings," Sophia said.

"Very good. I see you've been listening to my sermons. That shows you have great faith."

"Yes. Thank you," Dave said.

"I heard you wanted to go on my cruise."

"Yes we do," Sophia said, beaming.

"I want you to attend."

"We want to, but we can't afford it," Dave said.

Sophia looked at him puzzled. "Yes, but we're saving..."

"You don't have to worry about paying for the trip."

Their mouths dropped open.

"Seriously?" Dave asked.

"Reverend, you just made my day," Sophia answered.

"Don't go around telling everyone. I don't want them to think this trip is free for everyone."

"Okay, we won't," Sophia said, "but why are you offering us a free trip?"

"As I mentioned before, you give a lot to my church. This is a private cruise for special members only. We'll be taking my personal ocean liner."

"You have your own cruise ship?" Dave asked.

"Yes I do. The Lord has been real good to me." He showed a wry smile.

"That's impressive. Is that what the Lord gave you for tithing?" Sophia said.

He cleared his throat. "Something like that. You just keep giving like you do, and the Lord will bless you too," he said. He looked away with a smirk on his face.

"We will," Dave replied.

"There's one catch. Since you have such great faith, I would like the two of you to do something special."

"What?" Dave asked.

"You might think this is silly, but I want you to take the Water Walk."

"Water walk?" Dave said.

"What's that?" Sophia asked with feigned ignorance.

"It's an activity in which I have some members demonstrate their leap of faith to everyone else on the ship just like Jesus when he walked on water."

"We would be honored," Dave said.

Sophia thought about what Rita told her. Fear came over her. Her concern quickly faded and was replaced with excitement when she thought about how unreliable Rita is. *What a once-in-a-lifetime experience this trip would be,* she thought.

"All right. Now I have some business deals to tend to," he said abruptly.

This offer amazed Dave so much that he overlooked the reverend's eyes. He glared at them with eyes that looked like flames as if they could pierce their souls. The reverend's cold and clammy hand also went unnoticed as Dave shook it.

Sophia and Dave decided to splurge on their meager incomes by going out for brunch to celebrate.

"I'm so happy about Reverend Whitaker's offer. We've been saving up like crazy, and we still haven't saved enough even with my job, and your second one."

"I know. We've even given up our vices," Dave said.

"Now that we don't have to save for the trip we could use the extra money to make a living."

"We should buy new clothes with the extra money."

"But we need to get caught up on our bills," she said.

"Don't worry about it, hon. It'll all work out."

"We can use some of the money to buy swimsuits for our Water Walk I guess," Sophia said.

"You're right. We've lost some weight by cutting back, so we should look like models by then." He chuckled. "This has turned out to be quite a diet plan." They both laughed.

"Do you think Rita was right when she warned us about that water walk?" Sophia asked.

"Nah. I think she was just disgruntled about something in the church. Besides, she's the biggest gossip there. Everything that comes out of her mouth is exaggerated. Maybe the deacon didn't give her enough lovin'," he said as he chuckled again.

"Cut it out," she said as she chuckled. "You can be so silly sometimes."

"Seriously though, the reverend wouldn't do anything like that. He's a man of God," Dave said. "You know what?"

"What?"

"I bet we aren't saving as much because we keep giving more than we used to. I think the Bible only asks for ten percent. Let's say we only give the minimum instead of twenty percent. We could put the other ten percent into our savings."

"I don't know. I don't want to miss out on our blessings. Remember what Reverend Whitaker said..."

"You can't out give God," they both said in stereo as they smiled and gazed into each other's eyes.

An angry couple distracted them by complaining and yelling at a waiter. They demanded to speak to the manager who relented to their discontent by offering them a free meal.

"That's the oldest trick in the book," Dave said.

"I hope they were pulling a fast one, because I heard the food here was delicious. I don't want to be disappointed. We're practically spending our life savings to eat here."

"They were. Look at their plates. They ate quite a bit for people who didn't like what they had. Besides, my friends and I pulled this trick when we were in college."

"I see," Sophia said as she looked over at their table and shook her head.

Sophia and Dave ate like royalty. They both ordered the fancy brunch with mimosa and choice desserts.

"This meal should hold us for the day. That way I don't have to cook," Sophia said with a grin.

"I feel like this is our last meal before our execution," Dave said.

"Why do you say that?"

"You know how people on death row get a fancy meal before they're executed."

"That's morbid, Dave. You have a sick mind," she said rolling her eyes.

"Well it's true," he said as he chuckled. "How often do we get to eat like this?"

"It's our first time."

"Well, it could be our last. You never know."

"We might have more opportunities like this in the future when our money starts coming in."

"That's true, I guess. Maybe the food on the cruise will be this tasty too."

"That's what I like to hear," Sophia said.

"How's this: this food is fit for a king."

"And queen," Sophia said and smiled.

"Here's to you, your highness."

"And to you, your majesty."

They held their glasses of mimosa in the air and clanged them together before they took a sip. Then they smiled at each other and reached across the table. They pecked each other on the lips.

They paid for their meals with their credit card which was already near the limit. However, their concerns dissipated as they enjoyed each other's company. They felt excited about the trip, and the food tasted even better than they had anticipated.

Chapter 9

A Labor of Love

"Therefore, my beloved brethren, be ye steadfast, unmovable, always abounding in the work of the Lord, forasmuch as ye know that your labor is not in vain in the Lord."

1 Corinthians 15:58.

The news about Craig kept Zoe up all night.

That Sunday morning she went into her prayer room to read scripture and prayed before she had gotten dressed for church.

"Why? Why, Lord, did he do it? I told him about Jesus, and he came to church with me a few times. How could he be so selfish?" She cried out.

She felt sick to her stomach. Then she recalled a sermon that Pastor Thomas had preached as if God was speaking to her. He had spoken about faith being a spiritual gift. She paged through the Bible until she found 1 Corinthians 12:9.

Her commentary explained that all believers have saving faith. She understood that to mean everyday faith is a spiritual gift. She had gotten choked up as tears blurred her vision. "Maybe Craig lacked everyday faith, not faith in Jesus," she told herself.

She opened her prayer journal and wrote:

Dear heavenly Father,

Please give our family comfort over my nephew's death. Please especially give my sister Brenna and her family extra strength during this time. Let this tragedy bring her to you.

Thank you, Holy Spirit, for giving me saving faith and everyday faith. Thank you also for comforting me through your word. In Jesus' name I pray. Amen.

All of the kids raced to Zoe's car as she drove up, except Marvin.

"Hurry up, Marvin. I have to get to church for choir rehearsal. I'm already running late."

"You sing in a chair?" asked Little John-John.

"*Choir.* I sing in the church choir."

Marvin sulked and dragged his feet.

"What's wrong with you? Why are you so pouty this morning?"

"He doesn't want to come," Tamika said.

"Then why are you coming? I'm not forcing anyone."

"Our mama is makin' him," Phillip said.

"I wanna come," Little John-John said grinning.

"I can speak for myself," Marvin said.

"Whatever you decide, please do it quickly, because I have to get to church."

"Move over!" Marvin said to Phillip. He slammed himself down in the back seat.

"Hey! You're in a disrespect-free zone when you're in my car. Ditch the attitude."

He tisked and rolled his eyes. "Whatever," he said under his breath.

"Stop tisking. That's a sign of disrespect, and I told you I don't allow any disrespect in my car. This is my space, and you're mistreating people in it. That's unacceptable."

"I don't care," he said.

"Oooh! He said he don't care," Tamika said.

Zoe glared into the rear view mirror. She tried to lock eyes with him, but he looked out the car window.

Zoe sang to the music. Tears streamed down her face as she listened to a song that reminded her of her nephew. Then she smiled as the words eased her tension and gave her comfort as if God was speaking in her ear.

Zoe thought she had botched her solo. Her voice trembled as she sang. During some parts of the song the words wouldn't come out.

After the service many members of the congregation approached her. An elderly lady hobbled over to her, "You have a gift, young lady. Your singing touched my heart," she said with watery eyes. "I could see the Holy Spirit working through you."

Zoe smiled as tears watered her eyes.

One lady especially made her feel as if the Lord was using her. She had been a member of the church for decades. Zoe remembered that fateful period in Mrs. Baldwin's life when she became wheelchair-bound. Her leg needed to be amputated due to complications from diabetes.

"Great job singing this morning, Zoe," Pastor Thomas said. "You have quite a gift for the Lord. Your voice is like an angel."

She looked up at him and squeaked out a 'thank you'.

"Is something wrong?" he asked.

"Last night I found out my nephew took his life."

"I'm sorry to hear that. Did he know the Lord?"

"I'm not sure. I brought him to church a few times, and I told him about Jesus. His mother doesn't go to church, and she openly denounces Jesus."

"Hmm. That's too bad. What a tough situation. Do you have a minute?"

"Sure. Kids, you can go get some snacks in the fellowship hall. I'll be only a few minutes...Walk!" she said as they raced to the line.

"Let's pray about this. What was his name?"

"Craig."

"Didn't I meet him?"

"Yes."

"He seemed like a nice kid. Let's pray. Father God, we come before you on behalf of your dear child Zoe and her family. Please comfort her during this time of loss, and please help bring the family closer together in their time of sorrow. Give her the opportunity to comfort her family. Give her the right words to say when she lifts them up to you and consoles them. Help them to see Jesus in her, and help them realize the peace she has in you. Please use her to bring her sister to faith in you. In Jesus' name we pray. Amen."

"Thank you, Pastor," Zoe said as she hugged him.

"Anytime. Have a great week in the Lord."

"Thank you. You too."

"I'm widing sha gun!" Little John-John shouted. He trailed as the kids raced towards Zoe's car.

He gazed at Zoe with a twinkle in his eye while she drove.

"What are you looking at?" She asked as she smiled.

"Thank you for bwinging us."

"Did you enjoy Sunday school?"

"Yep!" He said as he continued to gleam at her.

Zoe's heart felt light.

As she arrived at their house she parked her car.

"Hold on, Marvin," she said. "I want to give you this."

She took out a pen and some paper and started writing.

"What's this?" He asked as he studied it.

"It's my phone number. Your mother already has it, but I want you to have it too. If you want to talk or you need me for anything just call me. I'm here for you."

"I won't need it," he said. He crumpled it up, but he put it in his pocket.

"You kids have a great day!" she yelled. "I love you!"

"Goodbye, Miss T," Tamika said.

"Bye!" Phillip said as he scurried away.

"I wuv you too!" Little John-John said. He hobbled back to her car and gave her a big hug. His eyes twinkled as he looked at her before he let go. She watched him and smiled as he limped away.

Marvin walked away without saying a word.

As soon as Zoe returned to her apartment she went into her special room. She wrote in her prayer journal:

> *Dear Heavenly Father, thank you for allowing me to edify worship today and inspire others as I sang praises to you.*
>
> *Thank you for giving me the opportunity to bring your little ones to church.*
>
> *I sincerely thank you for touching Little John-John's heart. I pray that Tamika and Phillip are getting to know who you are too. Please soften Marvin's heart with your Spirit. In Jesus' name I pray. Amen.*

After she left her prayer room she called her sister Onia.

"Where were you today?"

"I didn't feel like coming."

"Why not? I missed seeing you."

"My family is not in a good place right now."

"I know Ryan lost his job, but growing closer to God is especially important during hard times."

"I'm still in shock about what happened to Craig. I can't believe he committed suicide."

"I know. We're all sad about him. Has Ryan found a job yet?"

"No. I don't know what we're going to do!"

"Let's pray about it like we used to."

"That's not going to work. Nothing ever happens."

"Onia, you have to wait on the Lord's timing. His answers don't usually come overnight. Pray and surrender. In the world's terms, 'let go, and let God'."

"That's hard to do. I can't get a job to help out. No one's going to hire me. I have no job skills. I barely got my diploma."

"Matthew chapter six tells us to put God first. God also tells us not to worry."

"I don't need you to preach to me right now."

"Okay...Okay. Let's pray anyway."

"Oh, all right."

"Dear Heavenly Father, we humbly come before you on behalf of my sister Onia and her family. Dear Lord, you are Jehovah Jireh, our ultimate provider, and we trust you to continue to care for this family as you have promised. Please give my sister the faith to believe in your promises. In Jesus' name we pray. Amen."

"I hope it works."

"Trust in the Lord, Onia."

"You're preaching again. I have to go. Goodbye."

"Bye, Sis."

Zoe smiled as she set her cell phone down. She fixed herself lunch. Later that evening she wrote a prayer of thanks to God for using her to help her sister.

Chapter 10

Familial Woes

"Husbands, love your wives, and be not bitter against them."

Colossians 3:19

"This know also, that in the last days perilous times shall come. For men shall be lovers of their own selves, covetous, boasters, proud, blasphemers, disobedient to parents, unthankful, unholy, without natural affection, trucebreakers, false accusers, incontinent, fierce, despisers of those that are good, traitors, heady, high-minded, lovers of pleasures more than lovers of God;having a form of godliness, but denying the power thereof: from such turn away."

2 Timothy 3:1-5

Time had passed, and Ryan continued to mope around the house in his pajamas. He searched online for numerous jobs to no avail. With Onia's inability to find someone to hire her, their savings were nearly depleted. She rummaged through her purse to see what money she had.

"Ryan, I have to get some groceries. I asked Zoe if she could help us out." She pared down her shopping list when she saw how little she had left in food stamps.

"How dare you! I'm the provider in this household. What we have is just going to have to do until I find a job!" he said.

"Mom, can we go shopping with you?" Amber asked.

"Sure. But don't beg for things you want, because we don't have much money."

"Don't deprive the kids on account of me," Ryan said.

"I can't give them what we don't have."

"Sure, rub it in! I'm going back to bed."

"During the middle of the day? You just woke up."

"Don't nag me!"

"Can I come too, Mom?" Rachel asked.

"What's gotten into you? The last time you went grocery shopping with me you were...maybe nine."

"It's better than staying here with 'Grouchy Gus'."

"That's no way to talk about your dad. Show a little understanding. She put her hands on Rachel's shoulders and looked her in the eyes. He's going through a tough time right now. We need to be supportive."

"I don't have to be around him to be supportive, do I?"

"The same goes for me. Can I come?" Nathan said. "I'd rather be around Rachel than him."

Rachel licked out her tongue.

"Oh, all right. All of you get in the car."

"Thanks, Mom," they answered.

"Mom, when you were younger did kids talk back to their teacher?" Nathan asked.

"We didn't dare."

"So you basically did what you were told out of fear," Rachel responded.

"That was part of it. However, values were more important back then. We respected our elders. Most people cared about doing the right thing."

"That's weird. Kids don't care about that nowadays," said Rachel.

"They use cuss words too," Nathan added.

"I saw a boy and a girl having sex in the girls' locker room. The worst part about it was the teacher didn't do anything when I told her. She just shrugged her shoulders," Rachel said.

Onia shook her head and cringed as she drove on.

When they had arrived at the grocery store Amber asked if she could ride in the cart.

"I wanna ride too!" Aaron said.

"You both can't fit in there," Rachel said.

"I asked *first*!" Amber shouted.

"Well, now that you've announced it to everyone in the store, Aaron can ride in it," Onia said.

"That's not fair," Amber said and stuck out her bottom lip.

"Your lip is going to get stuck like that," Nathan teased.

"Shut up!" she shouted.

"Look, both of you stop right now, or I'll take you back home!"

Onia decided to get some nuts as a treat for Ryan. A man was sampling the bulk food items as if he paid for them.

"You should try this nut. It's delicious," he said to Onia. He helped himself to a handful of honey flavored cashews.

"No thank you," Onia said. She turned away and sighed.

"Mom, are we supposed to eat the food we haven't paid for?" Nathan asked.

"No," she answered and shook her head. "Those nuts aren't cheap either."

She decided to shop in another aisle while the self-indulgent man continued to pilfer. She heard a shrill scream, so she hurried to avoid the direction from where it was coming. Unfortunately, it met her in the aisle she rushed to as she witnessed a girl swatting at a woman and screaming.

"No! I don't wanna! You can't make me!"

"Jessica, put that down! You can't have that!"

"Yes I can! Stop yelling at me! I want it!"

"You don't need it, and I'm not buying it."

The girl flung herself to the floor and started kicking and screaming.

"Get up, Jessica," the woman said.

"No!"

She approached the little girl to scoop her up.

"Don't touch me, or I'll have you put in jail! You're not the boss of me! You're a bad mother!" the girl shouted in a tirade.

"Get up, Jess. You're causing a scene."

"I don't care! I want it! I want it!"

"What's all the commotion?" a manager said as she minced over to the aisle.

"My daughter wants a box of cereal, but I said she can't have it."

"I'm not your daughter!" the little girl yelled.

"Ma'am, I'm going to have to ask you to leave. You're disturbing the customers."

"Jess, get up!"

"No! Not until I get my cereal!"

The mother took a box of cereal from the shelf. The girl snatched it from her and put it in the cart. Then she put her nose in the air and strutted down the aisle.

"What's this world coming to?" Rachel asked. "Was I like that when I was her age?"

"Yes, only worse."

Rachel gasped. "What?"

"I'm just kidding, sweetheart. Too many parents let their kids run the household."

"What do you mean, Mommy?" Amber asked.

"Too many kids are turning against their parents. The kids want what they want and when they want it. Too many of them react the way that little girl did, and the parents give in."

"Did you see how mad that girl got?" Rachel said.

"Yes I did. Now don't you get the idea that's how to get what you want," Onia said.

"That was embarrassing," Nathan said.

Onia continued shopping after all of the drama, but her mouth dropped open when she arrived at the checkout counter. A sign read, "You must have your identification card in order to scan your groceries." A woman ahead of her pulled out an ID card that looked unusual. It had a five-pointed star inside a circle in the right corner. Her picture was inside what looked like a goat's head. She had to show the cashier in order to pay for her groceries.

"Ma'am, do you have a chip?"

Onia pulled her card out to be ready. She thought the cashier was referring to the woman's debit card until she witnessed something that caused her heart to sink. The woman set all of her groceries down in her cart. Then she gave her hand to the cashier to have it scanned.

"Look at that, Mom," Rachel whispered. "She's scanning her groceries with her hand."

"I see." Onia looked worried.

"Wow! That's so cool!" Nathan said.

"Ma'am, are you using government assistance?" the cashier asked Onia.

"Yes," she said looking down. Her cheeks turned red.

"Let me see your ID, and give me your hand."

"What?"

"ID, please," the cashier said.

Onia pulled out her driver's license. The woman examined her hand as she took the license.

"Your license is outdated, and you don't have a chip."

"I didn't know I was supposed to have one," Onia said looking worried. "I have my debit card."

"No ID, no chip, no groceries," the cashier said rudely.

"I didn't know I needed a them," Onia repeated.

Her heart beat fast. Her mind raced with emotions as panic and embarrassment overwhelmed her. She pleaded with the cashier.

"I need food for my family. My husband lost his job, so we need assistance. Please let me buy the groceries with my card."

"I'm sorry, Ma'am. No ID, no chip, no groceries...Next!"

"We need food! Please let it go just this one time," Onia begged.

"Mommy, what's going on?" Amber asked.

"They won't let me buy our food," Onia answered. "I need to speak to the manager."

The cashier called for the manager over the intercom.

"What's going on?" The manager asked.

"She doesn't have a chip in her hand and her ID is outdated."

"Please allow me to buy the groceries. My family really needs food," Onia said as her voice quivered. Tears streamed down her face leaving tracks.

"You need a chip put into your hand in order to buy your groceries when you're on government assistance," the manager said. "That's the law."

"But...I didn't *know*," she said as she continued to beg and plead.

"I'm sorry, Ma'am. We aren't equipped to take debit cards anymore."

Onia had to leave the groceries behind as she and her kids left the store.

Onia checked to see if Ryan was still asleep when she got home. She called Zoe. "Will you please help me?" Onia cried.

"What's the matter?"

"I can't buy groceries anymore with my government money card, and the kids are starving," Onia continued.

"What? Since when did this happen?"

"I don't know. I guess I have to go to the government office on Monday to have a chip put into my hand."

"Onia, don't do it! That's how the government can control you."

Onia chuckled. "That's nonsense. You've been watching too much TV."

"You know I don't watch TV."

"I'm worried, Zoe. By the way, the cashier said everyone will need the special ID soon."

"I'm not worried. I don't understand what's going on with Christians today. We're not supposed to live in fear. We need to be prepared to stand up against what's coming with the help of the Holy Spirit."

"All I know is my family is hungry, and we need food."

"I'll go to the hot bar and pick up some prepared food for you for today. Give me a shopping list, and I'll get those items tomorrow. Just don't get that chip put in your hand. When is a good time to bring it over?"

"Can I come to your place to get it? I don't want Ryan to know."

"I don't want to be sneaky, Onia. Be open with him."

"I don't want him to get upset."

"Maybe he'll work harder at finding a job when he sees that your situation has come to this."

"I guess you're right. I'll be home all day. I have nowhere else to go."

"Okay. I'll bring some food over. Is there anything, in particular, you'd like from the hot bar?"

"Anything is fine."

"All right. I'll see you in a little bit."

"Thank you."

"Anytime. That's what family is all about, especially believers."

Zoe did everything she could think of to prevent Onia from getting that chip implant. She continued to help her family throughout the weeks, even giving Onia money.

November came, and Onia invited Zoe over for a big Thanksgiving meal.

"Sorry for being late," Zoe said. "I had to scrape my car off and drive slowly. It's slick out there, and the snow doesn't seem to show any signs of stopping."

"Sounds like a song. Did you bring some corn for popping?"

"Ha, ha!" Zoe said as she gave her sister a big hug. "Mmm, it smells good in here."

"Thank you. Take your coat off and relax. Dinner will be ready in a few minutes."

"Okay. I'll do one better and take my boots off too."

"Remember the fun times we used to have during our Thanksgiving meals?"

"I sure do. If only Mom and Dad were still with us."

"Yeah."

"How come Brenna and Sophia aren't here?"

"I didn't invite them. They wouldn't have come all the way from Atlanta anyway."

"Have you heard from Brenna since the funeral?" Zoe asked.

"No. Have you?"

"No. She's still mad at me for giving Craig a Bible. She told me she didn't want junk like that in her house. I made her even angrier when I invited Craig to stay with me over the summer."

"What you go and do that for? You're most likely blacklisted for life for that stunt."

"It seems so. I just wanted to be a positive influence and tell him about Jesus. He was depressed and felt neglected."

"You shouldn't have meddled in her family affairs."

"I see that now. Thank you for letting me know about the funeral and how he died. I probably wouldn't have found out otherwise."

"You're probably right."

"Ryan! Kids! It's time to eat!" Onia yelled.

The kids raced to the table.

"Did you wash your hands?"

"Aw man -busted," Amber said.

"I did," Nathan answered.

"I did too," Rachel said.

"Ryan, turn that football game off, and come sit down to eat!"

"All right!"

"We've got good news," Onia said as Ryan sat down at the table. "Can I tell her?"

"I'll tell her. I finally found a job as a manager in a warehouse. The pay isn't as good, but I'm just happy to be able to support my family again." He winked at Onia.

They each held hands to pray. Onia noticed a bump on Ryan's hand.

"What's this?"

"What's what?"

"This thing on your hand."

"Oh, it's nothing. It's just a chip implant. All employees are required to have one put in. It's no big deal."

Zoe's jaw dropped as she glanced at Onia.

Chapter 11

The One that Got Away

"Marriage is honourable in all, and the bed undefiled: but whoremongers and adulterers God will judge."

Hebrews 13:4

A rare snowfall occurred in Atlanta early that December. Almost three months had passed since Craig's suicide. Brenna finally gathered enough courage to clean out his bedroom. However, her efforts were met with unexpected opposition from CJ who usually remained attached to the computer in his room. He snapped out of his cyber trance when he heard her moving furniture around.

"What are you *doing*!" he yelled as he barged in.

"I'm removing the furniture. While you're in here, come help me move this dresser."

"*No*! Why can't his stuff stay here? Nobody uses this room anyway."

"What do you expect me to do? Keep this stuff in here as a shrine? I can't bear the brunt of his memory anymore."

"Why does everything have to be about you? I want something around to remember him."

"Why the sudden sentiment? You never even spent time with him. You stay in your room doing God knows what with your computer."

"What I do in my room is none of your business. He was my *brother* for Pete's sake!"

"All right!"

Brenna dropped down on the bed and sobbed, each jerk of her body emitting more tears. CJ tried to fight back his own tears with futility.

"Mom, why did he do it?" he asked between sobs.

"I don't know."

As Brenna answered him she paused. She noticed a black book on the floor. She pulled herself off the bed and picked it up. She recognized it from a few Christmases ago. She opened it and saw a note written on the inside cover. It read: *To my dear nephew, May this book give you answers to life's questions. With all my love, Zoe.*

"I remember when Aunt Zoe gave him that." CJ said. "He looked happier than I had ever seen him."

The book was unusually thick. As Brenna fingered through it she found folded pieces of paper sandwiched between the pages. She opened one of them and gazed at the most beautiful freehand drawing she had ever laid eyes on. It depicted a scene of Moses on Mt. Sinai holding the Ten Commandments over his head. Each piece of paper revealed a drawing more intricate than the one before it. *My son was an artist, and I didn't even know it*, she thought.

One of the papers Brenna opened contained a diary-like letter. It read: *No one knows the hurt I feel at what my own father did to me. I couldn't tell anyone, because he told me not to. I am so confused. Part of me wants to hate him for what he did to me. Another part of me started enjoying it because there was no feeling left in my being. I forgive him, but I know what he did was wrong even though he would never admit it. Please help me, Lord.*

I'm confused about girls. Some of them like me. I like them too, but I have a stronger desire for men. Why did this happen to me, God?

Another one was similar except it appeared to be a poem. It read:

> *No one knows the hurt I feel at how my father treated me.*
> *Lord, I need your help to forgive him like Aunt Zoe told me.*
> *Please help me to forgive him just as you want me to do.*
> *For all your son has done for me, I know that's what I should do.*

Brenna burst into tears again as if the pain from his words had jumped from the pages and pierced her heart. She felt emptiness in the pit of her stomach. She didn't know how he felt until now, but it was too late.

Later that evening Chad came home. He had been gone for three weeks this time. He kept to himself which had become his usual routine for years. The remnants of charm he once appeared to have, had since abandoned him.

His relationships with his lovers had waned since his son's suicide. His "business trips" had reduced to nothing more than getaways for solitude. Most of his time away had been spent in hotels where he had engaged in adulterous affairs. However, lately, much to the surprise of the hotel staff, he had been staying overnight unaccompanied.

Occasionally he took a more extravagant trip to an island and lay on the beach alone, contemplating the freedom he used to have before he married. He often pondered what he had done to Craig and wondered if his actions were a contributing factor to his son's demise. Chad couldn't understand why the memories he had suppressed resurfaced. Yet he missed Craig terribly.

Monday morning Brenna dragged herself to work. She was an hour late, which had occurred more often than not lately. Devon still loved her, but he was puzzled as to why she struggled. She had wealth and lived in a beautiful area.

"Brenna, we need to talk," he said as he stepped into her office.

It reeked of alcohol.

"About what?" she said as she slurred.

He cleared his throat as he built up enough courage to speak. "For starters, your office smells like a bar."

She shrugged her shoulders and looked down.

He cleared his throat again. "What I really want to talk to you about is your lateness. You've been getting to work late too often. Is there something wrong?"

She paused before she started crying.

Devon felt uncomfortable and waited in silence.

"It's just that...it's my son."

"What about him?"

"He's dead." She started bawling.

He hesitated before he asked her what happened.

"My son Craig committed suicide about three months ago."

"I'm sorry to hear that. Why didn't you tell me before? Is there anything I can do to help?"

"I don't know. We found him hanging from the chandelier fan in our guest house the day after his birthday. The other day I thought I was ready to clean his room, but the whole thing struck me in the face again as if it just happened. I found a note that he wrote." She paused to collect herself. "It expressed the pain and confusion he had been feeling for a long time."

"Listen, I know it's been months since this happened, but why don't you take some time off to get yourself together. It seems like you've been through a lot."

She felt flush. She wasn't sure if it was the alcohol or his soothing words. She never met a man who was as understanding as he was. He seemed to understand her more deeply than anyone else. She regretted that she had been lured by charm and hadn't stayed with him. "Thank you, Devon. I really appreciate everything you've done for me."

"I told you that I care about you, Brenna. I would have married you had things not turned out the way they did."

She smiled at him with hungry eyes. "I wish I had better judgment of character back then. You're such a kind person. You should be mad at me for what I did to you. Instead you gave me a job and have shown me so much love."

"What can I say? That's the kind of guy I am."

"I like that about you. I'd like to have you over for dinner sometime to pay you back."

"I'd like that."

"What do you like to eat?"

He considered the proposition and realized his acceptance might perpetuate an ominous threat to her safety. "What will your husband think if your ex came to dinner?"

"He doesn't have to be there."

"I don't want to see you with another black eye, or worse yet –*dead*."

"That's not going to happen. Most of the time he isn't at home and Bertha will take care of him."

"Who's Bertha?"

"She's my gun."

"I definitely wouldn't want to be the cause of you taking someone's life."

"I was just kidding. It shouldn't come to that."

"Let's hope not. I especially like Italian, but anything you cook would be fine."

She smiled and winked at him. "I'll surprise you."

Brenna took much needed time off, but she didn't wait too long before her dinner date. She hadn't spent more time in a grocery store since her kids were little. Then she bought one of the best brands of white wine. She had to make everything just right.

She was so anxious for Devon to arrive that she felt like a schoolgirl anticipating her first date. She spent longer time than she had in years on her appearance. She kept rearranging the kitchen table to make sure everything looked inviting. She lit a couple of tapers to set the mood.

She had bedecked herself in one of her finest dresses. It was a black mini dress that fit snugly around her figure accentuating her womanly endowments. She took a much needed trip to the beauty salon to have her hair dyed and curled. She wore makeup, this time not to hide abuse to her face.

"What's going on, Mom? What's the occasion?" Charlotte asked.

"I'm having a friend over for dinner."

"Why are you dressed so fancy for a friend?"

"This is a special 1friend. We go way back to my college years."

The doorbell rang and Brenna quickly took her apron off and stepped into the bathroom to take one last glimpse, making sure not a strand of hair was out of place.

"You sure are making a fuss over this "friend" of yours."

Charlotte stared at Devon as Brenna opened the door. "He's handsome," she whispered in Brenna's ear. "Do you want to use the guest house?"

"No. But your father doesn't have to know about this, okay?"

"I won't tell," Charlotte said as she walked away.

"Brenna, you look gorgeous," Devon said.

Her cheeks felt rosy. "Thank you," she said with a smile. "May I take your coat?"

"Sure. What a beautiful home you have."

"Thank you. I'll show you around after we eat. Come sit down."

"It looks delicious," he said. "I didn't know you could cook."

"You haven't tried it yet," she said. She chuckled.

He sank his teeth into a forkful of linguini. "Mmm." He raised his eyebrows and ogled her. "It melts in your mouth."

"Let's toast."

They lifted their glasses of wine.

"Here's to good friends," he said.

As their glasses clanged together, they locked eyes. They smiled at each other with every bite.

"I have a surprise for you," she said as she broke their gaze and stood up.

"Oh yeah?"

She brought over a homemade red velvet cake.

"You remembered my favorite dessert after all these years?"

"I sure did."

"You know what they say, right?"

"What are you talking about?"

"The way to a man's heart is through his stomach."

"Is that so?" She set a piece on a plate for him. "I haven't heard that expression in ages."

They continued to eat and reminisced about their college years.

"Let me show you around."

Brenna showed him every room in the house except for CJ's. When she had gotten to Craig's room she hesitated before she opened the door. She felt a surge of nausea in the pit of her stomach. Devon could sense something was wrong, so he put his arm around her. She felt her body tingle as she melted in his arms. Her sadness was overcome with desire for him and a sense of unbridled arousal. She tried to ignore it, but the urge was too overwhelming.

She could no longer mask her lust for him. She turned to him, wrapped her arms around his neck, and pulled him into her. He wrapped his arms around her almost instantaneously and began to caress her. He groped her breasts. He worked his hands all over her body and squeezed her buttocks as he pressed her body against his. They locked in a long, passionate kiss. They spent the rest of the night in her dead son's bedroom.

The next morning they woke up in each others' arms, staring into each others' eyes. They continued to grope and caress each other when she heard footsteps.

"Did you hear that?" she asked.

"Hear what?"

"I heard footsteps."

A door squeaked.

"Get up!"

They scurried from the covers. She took him into the bathroom where they waited to see from where the noise was coming. Then they both heard a door shut.

"You have to get out of here."

"Last night was terrific."

"I know, but you have to go!"

He gave her a big kiss and hugged her tightly before he crept back into the bedroom to put on his clothes.

She chuckled. "You know what's funny?"

"What?"

"I was going to get rid of this bed before my son CJ had gotten upset with me."

"I'm glad you didn't."

The footsteps got louder.

She hurried to put her dress on before he kissed her again. "You better get out of here."

As they snuck down the stairs to the front door, Brenna heard the refrigerator door close.

"Goodbye," he said. She opened the front door and pushed him out.

Chad came into the living room as Brenna closed the door.

"Who was that?"

"Who was who?" Brenna said smiling. She brushed her fingers through her tousled hair.

"I clearly heard a male voice. I noticed an unfamiliar car out front too. That's why I came through the back. And why are you all dressed up?"

"I was in the mood for the holidays."

"Yeah, right. Don't lie, Brenna."

"Okay. I had breakfast with an old friend. But nothing happened. I was just showing him around the house."

"Who is he, Brenna?"

"You know him."

"Who *is* he?" he asked as he grabbed her arm.

"Ouch! You remember Devon?"

"Devon. Hmm. I can't say...oh, the guy I rescued you from."

"If you say so."

"What was he doing here, Brenna?"

"I told you I invited him over for breakfast. I was hoping you would be here too, so you two could talk."

"You're lying. I have nothing to talk with him about, and you know it."

"Okay, I saw him in the grocery store months ago, so I decided to invite him over to share some holiday cheer. You notice the beautiful decorations I put up?"

"Don't try to change the subject."

"You're never around anymore. I need someone to keep me company."

"I work long hours to provide for this family, and this is the way you repay me?"

"Come now, Chad, you don't expect me to believe you're working hard for this family when you're gone for weeks at a time."

"My job keeps me busy."

"Now who needs to tell the truth? How many women do you have on the side, Chad?"

"This is not about me."

"It's about both of us. We've drifted apart for quite some time."

"What are you saying?"

"I'm saying I want a divorce."

"You're my woman."

"I don't want to be married to you anymore."

"That's too bad. You belong to me."

Brenna glared daggers at him behind his back as she walked past him. She rued the day she met him.

Chapter 12

What's for Christmas?

"Wherefore do ye spend money for that which is not bread? and your labour for that which satisfieth not?"

Isaiah 55:2a

The doorbell rang one Friday evening as Sophia expected a rare visit from her sons. She pulled herself away from the TV.

"Hi, Mom, how are you doing?" Joshua gave her a big hug. Terry kissed her.

"Fine. Happy Holidays," she said. She gave both of them a kiss.

The two were a dichotomy. Joshua was the older of the two. He was lanky with curly blonde hair and brown eyes. His brother Terry was stocky with straight dark brown hair and brown eyes. Joshua played sports, and Terry dabbled in electronics. Joshua ran through girls like water. Terry was content with an occasional date, but he required alone time.

"I've got a present to put under your tree," Joshua said.

"Oh, thank you, sweetie."

He noticed a gaudy pine tree smothered with tinsel. It looked like a silver weeping willow. "I didn't know I needed to wear my sunglasses," he said as he placed the gift under the blinking lights.

"Ha, ha, ha. Real funny. I see you haven't lost your senseless, I mean sense of humor," she said, and smiled.

"I have something for you too," Terry said.

"Thank you, honey," she said before she gave him a big squeeze.

"Here's a card from both of us," Joshua said.

"To what do I owe this honor for all the goodies?" She tore open the envelope. She felt a lump in her throat as she read the words. "Thank you so much," she said and hugged them again. "Come sit down. Are you hungry?"

"I'm always hungry," Terry said.

"Great. I cooked a feast. I'll go check on it."

They noticed a man preaching as they sat down to watch TV. They eyed each other and rolled their eyes.

"Mom still watches this stuff?" Terry said. "When will she realize this guy is fake?"

"Shh! Here she comes."

"Why do you still watch those TV preachers?" Terry said.

"Where's Dad?" Joshua asked as he elbowed his brother.

"He should be home soon. You know he works two jobs now."

"Mom, why do you still watch...?"

"Don't start anything," Joshua whispered.

"Don't start what?" Terry asked as he shrugged his shoulders.

Dave burst through the door. Everyone's heads snapped toward him. Sophia jumped up and greeted him with a kiss.

"These are for you," he said.

"White roses with mistletoe! They're beautiful!"

"There are nine of them which represent eternal love."

"Oh, I love you too, sweetheart." Sophia plucked off some mistletoe and held it over Dave's head. They embraced and locked lips.

Joshua cleared his throat.

Dave reached into his pocket and retrieved a small, gift-wrapped box. "This is for you too."

"Thank you," she said as she gleamed into his eyes. "Can I open it now?"

"Sure. You're allowed one the night before Christmas."

"Oh, honey! It's beautiful!"

"Here, let me put it on you." Dave slipped a beautiful sapphire ring surrounded by diamonds on her finger.

"This is the wedding ring you never had, and sapphire is your birthstone."

"Thank you, but we can't afford this."

"We can now. Remember we don't have to pay for our cruise."

"Cruise? Did I hear you say 'cruise'?" Joshua asked.

"Yes you did."

"When? Where?"

"Late summer," Dave said.

"It's a Bible cruise put on by Reverend Whitaker," Sophia said.

"You can't be serious," Terry said.

"Why not?" said Sophia.

"That guy is a crook."

"Hey, watch your words, Terry!" Dave said with a scowl on his face.

"Where are you getting your information? Have you been talking to your aunt?"

"Aunt Zoe means well. She was concerned." Terry said. "We just want you to be careful."

"I have to agree with Terry on this," Joshua said.

"It's gonna be fun and exciting. Since we're one of his biggest contributors he selected us to go all expenses paid," Sophia said as she stuck her nose in the air.

"He's up to something. If it sounds too good to be true, it usually is," Terry said.

"How can you judge? You don't know him," Sophia said.

"I know enough from the complaints raised about him on social media."

"Oh, there's a reliable source," Dave said as he hung up his coat.

"People call him a money barnacle."

"They shouldn't talk about people they don't know," Sophia continued.

"Actually, a lot of people who criticize him *do* know him, and Aunt Zoe knows her Bible."

"Reverend Whitaker knows the Bible and he uses it to preach. Zoe doesn't know what she's talking about. She's the one you shouldn't be listening to," Sophia said.

"You not goin' to convince him, hon," Dave said.

"Just let it go," Joshua said as he nudged Terry's arm.

Everyone devoured their meal and cherished memories of past Christmases. They renounced their tradition and decided to open all of their gifts that evening.

"Well, we should be going," Joshua said.

"Take some leftovers with you. Otherwise it'll just go to waste."

"You don't have to twist my arm," Terry said, smiling. "Everything was very tasty, Mom."

"Thank you."

"Of course you would say that. You don't have to cook," Joshua said.

"True. At least I *can* cook."

"I cook a little. I just don't like to. That's what my girlfriends are for."

"What? I didn't raise you to have archaic ideas like that."

"I'm just kidding, Mom," he said and kissed her on the cheek. "Terry's right, everything was delicious."

Sophia packed enough food to feed them for the rest of the week.

"Where is Terry's stash?" Joshua asked.

"What? This is for both of you."

"Just kidding again," Joshua said as he smiled.

"You better be," Sophia said and smacked him on the shoulder.

"Bye, Mom. Bye, Dad," Terry said.

"We love you," Joshua said.

"We love you too," said Sophia.

"Stay in touch," said Dave as he walked them to the door.

He went to the refrigerator after they left. "Did you save anything for us, hon?"

"Of course."

"Great! Thank you."

"You're welcome. Can you believe Zoe? She has some nerve. Now I see what Brenna means about her."

"What does she say?"

"Zoe keeps telling everybody that Jesus is the only way to be saved. The thing is, she thinks she knows everything. Just because she finished college and became a teacher."

"It's Christmastime, Sophia. Where is your holiday joy?"

"You're right. I need to keep my mind on fun things in life like the cruise we're going on. We have two great boys. And I just love this ring you bought me. I love it, and I love you."

"I love you too. Merry Christmas."

"Merry Christmas, dear."

Chapter 13

A Fairweather Holiday

"Rejoice evermore. Pray without ceasing. In everything give thanks: for this is the will of God in Christ Jesus concerning you."

I Thessalonians 5:16-18

Nathan and Amber lay awake waiting for midnight to open their presents. He tip-toed into her room. "Let's go downstairs."

"Okay," she whispered. She rubbed her tired eyes and forced herself from the bed.

"Get out!" Rachel said. "Our room is off limits to morons...Mom!"

Onia staggered into their bedroom half sleep. "What? What's going on?"

"Tell Nathan to leave our room! I'm trying to sleep!"

Onia turned on the light. She squinted as she glared at Nathan with blurry eyes.

"Nathan, leave this room! I'm trying to sleep too! I have Christmas dinner to cook tomorrow."

"Okay. I'm leaving."

"What are you doing in here anyway?"

"Me and Amber were going to open our presents at midnight. I came in here to get her."

"Go to bed. You'll spoil the surprise."

"But it's Christmas at midnight."

"I tell you what. I'll wake you up when I get up to start cooking."

"When?"

"Seven, now go back to bed."

"Seven? I can't wait that long."

"Well, you're just going to have to."

"Why?"

"So we can open our gifts together, family style."

"Oh, all right."

"Ooh! Look what I got! I like it! Thanks, Mom," Amber said. She hugged and kissed Onia.

"I'm glad you like it. I was worried you kids wouldn't like your presents."

"What about me?" Ryan said with his arms open.

"Oh, yeah. Thanks, Dad," she said and gave him a big hug.

"You like that little old thing? I wouldn't," Rachel said.

"What's wrong with it? I *needed* a scarf. I can wear it with my snow pants."

"You've always been easy to please." her mother said, smiling.

"What? That's all I get is a pack of socks?" Nathan said after he tore open a box. "I put video games on my list. You don't love me," he cried. He threw them on the floor. Then he stomped over to the couch and pouted.

"I wanted a new cell phone, and that's all I got was some raggedy outfit," Rachel said.

"Kids, this is all we could afford this year with your dad losing his job."

"Next Christmas will be better," Ryan said. "I promise."

"It better be, or I'm finding a new family," said Rachel.

"Is that a promise? Why wait till next year?" Nathan said.

"If you're just going to complain and bad mouth everyone, you can go upstairs to your room," Onia said.

"Yeah, go to your room, slime ball," Rachel said.

"She was talking to you, pinhead."

"That's enough. I'm tired of you two fighting with each other. Peace and quiet; that's all I want for Christmas. And furthermore, if you don't like your gifts we could always take them back."

"Good grief. How did your kids become so ungrateful?" Ryan asked.

"My kids?" she said. She sighed and shook her head as she walked into the kitchen.

"I was just kidding, hon. Merry Christmas," he said as he grabbed her around the waist. He kissed her on the neck.

"C'mon now. I have to start cooking, and I have a headache."

"That can wait. I'm feelin' kinda frisky. Let's go back upstairs."

"What's gotten into you?"

"I'm in the Christmas spirit. Let me give you a Christmas present you won't forget."

They both giggled like two school kids.

"Where are you two going?" Rachel asked as they pranced from the kitchen.

"Don't worry about it. Go eat breakfast, or try on your new outfit, or something."

"Are you two going to do what I think?"

"You got it. We're married. You're not, so don't get any ideas."

Rachel rolled her eyes and shook her head.

"First they give us dumb gifts then they starve us to death!" Nathan said as he went into the kitchen to look for something to eat.

"Yeah! Wait, I like my gift," Amber said. "You like your gift too, don't you, Aaron."

"Yep," he said as he continued to play with his toy.

"That's because you two are weirdoes," said Rachel.

"You can be so mean," Amber said.

"You can be so mean."

"Stop mocking me!"

"Make me!"

Amber started panting as she glared at Rachel. Then she bull rushed her and knocked her into the Christmas tree. It fell and ornaments crashed and shattered.

"Oww!" Aaron shrieked as blood trickled down his cheek.

Nathan spilled his milk all over the floor as he raced back into the living room.

Onia and Ryan rushed down the stairs half-dressed. Broken ornaments, drops of blood, and puddles of milk speckled the floor.

"What happened?" Ryan asked.

Onia gave Aaron a big hug and rocked him as blood trickled down his face. "It's gonna be alright. It's just a scratch, sweetie."

He whimpered in her arms as she caressed him. She ordered Rachel to bring her a warm, wet towel. Everyone gaped in disbelief at the shambles that once resembled a room.

"You're gonna be all right." Onia said as she kissed him. She dabbed the towel on his cut and gave him another kiss.

Aaron calmed down and sat on the couch. He went back to playing with his toy. He rocked back and forth still sniffling.

"Who's responsible for this?" Ryan asked.

"Your little brat," Rachel said as she pointed to Amber.

"Shut up! You're so mean! You make me sick!" Amber said as she stormed away.

"Rachel, what happened in here?" her mother asked.

"I don't know. Maybe it was something I said."

"What did you say that could get her so upset?"

"You see, what happened was I called her a name. Then she attacked me."

"You're constantly picking at the little ones. She had enough, and so have I. I'm holding you responsible for this mess."

"What? Why?"

"You're too old to be picking on six year olds. Clean this mess up."

"Why do I have to clean this by myself? She was the one who knocked me into the tree."

"You're grounded during your entire Christmas break, if I hear one more word."

"Dad."

"You heard your mother, and I agree. Not to mention you ruined a perfectly good moment I had with your mother."

Rachel started laughing as she noticed what they had on. Her dad was wearing a pair of boxers with lips all over them. Her mother was wearing a short negligee, the back of which somehow had gotten stuck in her underwear. They looked at each other and joined in. Nathan turned away to go finish the remnants of his breakfast.

"I'll help you clean this mess, and you help me cook," Onia said.

"Okay."

"Everyone should learn how to cook anyway."

"I said okay, Mom."

"You need to apologize to Amber when she calms down."

"I'll go do it right now."

"Oh no you don't. You clean up this mess first." Onia lifted up the silver tree.

"You could be nicer to your siblings."

"It's hard," Rachel said as she swept up the broken ornaments.

"Why is it so hard? They're a part of the family."

"I don't know. I try to be nice, but something comes over me and makes me pick on them."

"That sounds like an excuse. What's the real reason?"

Rachel hesitated for a few minutes. "Why did you decide to have them? Everything was fine until they came along."

"I can't believe what I'm hearing. Are you really that selfish?"

"I'm just saying everything was better when I had you to myself."

"How can you say that? I had Brett first anyway."

"Yeah, but you paid more attention to me, and I felt like daddy's little princess. Things aren't the same now."

"Of course they aren't. There are more people in this household for you to learn to love."

"I never thought of it that way."

"Well, I love you just as much as I love them."

Onia walked over and put her arm around Rachel. "You're my first girl. Maybe we can spend more time together, if you can take some time away from your friends."

"I'd like that."

"Good. We can start by tackling Christmas dinner and desserts."

"I always wanted to learn how to make your stuffing."

"All right. Let's get to it."

"Hi, Zoe. Come on in."

"Hi, Aunt ZZ," Amber said.

"Hi, sweetie!" She hugged Amber. "Something smells really good in here."

"I'll take your coat," Onia said.

"Aren't you going to hug your big sister first?"

"Of course. Merry Christmas, Sis," she said as she hugged Zoe.

"Merry Christmas, everyone! I come bearing gifts."

"What did you bring me, Aunt ZZ?"

"Close your eyes. It's a big surprise" Zoe dug through her bag and pulled out a box. "Sorry, I didn't take the time to wrap the presents. It's such a waste of paper anyway."

The box revealed a beauty kit and some dolls. "I love it! Thank you," Amber said. She hugged her aunt so tight that Zoe winced.

"This is for you, Aaron," Zoe said. She handed him a puzzle.

Zoe turned to Onia. "Is there anything I can help you with?"

"You can help me set the table."

"So how's everything?" she said as she placed cups down.

"Much better than the last time you came over, but they're still not good."

"What's going on?"

"Everything. The kids constantly fight with each other. I don't feel good half the time, and we can never stay ahead of the bills."

"Maybe you're pregnant."

"Bite your tongue! The last thing we need is another mouth to feed."

"God will provide."

"That's what you always say, but I have yet to see it," Onia said. She retrieved a chipped plate from the cabinet. "See."

"I see a plate that isn't perfect, but it's still usable just as we are in God's eyes."

"Did you go to church this morning?"

"Of course. The choir sang. The service was wonderful. You should've come."

"I had too much to do with getting ready for Christmas. It's a tradition, you know."

"All right, Martha."

"Whatever."

"What did you get me, Auntie Zoe?" Rachel asked as she barged in.

"Let me go check my bag. Nathan this is for you."

"Oh, boy! Video games! Just what I wanted. Thank you." he said as he grinned from ear to ear.

"What about me?" Rachel asked again, looking like a hungry puppy.

"Aren't you too old for presents, especially from relatives?"

"I didn't think so," she said as she looked down at the floor.

"Well, I don't think so either. I was just teasing you. Here, open it." Zoe handed her niece a box the size of an adult hand.

"It's kinda small."

"Just open it."

A loud squeal permeated the room as Rachel opened it. "Oh my God! Thank you so much!"

"You're welcome."

"I can't wait to tell my friends! This is just what I wanted. It's the latest model too."

"You can use it with the plan you already have."

"Sweet."

"Dinner is ready everybody," Onia said.

"I'm famished," said Zoe.

"Mmm! This is delicious, honey," Ryan said as he sank his teeth into the stuffing.

"Wait, honey. We didn't say grace."

"I'm starving," Ryan said.

"I helped her make the stuffing and the pie," Rachel said.

"I'm so proud of you. I can't wait for dessert to try your pie."

"Let's say grace," Onia said.

"I'll do it," Rachel said.

Everyone gawked at her.

"*What*?" Why does everybody look so surprised?"

"I didn't expect you to volunteer," her dad said.

"I'm just really happy thanks to Aunt Zoe." She looked at Zoe and smiled. "Thank you, God, for this food. Amber, I apologize for how I treated you this morning. I apologize to everybody for being so mean. And thank you, God, for the best aunt in the world. Amen."

"I'm proud of you for apologizing in front of everyone when you could have done it in private. That took courage. We all forgive you, don't we?" Ryan said.

"Yes," everyone answered.

"The students at my school could take a chapter from your book," Zoe said.

"Oh?" said Onia.

"Rachel owned her mistake. You can't really tell that I teach at a Christian school most of the time. Kids use foul language, and the disrespect is out of control. They find ways to skip class. They just don't care to learn much these days either."

"It's come to that?" Onia said.

"And then some. I had to reprimand this one kid the other day for disrespect. He gave a teacher the finger behind her back. The teacher simply told him to stop bouncing a ball in the hallway. Then I heard him say he hated her and called her a bad name."

"You're just not with the times," Rachel said.

Onia glared at her. "Excuse me?"

"Okay, I'm sorry. I'm starting again."

"I'm going to hold these kids accountable for their behavior whether they like it or not. I'm not going to keep up with the latest filth and depravity and pollute my spirit either just to relate to the kids like some teachers do."

"And you shouldn't have to, but aren't you being just a bit judgmental?"

"How?"

"Do you know what the other teachers do? Maybe they just relate to the kids better than you."

"Ouch! By the way, where's Brett?"

"He chose to spend Christmas with his girlfriend's family. He found fresh meat to bum off since we don't have anything to give him anymore."

"How are things going with the two of them?"

"Oh, I didn't tell you? They have a kid on the way."

"Are they planning on getting married?"

"Not that I know of."

"Are you okay with it? I mean, doesn't that bother you?"

"It does, but they're grown. I was around his age when I had him. As long as they can afford it, it doesn't bother me. Lola's parents make good money, and she has a good job."

"That's not how God tells us to live."

"That's true, but hardly anybody pays attention to that these days. We do have a free will."

"Yes, but God tells us everything that is allowable is not necessarily good for us."

"Must you bring up scripture all the time? You talk like a walking Bible."

"That's the only way to live."

"Sometimes you can be too zealous. Maybe I should start calling you Zoe the Zealot."

"Ha, ha, ha!"

"Are you going to Uncle Jerry's New Year's Eve party?"

"I didn't know anything about it."

"I was thinking about it. I just don't know what to do with the kids."

"I can babysit them," Rachel said.

"I don't have to go. I can watch the kids," Ryan said with a big smile on his face.

"I want you to come with me. I don't want to go alone."

"Don't you trust me?" Rachel asked. "I said I could babysit."

"I don't know. You have to prove to me that you can be trusted with your siblings without any drama."

"I promise. This will give me a chance to work on being nicer to them."

"You have this week to prove that you can handle it. One slip up and you can forget it."

"All right. You'll see."

Onia coerced Zoe to attend Uncle Jerry's party as a relative, yet uninvited guest. His place reeked of alcohol and stogie like a casino. Guests poured in as they anticipated the inauguration of the New Year.

"These hors d'oeuvres are delicious," Onia said.

"How can you taste them with this overwhelming stench? I can't believe I let you talk me into coming to this cesspool."

"Quit being so uppity and try to enjoy yourself."

Uncle Jerry staggered over. "When did you get here? You're Katherine's daughter, right?" He looked at Onia.

"Yes. I'm the youngest."

"Where are my other two beautiful nieces?" he asked as he hugged her and sat down.

"Who? Sophia and Brenna? They haven't been here since college except for an occasional visit."

Coughing, Zoe said, "Hi, Uncle Jerry." She waved her hand to fan the cigar smoke.

"Who are you?"

"I'm Zoe."

"I don't remember you. Did your parents have you locked away in a closet or something?" he said and laughed.

She ignored him and looked away.

"I remember when Katherine had you. You had a head full of beautiful blonde curly hair," he said. "You look just like her. I remember Brenna and Sophia too. They look like their dad. Where do they live?"

"Atlanta."

"Hi, I'm Maggie, your uncle's third wife. They say the third time's a charm," she said. She giggled and gazed at him. "We just recently got married."

She had big blond curly hair which draped across her head like a mop. She wore a long gown that glittered like a chandelier. It brought out her physical bulges and endowments and left nothing to the imagination. She wore heavy makeup with false eyelashes about half an inch long. She held a cocktail in one hand and a cigarette in the other. She looked young enough to pass for their sister.

Zoe, with her mouth agape, studied the woman.

"We made it quick and snappy at the courthouse. We can't stand being in a church with all of those icons and idols. It's against our religion anyway," Uncle Jerry said.

"What religion is that?" Zoe asked.

He ignored her as if she was invisible.

Maggie scoffed at Zoe as she noticed the cross necklace around her neck as if it offended her. Zoe could feel Maggie's eyes piercing her soul when their eyes met which sent a shiver down her spine.

"I'll bet she married him for his money," Zoe said when the couple meandered away.

"That could be. I wouldn't be surprised. He was overly friendly with me when we were kids. I know he likes blondes."

"What does that have to do with anything?"

"I'm saying he seems to have a weakness for young blondes. What would stop him from buying some young, blonde floozy?"

Onia and Zoe mingled with family members - some of whom they recognized, others whom they never knew existed, and ones they wished they hadn't.

Zoe held her head up despite the scorn and ridicule she encountered from most of the family besides her aunt and uncle. As she observed the crowd and listened to their godless banter, she perceived the ornament around her neck to be the culprit for being ostracized. She tagged along, hiding behind her sister's congeniality as if she was a little girl. She prayed for inner strength to withstand the barrage of emotional abuse and loneliness she felt as the party dragged on. As Onia socialized, she anticipated the final moment to bring on the New Year, so she could leave this platform for rejection and return to her respite called home.

Chapter 14

The Invitation

"And when he had opened the fourth seal, I heard the voice of the fourth beast say, Come and see. And I looked, and behold a pale horse: and his name that sat on him was Death, and Hell followed with him. And power was given unto them over the fourth part of the earth, to kill with sword, and with hunger, and with death, and with the beasts of the earth."

Revelation 6:7-8.

The New Year had commenced. Brenna and Devon had rekindled their relationship as she had hoped. Their lust for one another warranted no need to make their encounters private. They continued their escapades having disregard for potential disclosure with her children. CJ had noticed him leaving after their first morning and had interrogated her. She circumvented his interrogation with her usual deception. Chad was never around anyway and she needed to gratify her libido.

Brenna found a strange envelope in the mailbox one brisk morning after an intense night of ecstasy with Devon. It was an invitation with an unfamiliar return address. She wondered if it was a joke. She opened it anyway.

It read:

> *"You are cordially invited to a family reunion. It will be out of this world and the most memorable occasion you have ever experienced. Come join us for food, fun, and fellowship before it's too late. It will take place sometime this summer. More details are forthcoming.*
>
> *With all my love, J.C."*

"Too late? J.C.? I don't know a J.C."

She tore it up and threw it away.

"Honey, I'm home." Dave said.

"Hi, sweetie," Sophia said before she kissed him.

"I've got something for you."

"Another diamond ring?"

"Ha, ha. No. I've got mail."

"For me? That's weird. I never get mail." Sophia tore the envelope open like a child opening a Christmas present. "That's odd. It doesn't say who it's from."

"Check the return address."

She pieced the envelope back together. "Oh, here it is. It says J.C."

"That's odd, honey. Who's that?"

"I don't know," she said looking perplexed.

"What does it say?"

She read it out loud. "Before it's too late? Is this some kind of joke?"

"I dunno."

"Yes you do. You're playing a joke on me. You wrote this."

"No I didn't," he said, smiling. "Although I like the idea and wish I had thought of it."

"I wonder if Josh sent this to me as a joke."

"Maybe. Those are his initials."

Sophia texted her older son to see if he could help her reveal the mystery.

"Josh texted back. He didn't send it. I don't know who else would have."

"What about one of your sisters?"

"It doesn't make sense. Why would they leave it anonymous?"

"I'm just trying to help."

"I know. And I appreciate it. I'll give Brenna a call."

"You two don't keep in touch like you used to. It'll do you some good."

"I'm not so sure about that. We always argue when we talk."

"Why is that?"

"She always brags about all the money her husband makes when she's the saddest person on the face of the earth."

"Big Daddy's gonna come through for you soon."

"Big Daddy? Is that your new nickname? You're too funny," she said as she smacked him on the shoulder.

"Hey, Brenna. It's me, Sophia. How are ya doin'?"

"I'm doin' great. What's up?"

"I called to see if you received a strange invitation in the mail."

"Yes I did. I threw it away."

"Why? Aren't you curious about it?"

"I can't be bothered with that," she said while she fixed her eyes on the news.

"I think it's exciting."

"You would," she said as she turned up her nose. "Hey, look. Have you been watching the news?"

"No. Why?"

"There's some serious stuff going down. People are dropping dead all over the world."

"From what?"

"The doctors haven't figured it out yet. It happened so fast they got caught off guard. Some speculate it's from pollution. It's happening to animals too...Oh my God, you should see this. Body bags are everywhere in this one town. They're saying it's in the air and the water. This is scary."

"Is it happening here?"

"I don't know. I don't think so. It sounds like it's coming though. They're saying it's spreading. I noticed a film in the sky lately, especially in the morning."

"You're making me scared. That's why I don't watch the news."

"So many people are getting killed by random shootings too. Everybody is rioting and looting streets. There's lots of juicy stuff to watch."

"You have your shows, and I have mine. Anyway, about this invitation," Sophia said, "It sounds interesting. Don't you love the intrigue?"

"I lost that long time ago. Well, I take that back -not entirely," she said as she smiled at the thought of her love affair with Devon. She continued to watch the news for entertainment.

"What do you mean, 'not entirely'?"

"I've decided to take care of me lately, that's all."

"What does that look like with your grown children still living with you?"

"Don't start that again. Besides, I hardly see them. They have their own lives."

"What about Chad?"

"He's never around, but I already have a remedy for that."

"What did you do, get a dog?" Sophia said as she chuckled.

"Something like that, only better."

"Oh, okay. Are you going to keep me in suspense?"

"Yes, for now."

"Well, are you going to the reunion or not?"

"I told you I threw the invitation away."

"I would love to go. You could come with me as a guest."

"I'd rather not. What about Onia? Do you know if she's going?"

"No. I haven't called her."

"So I'm the lucky one?"

"Well we live in the same area, so I thought I'd call you first. Say, why don't we get together sometime? Start fresh for the new year."

"Um..." She sighed. "I guess we could."

"You guess? I'm your sister, and I want to amend our differences."

"When is a good time for you? I started a new job a few months ago, so I'm not as available as I used to be."

"What about this weekend?"

"I'll have to check my schedule."

"Okay. Let me know."

Brenna sighed again. "I will," she said as she fixed her eyes on the newscast.

"Goodbye, Brenna."

"Bye."

Keys jingled and the door rattled as Onia lay napping on the couch. She sat up.

A shadow appeared in the doorway.

"Ooo, you scared me," she said as Ryan approached her.

"Hi, is dinner ready?"

"I'll throw something together." She yawned. "I dozed off longer than I planned."

"Where are the kids?"

"Upstairs."

"I picked up the mail. There's something for you."

"Huh, I wonder who from."

"Here, open it and see," Ryan said. He handed her the envelope.

"J.C. I don't recall a J.C. in the family. I'm confused."

"Well, you don't have to go. It could be a hoax or a scam."

"What do you mean? Wouldn't you go with me?"

"No. Most likely I'll have to work."

"I'll call Zoe. Maybe she knows about it."

Before she could make the call her cell phone rang.

"Hello...Really? I just saw him a few weeks ago."

"Who is it?" Ryan asked.

"Shh." She held her hand up. "How did it happen?...That's too bad. When and where is it?"

She grabbed a piece of paper and a pen. Ryan looked over her shoulder as she jotted down information. "Okay. Thank you for letting me know. Goodbye."

"Didn't you just go visit him?"

"Yes. It happened so sudden."

"How did he die?"

"He had a massive heart attack."

Ryan whistled. "That's rough."

"I better call my sisters to let them know."

Zoe's cell phone rang as she was juggling groceries. She tried to unlock her apartment door. "What next?" she asked herself. She flung her groceries on the couch. "Hello?"

"Hi, Zoe. Did I catch you at a bad time?"

"No. I just got home."

"You sound out of breath."

"I had groceries in my hand. What's going on?"

"I have bad news and interesting news."

"All right, give me the bad news first."

"Uncle Jerry died."

"What? We just saw him a few weeks ago. What happened?"

"He had a massive heart attack."

"Wow! How did it happen?"

"I don't know. Maggie didn't give me all the details. Besides, she sounded a little hysterical."

"I'll bet. More like excited; now she can cash in."

"Quit being so judgmental. Anyway, the other thing I called you about is to see if you know J.C."

"Who?" Zoe smiled.

"J.C. I received an invitation to a family reunion from a J.C."

"You sure that's not related to the funeral. I think those are Uncle Jerry's initials."

"Oh. That makes sense. Wait a minute...why would it have said to RSVP?"

"I don't know. I didn't get one."

"That's strange."

"Not really. I'm always the last to know what's going on, if I find out at all."

"I was talking about the invitation. On the other hand, quit feeling sorry for yourself."

"Somebody has to. I always get left out."

"The invitation was worded kinda weird. It said something like RSVP before it's too late. What do you suppose that means?"

"I don't know." Zoe smiled again. "When did you get it?"

"Today. Maybe yours will come later today. Some mail carriers are slower on their routes than others."

"My mail usually gets delivered by now."

"Why don't you go check?"

"I'll check later. If it was from Uncle Jerry I won't get one. You saw how he treated me at his party."

"Maybe yours just didn't come yet."

"Sure. That's it." Zoe said. She chuckled.

"Maybe he didn't get around to sending everyone's out before he died."

"True. When is his funeral?"

"Next Saturday."

"That's over a week from now."

"Maggie said they wanted to give the family some time to travel from all over."

"When is the family reunion?"

"I don't know. The invitation said it'll take place sometime this summer."

"That's it? It didn't give a date?"

"Nope."

"That's really weird. Well if it's from Uncle Jerry, the poor old fart kicked the bucket before he could have it."

"Zoe, I'm surprised at you."

"What?"

"What happened to that Christian walk and talk?"

"I'm forgiven, not perfect."

"Touche'."

"Thank you for letting me know, but I have some groceries to put away and some papers that aren't going to correct themselves."

"All right. See you at church?"

"Of course. Talk to you later."

"Bye."

Chapter 15

Love Personified

"Beloved, let us love one another: for love is of God; and every one that loveth is born of God, and knoweth God."

1 John 4:7

Zoe arrived at the kids' house later than usual one cold and snowy morning. She had spoken with their mother the previous night to make arrangements for a special lunch with them. She didn't plan for blizzard-like conditions.

"How are you doing this morning?" she said smiling as they shuffled through the snow.

"You're in a good mood this morning," Marvin said.

"I'm usually in a good mood. But I'm in a better mood because I have something special planned for you after church."

Marvin rolled his eyes.

Little John-John said, "What is it?"

"It's a Valentine's Day surprise."

"Can you give us a hint?" Tamika said.

"No can do."

"Aw, man." she said.

"It's probably something stupid." Marvin said.

"Whether you think it's stupid or not you still have to wait until after church."

"Whatever."

"Hi, Onia."

"Hi, Sis."

"Where's the rest of your family?"

"They went to St. Mattress with Pastor Pillow today."

"Huh? Oh, I get it." Zoe said. She laughed. "I guess a lot of people didn't show up today because of the weather. The attendance sure was pretty sparse."

"I can't believe how many people are dying in this church."

"Pastor had a long prayer list this morning, didn't he?"

"He sure did. They're not that old either, like Laura Westbrook."

"The pestilence is upon us."

"What do you mean?"

"Sickness and disease is a sign of the end times."

"Don't talk like that. You're scaring me."

"Why be scared? You know you're going to heaven."

"That's just it. I'm not sure."

"You worry too much."

"Really? Nobody can be sure."

"I'm sure."

"Yeah right."

"I *am*. The Holy Spirit gives us the faith to believe. Don't you believe that?"

"I guess so."

"Certainly you believe that Jesus is your Savior."

"Yes, but I have doubts sometimes."

"I pray that changes."

"There you go with that prayer talk again. You talk too much about Jesus."

"That's the only way to talk. That's the only way to live, too, for that matter. Do you remember that song 'For Me to Live is Jesus'?"

"If you say so. I don't believe all of that song though. The next line says to die is gain. How do I gain anything from dying?"

"Death is our gateway to heaven."

"Death is scary. That's what it is. The process is even scarier. I hope I don't get cancer and rot away."

"I agree to disagree with you about death along with your worry about money and the future. Maybe you should talk to the pastor about your concerns."

"Absolutely not!"

"Do you read the Bible on your own?"

"No. I come to church often. That's enough for me."

"Good thing you go to a church that teaches straight from the Bible or you could be fooled into believing whatever a preacher tells you, like Sophia."

"I guess. I still think death is scary and we can't be sure whether we go to heaven or not."

"I can only hope and pray that you have a change of heart."

"Can we go?" Marvin said.

"Lovely child you got there," Onia said.

"I'll talk to you later."

"It's about time," he said.

"Watch your respect and patience."

Zoe ordered pizza and had it delivered while she and the kids made Valentine's Day cookies.

"Oooh!" Phillip said as he noticed her sifting flour. "That looks like the stuff I see in lines on our table at home."

"Shut up, big mouth!" Marvin said. He punched Phillip on the arm.

"Ouch!" He tried to hit Marvin back.

Zoe jumped between the two of them before he could. "That's enough! You're family. What's wrong with you?"

"I didn't want to come here, no way," Marvin said.

"That's beside the point. You don't just go around hitting people when they say something you don't like."

"I don't care! Take me home. I don't wanna be in this stupid house."

"I'll gladly take you home when we finish these cookies."

"Bro, I want to go home now!"

"You can call your mother to come pick you up then."

Marvin stormed from the kitchen and flopped onto her couch. He targeted a magazine on the table and tore it up. Then he slammed his back against her couch repeatedly as he pouted.

"Why was he so upset about what you said?" she asked Phillip.

"I guess because he didn't want you to know."

"What is he trying to hide?"

"I guess he doesn't want you to know about the stuff that happens at our house. He brings the money in."

"What does that mean?"

"I'm not sure. I just know our mama yells at him to go make that money if he knows what's good for him."

"Hmm...interesting," she said under her breath.

A timer dinged while they played flashcard games.

"Yay! The cookies are done!" Little John-John said.

Zoe took them from the oven.

"They smell good," Tamika said.

Phillip said, "They look good too."

"We have to let them cool off before we decorate them. Speaking of cooling off, I'm going to check on Marvin. Stay away from those cookies until I come back."

"What are we supposed to do?" Phillip asked.

"Play some of these games." She took some board games from a shelf. "Eat some more pizza."

"Okay," they said and smiled.

Zoe noticed paper strewn all over the floor. Then she spotted Marvin folded over the arm of her couch with his head buried. His body was shaking, and she thought she heard sniffling. She sat down next to him and put her hand on his shoulder.

"Leave me alone," he said. He jerked away from her.

She pulled back. "Would you like to come decorate some cookies with us? They're done."

"No. Just leave me alone!"

"I can't leave you alone, because I care about you."

"Yeah, right."

"I do. In fact, seeing you like this hurts my heart."

Marvin sat up and leered at her. "Nobody cares about me."

"I do. Your mother does."

"You don't even know me, and my mama only thinks about herself."

"Are you embarrassed because of what Phillip said?"

"No. I just don't like him tellin' our business, that's all."

"Tell me this. If it was something you were proud of would it be okay for him to tell?"

He clammed up.

"If you don't want to talk about it anymore, I understand."

Tears streamed down his face as he choked out his words. "My daddy...I only met him twice. My mama won't let me see him. It ain't fair. The other kids get to see their daddies," he said as he noticed something on her table.

Zoe's eyes blurred as she listened.

"Ooo!"

Zoe hurried to the kitchen. "What's the matter?"

"Phillip just..."

"Shut up!" he said.

"Phillip *what*?"

"He just ate a cookie."

"That's what all the commotion is about?"

"You told us to wait 'til we decorated them," Tamika said.

"Can we paint the cookies now?" Little John-John asked.

They all laughed. "Yes, sweetie, we can paint the cookies," she said.

Marvin dragged himself into the kitchen.

"I'm glad you decided to join us," Zoe said.

"Ooo, sprinklers," Little John-John said.

They gawked at each other and laughed again. Then they noshed on the cookies and washed them down with hot cocoa.

Marvin checked his cell phone. "We have to go," he said.

"What's the rush?"

"My mama texted me. She wants us back home now." he said. He took what was in his hand and slipped it into his pocket. "I have some money to make."

She packed some extra cookies for them to take home.

"Thank you," they said except for Little John-John. He clung on to her.

"I wuv you," he said.

"I love you too, sweetie. I love all of you." She hugged each of them with reciprocity except Marvin who stood like a statue.

Zoe went directly to her prayer haven after she took the kids home. She wrote each of their names on a separate post-it and placed them on her bulletin board. She prayed over each one.

Chapter 16

The Family Gathering

"Fear thou not; for I am with thee: be not dismayed; for I am thy God: I will strengthen thee; yea, I will help thee; yea, I will uphold thee with the right hand of my righteousness."

Isaiah 41:10

"Wasn't that a beautiful service?" Sophia said as she smiled.

"Are you serious? There's nothing beautiful about funerals. I hate 'em," Brenna said as she scowled.

"Welcome back to Milwaukee, ladies. It's so good to see you." Onia said as she hugged her two siblings. "We have to stop waiting for funerals to get together."

Sophia and Brenna looked at each other and shrugged their shoulders.

"Did you two fly together?"

"Yes we did. I forgot how cold it gets here." Brenna said.

"From what I saw on the news, Atlanta wasn't looking too warm either these days."

"True," Sophia said, "but Atlanta's cold days are more bearable than this, and they go away faster."

"Let's find a place to sit, so we can talk about old times," Onia said. "Oh, there's Zoe," she said. She noticed her sitting by herself eyeing the crowd.

"Hi, Zoe," Sophia said.

Zoe stared at a slightly oversized lady who resembled her older sister.

"Sophia, is that you?"

"All one hundred ninety-six pounds, but I lost about fifty," she said. She giggled.

"What happened? I mean...How did you lose so much weight so fast? I just saw you a few months ago at Craig's funeral?" Zoe said as she hugged her.

"It's been four months. I ended my love affair with donuts."

They laughed. "Well you look great."

"Thank you. I need to lose fifty more by August."

"I'm sure you can do it. Hi, Brenna," Zoe said.

"Why do you wanna sit here?" Brenna said. She turned up her nose. "Let's sit at the table closer to the food."

"What's wrong with this one?" Onia said.

"I don't like the atmosphere. Besides, it stinks at this one."

Onia sniffed and then shook her head. "It smells good to me."

"Here, Sophia, you sit next to me. Onia, you sit on the other side," Brenna said.

"Come join us," Onia said to Zoe.

Zoe placed herself on the other side of Sophia.

"So, how are my two lovely sisters doing?" Brenna said.

Onia and Sophia looked at each other in confusion. "What about Zoe? You can't possibly be mad at her after all this time," Onia said.

"Try me. It's all her fault."

"What's her fault? Jerry's death?"

"No!" She said with a sneer.

"Then what? Quit beating around the bush and say what you have to say," Sophia said.

"It's her fault that Craig took his life."

Her sisters' mouths dropped open as they stared at each other.

"Now wait a minute! How can you blame me for what happened? I hardly ever saw him, and I live nowhere near you," Zoe said.

"You're the one who gave him that stupid Bible. It confused him."

"I don't believe this. I try to do something thoughtful and you twist it around. That's so like you."

"I told you I didn't want you bringing your Jesus paraphernalia around my house, and you did it anyway behind my back."

"How was it behind your back? You had to see it when he opened it up at Christmastime."

"Yeah, you were very sneaky. You had it wrapped up."

The sisters chuckled. "That's what you do with Christmas presents," Zoe said.

"Don't talk to me. You went against my wishes."

"You came all this way to pick a fight?" Onia said.

"No. I came for Uncle Jerry's funeral. She just happens to be here too. Why I don't know. She thinks she's too good to come to other gatherings."

"I'm always the last to know."

"There you go feeling sorry for yourself. I've heard your sob story hundreds of times."

"If Onia hadn't told me about Craig I would have missed his funeral."

"I would've preferred it that way."

"You're so wrong, Brenna," Onia said. "She's your sister whether you like it or not."

"Well I don't. I never could stand that...She doesn't even look anything like us. She's a misfit."

"You're mean, Brenna," Onia said.

"Hello, ladies, I'm glad you could make it," Maggie said.

"Hi," Onia said.

"Who is she?" Sophia asked Zoe.

"That's Uncle Jerry's wife. Onia and I met her at his New Year's Eve party. She made a point of letting us know she was his third one."

"She looks kind of young," Sophia whispered as she studied the woman.

"She is. I'd say she's about your age."

"You can go grab a bite to eat," Maggie said as she sat at their table.

"I'm curious. What caused his heart attack? We just saw him, and he looked healthy as an ox," Zoe said.

"I can't tell you. It's kind of private."

"Private? He died of a heart attack. What is pri...oh...I get it." Onia said. She started to turn red. "I'm having a hot flash," she said. She chuckled and started fanning herself with her funeral program.

"I don't get it," Sophia said.

"Me either," said Zoe.

Onia winked at them. "He died of a heart attack, and it's private how he had it."

Brenna grinned from ear to ear.

"Ohhh," they both said.

"I knew what she meant all along," Brenna said as she flung her hair back. "Women can have that effect on men."

"How would you know?" Sophia said. "Are you harboring a secret?"

"Maybe. I just know that I've had a similar effect on them."

"Oh really? When? Who?...Chad?"

"Chad isn't the only guy I've been with."

"What young buck could you have seduced who would nearly have a heart attack before you dated Chad? You were young back then." Onia said. "There's something you're not telling us."

"Yeah. C'mon, spill the beans," Sophia said.

"All right. I dated a guy in college before I met Chad."

"What was wrong with him that he could have a heart attack in college? Was he obese? Did he have a condition?" Onia said.

"What's with the third degree?"

"You brought it up. Inquiring minds want to know," Onia said.

"A woman has needs just like men. That's all I can say."

Maggie smiled at the banter before she left to mingle with other relatives.

Onia's stomach growled. "I don't know about you ladies, but I'm going up to get some food."

"I'll come with you," Zoe said.

Zoe appeared to be fighting her emotions, so Onia asked her if she was okay. "No, but I will be." She sniffled as she daubed her napkin on her eyes. "I just don't understand why Brenna hates me so much."

"You intimidate people."

"What? How?"

"You're beautiful, and you're sure of yourself."

"She's beautiful."

"She might be a little jealous of you. You have a successful career which is something she gave up for a man. She could be bitter and resentful, so she's taking her failures out on you."

"Wow! I can't believe my own sister would treat me like this."

"It's part of who she is. She's mean-spirited."

"Thank you for helping me understand."

"Of course. She's not much nicer to the rest of us anyway."

"I didn't want to say anything while miss holier-than-thou was around," Brenna told Sophia. "I ran into my first college boyfriend in a grocery store about six months ago. We got together and we've been sleeping around for quite some time. I've never felt so alive."

"You're having an affair?"

"I wouldn't call it that."

"What would you call it then?"

"Sexual gratification. Chad is never around much and I have needs."

"How could you do this? Mom and Dad raised us better than that."

"I told you Chad has hardly been around to satisfy me. Besides I love Devon."

"Don't you love your husband?"

"Not really. Our marriage was based on lies, and we've drifted apart a long time ago. I'm sure he's cheating too, because he's never home."

"That's pretty daring. You better be careful. That could backfire."

Brenna rolled her eyes. "Look at my sister trying to tell me about life."

"Mom and Dad also wouldn't approve of how you're treating Zoe either."

"You shared some things you don't like about her too, so who are you to tell me?"

"Yes, but you're coming on too strong with your attitude. I heard what you called her under your breath. She may have heard it too. You need to lighten up and let go."

"What is this, pick on Brenna day?"

"Treat her the way you would want to be treated. She means well and she is our sister."

"They always favored her. I had to work my butt off to earn my way to college, and she got a handout."

"That's what this is about? So you're jealous of something that happened eons ago?"

"They let her go to that prep school when we had to go to public school."

"No we didn't. They let us decide, and that's where Zoe wanted to go. Did you want to go there?"

"Absolutely not!"

"Well then, quit griping about something that can't be changed anyway."

"All I know is, they wouldn't let me go, if I wanted to."

"You don't know that, and you're being petty."

"Look, I don't have to sit here and take this, especially from you. I'm going to get some food."

Onia and Zoe came back to the table with their plates overflowing.

"Aren't you going to eat, Sophia?" Onia asked.

"Brenna's attitude kinda spoiled my appetite. Did either of you get an invitation to the family reunion?"

"Yes, but I don't know who J.C. is. Do you?" Onia answered.

"No. I was wondering the same thing. I want to go too, but I can't. Dave and I'll be on our cruise during that time."

"A *cruise?*"

"Yes. We're going on a Bible cruise this summer. We can't afford to miss that."

"Couldn't you do both?" Zoe asked.

"We don't know when the reunion is, and we can't risk missing the cruise. This is a once-in-a-lifetime venture for us."

"Aren't cruises expensive?" Onia asked.

"Ours is free. Our preacher has his own ocean liner. We can't pass on this for some mysterious reunion."

"That sounds too good to be true," Onia said, munching on a dinner roll.

"It is."

"What is?" Brenna chimed in as she returned with a plateful.

"I already told you that Dave and I are planning a Bible cruise this summer. We can't afford to miss that."

"You can't afford to go. Where'd you get the money?" Brenna said.

"What concern is that of yours? You said you weren't going anyway."

"That's right. You couldn't pay me to go to that reunion. What I don't understand is why you're so set on going on this cruise? I mean, it seems like you're so obsessed with this particular cruise when you can go on a cruise any time."

"Easy for you to say…we can't afford it, remember? For your information the reverend is letting us go for free, so we can't pass up this opportunity."

"Now that's almost worth going to church for."

Onia leaned over to Sophia. "I think Brenna has a few screws missing."

"She's probably still grieving," Sophia whispered. "Now, if you'll excuse me your food smells too good for me to wait any longer," she said before she finally went to fix her plate.

"Ryan and I would go, but there isn't enough information," Onia said. "It doesn't give the date, and I find it strange that the host is so obscure."

"I would love to see you there," Zoe said.

"Did you finally get an invitation?"

"Well, no, but I could have tagged along with one of you."

"What makes you think you're going to get one?" Brenna said.

"Look, I've had about enough of your brutality!"

"Are you getting angry? And you call yourself a Christian."

"Just ignore her," Onia said.

Sophia sat down and started gobbling her mountain of food.

"Why are you eating so fast?" Brenna said.

"I didn't realize how hungry I was. Besides we have to get going soon so we don't miss our flight."

"You're right for once," Brenna said.

Sophia looked up just enough to sneer at Brenna before she stuck her nose back into her plate.

"How are your kids doing, Onia?" Sophia asked between bites. Her sisters looked at each other in disgust as they watched her lick her fingers and smack her lips.

"They're doing alright except for Rachel. She's been lying to us more than usual lately. She's also been breaching her curfew by sneaking out with that friend of hers."

"She's a teenager. They do that." Brenna said.

"She's barely thirteen, and her behavior is not okay. Anyway, we grounded her indefinitely."

"You're too hard on the poor girl," Brenna said.

"I didn't tell you how to raise your kids. Please don't tell me how to raise mine."

"Excuse me."

When Sophia finished guzzling her portion, she and Brenna wasted no time to depart as if staying any longer would have been a nuisance to their agenda.

Zoe's eyes watered as she munched on remnants of her meal. Her feelings betrayed her. She wasn't sure whether she was more upset about Brenna's animosity towards her or her sisters' refusal to acknowledge the importance of a reunion invitation that appeared to be designed especially for them.

"You look sad," Onia said.

"I just have a lot on my mind."

"I can certainly relate to that. Rachel has been giving us more trouble than I cared to mention."

"More than usual?" Zoe said.

"Yes. I didn't want to say too much around Brenna and Sophia, but she ran away from home last week."

"Really?"

"Yes. She went to her friend's house. She's been lying about where she's been going too."

"Have you tried talking to her to understand what she might be going through?"

"No. I'm afraid. I think she has a boyfriend, and we told her she has to wait until she's at least sixteen. She's been wearing new outfits we hadn't bought her, and she also seems to have money. I have no idea where she's getting it from, because she doesn't have a job."

"I think you should ask her where she's getting all her stuff."

"Okay. I will."

She prayed with Onia before they said their goodbyes.

Zoe entered her apartment and hurried to her little room to meditate. Her heart was loaded with feelings of rejection. She happened to open her Bible to Matthew 11:28 which read: "*Come unto me all ye that labour and are heavy laden, and I will give you rest.*" Her eyes began to water as she prayed.

"Dear heavenly Father, You are so awesome. Finding this passage was no coincidence. I heard your voice as I read it. You know my heart is sad. I feel so alone around people at times. I don't know what's going on with my sister, but you do, O Sovereign of the Universe. Please touch her heart with forgiveness for her sake. And dear Lord, if it is your will, please let my sisters change their hearts and believe in you.

I'm so blessed to know you and to be called your child. You make my life complete and give me worth. Thank you for the confidence I have in you to endure.

In Jesus' name I pray. Amen."

Chapter 17

THE SINISTER MINISTER

"No man can serve two masters: for either he will hate the one, and love the other; or else he will hold to the one, and despise the other. Ye cannot serve God and mammon."

Matthew 6:24

"Hi, Dave. Hi, Sophia. Come have a seat," Reverend Whitaker said as he welcomed them into his office. The ambience had that same eeriness they had noticed before. "Did you bring the paperwork I asked for?"

Dave's hand felt heavy as he relinquished a manila folder. The Reverend opened it with the eagerness.

"Excellent!" he said as he perused its contents. "You did a good thing."

"What do you need it for?" Dave asked, worried.

"Don't be silly. Our church could always use a little extra. I couldn't be happier that you made us your beneficiary. Don't you remember? This is part of our deal as a prerequisite for the free cruise."

The couple looked at each other as if they had signed their life away.

"Why is it so cold in here?" Sophia said, rubbing her arms. "It feels like a refrigerator."

"Nonsense. It's just right. We store the band instruments in the back room. The temperature has to be cool, so they don't warp."

"Oh." Dave said as the door squeaked open.

"We've got another one for you. Oh, I'm sorry. I didn't know you had company," a bean pole of a man blurted. He looked as if he may have played basketball in his younger years except for the bay window which hung over his belt. He wore clothes that were outdated, pants legs high above his shoes. He had a van dyke with a handlebar mustache and long stringy hair that looked like it yearned for a good shampoo.

"Don't you ever come in here unannounced again!" the reverend said.

"Sorry, sir."

"You should be. Now leave! I'll deal with you later."

"Yes sir. Do you want me to put it in the back room?"

"Of course, now go!" The reverend escorted him to the door.

Dave nudged Sophia and stared at her. "Maybe we should go," he said.

"Why? We aren't finished yet."

"I don't like the way he talked to that guy. Something's not right."

"You're overreacting."

"Overreacting about what?" the reverend said.

"Oh, nothing. We were talking about my sister. She's upset, because she didn't get an invitation to our family reunion."

"Oh? When is that?"

"It's this summer, but we already decided we aren't going. We're too excited about this cruise."

"Good. Now all I need you to do is sign off on the policy, so we can take your...the church can officially be your beneficiary."

"Ugggghhh."

"What was that?" Dave asked.

"What was *what*?" the reverend said wringing his hands.

"Reverend, you had to hear that."

"I don't know what you're talking about. Just sign right here, and we can be done."

"I don't know," Dave said. He shook his head.

"It's okay, honey," Sophia said. "We trust you Reverend."

"That's what I like to hear."

"Ugggghhh."

"There's that noise again." Dave said.

"Thank you very much," the reverend said. He rose and extended his hand. "I'll see you in church." He hurried them to the door. He slammed it behind them, sighed, and then raced to the back room.

Dave looked puzzled as they walked away. "I feel like I was just brushed off like a piece of lint on a suit coat."

"Why do you say that?"

"That whole thing with that man was weird. I'm having second thoughts about this cruise," Dave said. "Something's not right."

"Don't be silly, honey. You're just being paranoid."

"Paranoid? Did you hear how he talked to that guy? It was like he took on a whole different personality from the reverend we know."

"It's gonna be fine." Sophia rubbed his shoulder. "That's just the devil trying to steal our joy and turn us away from having fun. You know the devil is a joy robber."

"That's true. But what was that moaning noise? It sounded like someone was in pain. I know you heard it."

"I did, but that had nothing to do with us. It'll be alright. What happened to your excitement?"

"I guess I have reservations about turning our death benefits over to some minister instead of to our kids. He's starting to make me think he just wants our money."

"Our sons have good jobs. We don't need to take care of them. They can take care of us."

"I suppose. That's why I love you so much, dear. You have a way of putting everything in such a positive light."

"I love you too, hon." They kissed and walked hand in hand to their car.

Despite Sophia's encouragement, she looked pensive. She turned away so Dave wouldn't notice. She knew he was right to be suspicious, but she wanted to go on this cruise more than anything. She pondered what Zoe had warned her about. Could Reverend Whitaker be a false prophet? Something didn't feel right, but she and Dave were in too deep with relinquishing their life insurance policy. She also had convinced herself that this trip was a once-in-a-lifetime adventure for them.

"What's going on here?" Reverend Whitaker said to the strange man. "You almost blew our cover."

"I'm sorry sir, but this body decided to moan as I was putting it on the table."

"Just be more careful next time, and don't come barging into my office without knocking first."

"Yes sir."

"Where did you get this one?"

"There was some vagrant lying on the street half dead already. I helped him along."

"Make sure you clean it and refrigerate it to prepare it for the ritual."

"Okay."

"We'll have our meeting at seven and then have our monthly ritual as an offering to Mammon."

"All right, Sir."

He left the man with the corpse. The man had his way with it before he cleaned it and refrigerated it.

All of the men met at the church before they carpooled to a remote cabin. Reverend Whitaker ran the meeting which consisted of the strange man and board members from his congregation.

The strange man was a mortician with a fetish for necrophilia. He acquired the corpses for the rituals from the homeless and from loved ones who were not given a proper funeral due to the expenditure. Their bodies were sometimes donated to science, but the paperwork somehow disappeared.

"This meeting is now in session." Reverend Whitaker said. "How many of you were able to get people to part with their insurance policies this week?"

A few hands went up.

"Come on, gentlemen. We've got to do better."

"I was able to convince my dying grandmother she would get to heaven if she turned hers over to the church," one man said.

"Very good, but we must do better for Mammon."

"Yes sir," they all said.

"Give me what you have, and I'll put them away."

After he collected them, the strange man said, "Come let us have our way with the body."

One by one each man gratified himself by defiling the corpse while the others cheered. When they were all finished they chanted, "All hail to Mammon! He is god above all gods!" They continued the chant to a rhythm as two men hoisted the corpse in the air. They carried it to a fire pit outside as the rest of the men marched along. The two men threw the body into the pit while two others gathered firewood. They desecrated the body with sticks and branches. Then they resumed their chant as it crackled in the flames until its mortal remains were reduced to bone fragments and ashes.

"Well done, Gentlemen," the reverend said. "All praise to Mammon!"

"All praise to Mammon," they all said.

"Until next month, gentlemen," said Reverend Whitaker.

Chapter 18

Renegade Rachel

"Honour thy father and thy mother: that thy days may be long upon the land which the LORD thy God giveth thee."

Exodus 20:12

"Mom, can I go to Ellen's birthday party this Friday?"

"I don't know. I have to talk with your dad about it. You've been very difficult with us lately."

"How? What did I do?"

"Right, what have you been doing? You haven't been turning in your homework. You haven't been doing your chores. The only thing you *have* been doing is arguing with us and disobeying us."

"Please, Mom. I'm sorry. I promise I won't talk back, and I'll do my schoolwork and chores."

"Those things are expected of you and not up for negotiating. As I said, I will talk with your dad. That's my answer. Take it or leave it."

"I'll leave it," she said under her breath.

"What did you say?"

"Oh, I said I don't believe it."

"Uh, huh."

"I gotta get to school to do that schoolwork. See you, Mom," Rachel said as she kissed Onia. "I love you."

"You don't have to try and butter me up, but I love you too."

Rachel met Ellen outside of school.

"What took you so long?" Ellen asked.

"I had to butter my mother up."

"Did it work?"

"Yes. She said I could go to your party."

"Way cool," Ellen said as she grinned. "You're gonna have a good time."

"I can't wait."

A man pulled up in a lustrous, red jaguar convertible.

"Hey, Ladies, care to go for a ride?"

"Hi, Kyle," Ellen said. "Sure."

"How come you know this guy?" Rachel asked. "I don't recognize him."

"That's because I was waiting for the right time to tell you about him. He's just a friend. He's the one who's been giving me the nice clothes that I let you have. We'll be together. Where's your sense of adventure?"

"I left it at home. We're going to get in trouble for skipping school."

Ellen chuckled. "School will be here when we get back." She hopped in the back seat and stretched out leaving Rachel no choice but to sit in the front.

"You look good," the guy said.

"Thank you," Ellen said. She smiled.

"I was talking to your friend."

"Oh."

"Thank you," Rachel said.

"You look good too, Ellen."

"Thanks."

"I love that shirt you're wearing," he said as he examined Rachel's developing cleavage and midriff.

Kyle drove them around like a tour guide showing them what he called hot spots in the city. As the morning turned into noontime he found a fancy restaurant and treated them to lunch. He interrogated Rachel by bombarding her with numerous questions about her family. The attention made her feel like a princess.

"Are you the oldest?" he asked.

"No. I have an older brother, but I hardly ever see him."

"Ellen, you're the oldest right?" he said as he put his hand on her knee and caressed it.

She smiled at him and nodded.

"We're going to the mall after we eat. I want you two to look good for me, I mean, for your friends, like me."

"I have to use the bathroom," Rachel said. "Come with me, Ellen."

She gawked at Rachel before she followed her.

"What is this all about? Why is this guy buying us all this stuff? Is he rich or something? Doesn't he know what to do with his money?" Rachel asked.

"Something like that. I wanted you to meet him, because he's going to be at my party with some friends of his."

"He's good-looking, but he's kinda old."

"He's not that old. He's in his twenties."

"That's old. I like guys, but I was thinking about guys our age not some dinosaur."

Ellen chuckled. "There'll be guys our age at the party too, don't worry."

"There's something you're not telling me."

"Don't worry. You'll have fun."

"Are you trying to set me up with him?"

"Yes."

"I don't know, Ellen."

"Just go with it and enjoy. I know how you like nice outfits, so that's what I told him."

"Where did you meet this guy?"

"I met him with a friend of his after school one day a few weeks ago. I've been with my friend since then."

"Is he as old as this one?"

"Yes. He's just as good-looking too."

"Does he have money?"

"Of course. Where do you think I've been getting the money I share with you? He buys me clothes too."

"All right. Let's not keep the man waiting."

As they strutted from the bathroom Kyle was paying for the meal. "Are you ladies ready?" he asked as he smiled.

"Yes," they said.

"Let's go." He grabbed each of their arms and escorted them to his car.

"Thank you," Rachel said as they left the mall. She smiled at Ellen.

"You can pay me later," he said.

"What's that supposed to mean?" Rachel asked.

"I'm kidding. It's just an expression."

"Oh."

"School is over by now. I'll take you ladies home."

"I can catch the bus," Rachel said.

"C'mon. You already missed it, and it's getting late."

"I dunno," Rachel said. "I'll get in trouble if my mother sees me getting out of the car with you."

"Quit being a scaredy-cat," Ellen said.

"All right."

"You can take me home first," Ellen said. She winked at him.

Rachel glared at her. She swung at Ellen and hit her on the shoulder with the side of her fist. Ellen leaned back and giggled.

"I'm coming home with you," Rachel said when Kyle dropped Ellen off.

"You can't. I mean...how are you going to get home from my house?" Ellen said. She stepped out of the car and quickly shut the door.

Before Rachel could answer Kyle pulled off.

"Don't worry. You're in good hands with me," he said. He noticed Rachel squirm. "Are you going to be okay?"

"I guess so." She looked away.

"You don't sound convincing." He pulled over and looked at her. He took one hand and put it under her chin to turn her head towards him. "Look at me. I'm here to help you."

"Okay," she said trying to smile.

"You don't have a job do you?" he asked.

"No. I'm not old enough."

"I know how you can earn some money to buy your own outfits. If you feel obligated, you can pay me back with some of your earnings. Otherwise this first one's on me."

"Why are you being so nice?"

"I'm rich, and generous. That's a winning combination to someone such as yourself, isn't it?"

"How can I get a job at my age?"

"I can pull some strings. I have connections."

"Oh?" she said as they arrived at her house.

She bolted from the car as he said, "I would like to see you again."

She ignored him and skipped stairs to reach the front door. He eyed her every move before he drove away.

"Hello?" Rachel said as her phone rang.

"How did it go?" Ellen asked.

"How do you think it went?"

"Well, did you hit it off with him?"

"No. I was so nervous the whole time. How could you leave me with him?"

"Rachel, is that you?" Onia asked.

"Hey, I gotta go."

"Okay. Talk to you later," Ellen said.

"Yes, it's me, Mother."

"Where have you been? You should have been home by now."

"I'm here now."

"You didn't answer my question."

"I was with Ellen."

"Do you realize the school calls when children are absent? I received a phone call wondering why you weren't in school. I would like to know as well."

"I was with Ellen."

"So you both decided to skip school? And what is in that bag you're carrying?"

"It's a new outfit."

"Where'd you get the money to buy it?"

"Ellen bought it for me."

"She bought *you* something for *her* birthday? That doesn't make sense."

"She's a generous person."

"You've helped me make my decision about the party on Friday. You're not going."

"Why?"

"You're lying, Rachel, and you skipped school. That's not okay."

"Whatever," Rachel said. She rolled her eyes and turned away.

"Go upstairs. Your father and I will deal with you later."

Rachel stormed away in a huff.

Rachel blasted her music and barely heard a knock on her bedroom door.

"It's time for dinner," Nathan said.

"Go away!"

"Dinner won't be the same without you."

"Go away, I said."

"We're your family, and we love you."

"I want a different family anyway."

"You're being a selfish big head."

"I don't care! Go away!"

"Mom, Dad, I tried," he said as he trotted down the stairs. "She won't listen."

Both Onia and Ryan crept up the stairs. They burst into Rachel's room. "We've had about enough of this," her dad said. "Your mother told me how you've been acting. You have to accept the consequences of your actions as a member of this family."

"That's just it. You're never around to know what's going on. She never lets me do anything. It's not fair!"

"I'm sorry, honey. I have to work to provide for you all. My job demands a lot from me. They track my every move with this chip in my hand. I feel like a parolee who has to wear a tether."

"What's that?"

"It's a tracking bracelet. I want to spend more time with you, but they treat me like they own me. It can only get better. Give me some time to get seniority."

"I could be grown up by then. You don't care about me. That's all you care about is making money."

"I *do* care. It's just that, I have to provide for the family. I don't make as much as I used to, so I have to work longer to make more. There's no other way right now."

"Will you at least let me go to Ellen's party?"

"No. I agree with your mother. You're on punishment for two weeks. One week for skipping school and one for being dishonest."

"That's not fair!"

"Fair or not, we've made our decision. We love you despite all of this."

"I don't care."

"Rachel, you'll come down and eat dinner with us."

"I don't want to."

"Do you want a third week for being defiant?"

"I hate this family," she said as she jumped from her bed.

"You're being ungrateful. We do everything we can to provide for you which doesn't mean you always get your way."

"We'll give you five minutes to get yourself together. You're a part of this family, and we love you regardless," Onia said.

"I don't want to."

"Three weeks," her dad said.

"Oh, all right. I'll come down, but I won't like it, and you can't make me eat."

Rachel gave everyone the silent treatment during the rest of the week. That Friday morning she smuggled a few outfits into her backpack. She met Ellen at school hoping to celebrate her birthday and stay overnight.

Onia had dozed off when she was awakened by her phone alarm. She hurried to school to pick up Rachel. She waited in the car for fifteen minutes watching students pour out of the building until only a few trickled behind. Rachel wasn't with any of them. She saw no signs of Ellen either. She couldn't imagine Rachel skipping school again knowing she would have another week added to her previous consequence. She called Rachel's cell phone. There was no answer, so she decided to talk to the principal.

"Rachel wasn't with the other kids because she was marked absent today. I tried calling. I left you a voice message."

"Not again."

"This is the eighth absence this month. She'll get suspended if she has another one."

"I'm not concerned with a suspension right now. I want to know where she *is*."

"Sorry, Mrs. Fairweather, I can't help you with that. If I knew I'd be happy to let you know."

"Can you check to see if her friend named Ellen McCrory was in school today?"

"I can't tell you about other students. It's against school policy."

"Can you bend the rule just this one time? I'm worried that something may have happened to my daughter, and Ellen is her best friend."

"I'm sorry, Mrs. Fairweather, I can't."

Chapter 19

Teenage Terrorism

"An evil man seeketh only rebellion: therefore a cruel messenger shall be sent against him."

Proverbs 17:11

"Zoe, it's me, Onia. Sorry to call so late."

"What's up?"

"I need your prayers." Her voice quivered.

"What's going on?"

"Rachel is missing again. This time we don't know where she is. We checked with all her friends. None of them saw her in school today."

"Oh my goodness, I sure will. Where are you?"

"Ryan and I are at the police station. I tell you, if it's not one thing it's another."

"That's true. Though kids are a blessing, life is more stressful with them. I'm praying with you right now. Dear heavenly Father, We come before you lifting up Rachel. Lord, we know she's been rebellious lately, but we pray for your grace and mercy. Please spare her life wherever she is and bring her back to us. Comfort us and give us peace as we wait for your timing. In Jesus' name we pray. Amen."

"Thank you. I appreciate it even though it doesn't always work."

"Anytime. I hope God will give you peace. I'll keep you in my prayers. Keep me posted."

"Okay, I will."

"I have another favor to ask you," Onia said, biting her index finger.

"What?"

"Can you come to the police station?"

"Why? Which one?"

"I'm at the one near our house. I could use some moral support."

Zoe sighed. "Sure. Let me throw something on."

"Hello, I'm Detective Warren. I'll be handling your case."

Zoe walked in as the detective shook Ryan's hand. Her hair was mussed which made her look more down-to-earth than usual. The detective's mouth dropped open, and he beamed from ear to ear. "Hello, my name is Jim Warren." He let go of Ryan's hand and took hers. She shook his hand; however, he made her feel uncomfortable as he ogled her.

"Hi, my name is Zoe. I'm Rachel's aunt. If you don't mind, I would appreciate it if you would stop staring at me."

He shook his head to snap out of his trance. "I'm sorry. I just haven't met anyone as beautiful as you are."

"Will you please focus on my missing daughter?" Ryan said.

"You're right. That was so unprofessional of me. Let me start over. My name is Detective Warren, and I'll be handling your case."

"You said that already," Ryan said.

"Are you sure you're up to the challenge? I mean no distractions will get in your way will they?" Zoe said.

"I did apologize for how I came across. Can you show some understanding?"

"Okay. I just wasn't expecting attention being drawn to me. We have a serious circumstance on our hands, detective. My niece is missing."

"You're right. Can I make it up to you over a cup of coffee?"

"I don't drink coffee."

"How about tea, or any drink of your choice."

"I'll tell you what. You find my niece, and I'll take you up on the offer."

"Great." He looked at Ryan and Onia. "When was the last time you saw her?"

"This morning," Onia said.

Detective Warren looked into this case with unyielding eagerness. He felt like a child on a scavenger hunt as he searched for leads with persistence, a date with Zoe being his inspiration.

He went to Ellen's home which he thought was the best place to start.

"Hello, Ma'am, my name is Detective Jim Warren. I'm here to see your daughter Ellen."

"What do you want with her?" Ms. McCrory asked with a cold glare.

"I came here to ask her a few questions about her friend."

"She has lots of friends. Which one?"

"Rachel Fairweather."

"Well, she's not here," Ellen's mom said and slammed the door.

Rachel woke up groggy and sweaty, her vision blurry. She sat up and studied her surroundings with what remained of her faculties. The place reeked. The only illumination came from a gaudy red light. There were dirty mattresses lying all over a cement floor.

She noticed what looked like deflated balloons strewn everywhere. Where am I? She wondered. Across the room she noticed two people on one of the mattresses. One was moving around while the other lay motionless.

She heard footsteps. Then she felt a hand smack her across her face. She fell hard on the mattress. A man who stank of alcohol lay on top of her. He slobbered on her face and panted as he unzipped his pants. She realized she wasn't wearing any underwear when he penetrated her private. She was too dazed to scream.

She was glad when he was finished only to discover the nightmare wasn't over. The horror continued as more men swarmed her. Some couldn't wait their turn and sought pleasure from her behind. She thought she was going to die. Worse yet, she thought she had died and gone to hell. Where am I? She wondered again. How did I get here? She asked herself. Then she passed out.

The next morning she woke up hoping she had been dreaming. Everything was the way it had been the night before, only light tried to peek through the dingy room. The mattress was soaked where she lay, and it reeked of urine. It had a pungency she didn't recognize.

"Get up and clean yourself, you nasty slut!" a man yelled.

She looked up at him. His face looked familiar. She couldn't remember where she had seen him until someone called him.

"Kyle, get over here! We lost one."

"Don't just stand there. Dump the cadaver."

Rachel's mouth dropped open. Tears filled her tired eyes. Her heart raced. She recognized the body as the girl who lay motionless the night before.

"Kyle?" she said.

He slapped her with the back of his hand. Her head slammed on the mattress.

"Don't call me that. I'm your big daddy. You belong to me."

Rachel gawked with astonishment.

"What are you staring at, whore? Get up and clean yourself up!" he said as he yanked her by her hair.

"Oww!" she cried.

He dragged her until she managed to get to her feet. Then he pushed her toward a door. She opened it and discovered a toilet and a sink both covered with brown rings. She knelt down on a floor laced with debris and vomited.

A few minutes later the man opened the door and threw clothes at her as he said, "Try to make yourself presentable for your company."

Rachel's head was spinning. Everything was happening so fast. She struggled to her feet. She washed and scrubbed herself until her skin felt raw, yet she still felt dirty.

She put on the outfit and tried to style her mussed hair with her fingers. Tears streamed down her face as she eyed herself in the dirty mirror.

"What's taking you so long? I've got a schedule to keep."

She trembled as she tried to hurry.

"Now you look like one of my prize whores. My friends are going to love you," he said. "We have a few errands to run. You're going to get a tattoo, so you know you're mine."

Rachel kept rubbing her arm after getting the tattoo. It looked puffy and swollen, but she knew she dare not say anything.

Kyle took her around town. Many of the places resembled the tour he gave her earlier during the week. She thought about that day which seemed a distant memory. She thought about Ellen. She missed her friend and her family. She had to convince herself not to think about them. The thought of never seeing them again was too much to comprehend.

Kyle drove into a motel parking lot. He checked them in and took her to a room. He pulled a syringe and needle from a duffle bag and showed her how to use it. He then made her take her clothes off and violated her. As she lay there he made a few phone calls. Before her stay had ended five other men had taken advantage of her.

Kyle took her to get something to eat before they returned to the room with the red light. As she staggered past other girls she thought she saw Ellen. She whispered her name. The girl looked through her as if she was in a trance.

"I'm gonna give you another dose of this stuff I gave you earlier. You have a night shift to make it through."

As Rachel lay on the mattress in oblivion a line of men came to be with her violating her throughout the night. She passed out only to be awakened and startled by a scream. Through blurry eyes she could see a girl getting beaten. The girl resisted until her lifeless body lay on the floor. Rachel cowered and whimpered...shivering... tears drenched her face. She screamed, let me out, but no sound came from her lips. She was trapped...trapped in her surroundings... trapped inside her body, feeling terror, but too paralyzed to express it. She needed a hit. She needed anything to escape.

Ryan had to prepare meals for the family more often than not. Onia spent most of her days in bed since Rachel had disappeared leaving him and the kids to carry out the chores.

"We're having pancakes again?" Nathan asked.

"There's not much else I can make."

"Can we have pizza instead?"

"Maybe tomorrow. Go get your mother."

"Mom, it's time to eat!" Nathan yelled.

"I could have done that," Ryan said.

"Pancakes? That's Rachel's favorite," Onia said when she dragged herself down the stairs.

"Can you make some scrambled eggs to go with the pancakes, sweetheart?"

"Sure."

After Onia scrambled the eggs she set six plates on the table.

"You have too many plates," Nathan said.

Everyone stood motionless.

"Oh, I guess I do."

She sighed and her hands began to tremble.

"It's okay, honey. It's going to take some getting used to."

"What do you mean 'getting used to'? Are you giving up hope?"

"I'm sorry. I meant for now." He cleared his throat. "Let's eat," he said.

"I lost my appetite," Onia said and went back upstairs.

"What's wrong with Mom?" Amber asked.

"She's a little under the weather."

"Huh?"

"She's not well."

"She's been acting weird lately. When will she get better?"

"I don't know. What I do know is we have to be patient and understanding."

"I miss Rachel too," she said.

"That's good to hear, especially seeing how she always picked on you."

"It's not the same without her. I kinda got used to it anyway."

"Do you think she'll show up, Dad?" Nathan asked.

"We can only hope."

Ryan plodded up the stairs with a plate of food for Onia. She was crying which became her usual pastime. "Hi, Honey, I brought you something to eat," he said.

She didn't respond at first, so he shook her. She appeared to have aged many years in a few weeks. Her face had more lines, and her eyes sagged.

"Oh, thank you. Any word on Rachel?"

"No. Sorry, honey, we all are worried about her, but we have to get on with life."

"I can't believe you're saying this."

"We can't make what happened go away by hiding from it and pretending it didn't happen."

"You have your way of dealing with it, and I have mine."

"You're only thinking of yourself. There are other members of this family who miss Rachel and care about you too. You have a family with other children and a husband who needs you and misses you," he said as he caressed her shoulder. "We can make arrangements for you to talk to someone about it."

"Like who? You're not implying that I need to see a psychiatrist, are you? I don't need counseling! I just need my daughter."

"I need your help around the house, and I need you to be strong for our other kids," he said. "I'm running out of excuses to tell them."

"Then tell them the truth."

"Tell them that their mother has given up on life, because her daughter is missing? I can't do that. I won't do it."

"I haven't given up on life."

"What do you call it?"

"I just need some time to think, that's all. What would you have called how you acted when you lost your job?"

"Don't go bringing that up. We're talking about you. You've had almost a month to sort things out. If we have to keep living like this, what's the point of you being in the kids' lives?"

"What are you saying?" she asked as she sat up.

"I'm saying that I have to be the mommy and the daddy around here. If you don't snap out of this, and you don't want to get help, I have to take the kids and move out."

"You would do that to me?"

"Yes. You have until the end of the week to snap out of it, or agree to get help."

"But..."

"Now I love you, but I have a household and a job to maintain with or without you."

He kissed her on her forehead. "Is there anything else you need in the meantime?"

"No. You've given me enough to chew on."

Rachel woke up groggy and sore. She had bruises on her body, and she was naked from the waist down. She saw Ellen's doppelganger again. This time the girl lay on the mattress next to her. She crawled over to get a closer look. She recognized her blonde hair and blue eyes. She spoke her name, but the girl turned away.

"What are you doing?" Kyle asked.

"I thought, I thought I saw my friend Ellen."

"I don't permit you to think. You're here to perform, and that's it. She isn't allowed to talk to you anyway, so don't try unless you want your tongue ripped out."

Rachel gasped and crawled back to her mattress.

"Put some clothes on, whore. I expect my girls to look presentable in my presence."

Rachel searched for the rest of her clothes. She found them thrown in a corner. She hurried to get them only to find them covered with blood.

"I can't wear these...," she said. Before she could finish, Kyle dragged her across the mattress.

"Since you can't wear them I'll give you a reason not to put them on," he said before he violated her. "I have a project for you. You're my prize whore, so I want to show you around. Go clean yourself up!"

Rachel tried her best to clean herself from the filth that consumed her inner being. Before she could finish scrubbing herself, Kyle opened the bathroom door and threw another outfit at her to change into. It baffled her because it only had straps. She came from the bathroom drawing attention and a few laughs.

"Go show her how to wear that thing," he said to one of the more experienced women.

"Where's the rest of it?" Rachel asked.

The woman chuckled, "This is it, honey. Kyle must really like you. He's going to make you a star. Put this sweat suit on over your outfit."

Rachel looked mystified, "A star? In a place like this?"

The woman smirked. "I'll let Kyle surprise you."

Kyle drove her around town again. This time he blind-folded her. When he took it off, they were in the country. "I'm taking you on a special ride," he said.

"I get sick on long trips," she said.

"You crazy sluts and your motion sickness! Here, take this." He gave her Dramamine.

When they arrived in another city and state, he checked them into a hotel suite. There were other girls dressed like her in the room. Cameras and lights were everywhere. The cameramen made her pose in different ways. She posed in her outfit, but Kyle coerced her to pose nude in other shots.

Onia decided to creep down the stairs the next day.

"Mommy!" Amber yelled. She pounced on her like a cat. "You're better!"

"A little bit. How's my girl?"

"Fine. I'm sure glad to see you."

"Good morning, honey," Ryan said. He hugged and kissed her. "Welcome back."

"It's good to be back."

"Hi, Mom," Nathan said.

"Hi, sweetheart." She kissed him.

Aaron looked at her as if he had seen a ghost. They locked eyes before Onia told him to come. She opened her arms, and he ran up to her. They embraced.

"I cooked breakfast. Come join us," Ryan said.

"What did you make?"

"My usual."

"I have good news! Rachel will love it. She's upstairs. I heard her this morning."

Her family stared at each other in bewilderment.

Ryan motioned for her to be quiet. "Let's eat," he said.

As they sat down to eat Onia said, "I don't know why she's not coming down to join us."

"Who, Mom?" Nathan asked.

"Rachel. Go see what's taking her so long, would ya, hon?" she said to Ryan.

"Kids, why don't you go into the backyard to play? Your mother and I need to talk."

"But I didn't finish my breakfast," Amber said.

"You can finish it later."

"It'll be cold then."

"I can warm it up. Now go."

Ryan put his arm around Onia after the kids left. "Honey, I know this is hard on you, but you have to be strong for the kids remember?"

"What are you talking about?"

"You have to accept the fact that Rachel isn't with us right now. We don't know where she's at."

"Sure we do. She's upstairs."

He put her face in his hands then looked into her eyes. "She's not here. Everything's gonna be all right though," he said. "We have a detective looking for her." He kissed her on the forehead.

"You're wrong. I saw her this morning. I'll show you."

They walked upstairs to Rachel's room. "See, there she is," Onia said as she pointed to a picture in a frame.

"This is hard for me, but I need to go make a phone call," he said.

Onia walked over to the picture and caressed it. "It's okay, Rachel. He doesn't understand. It's a girl thing." Then she chuckled.

Chapter 20

Caught in the Act

"For nothing is secret, that shall not be made manifest; neither anything hid, that shall not be known and come abroad."

Luke 8:17

Brenna and Devon continued to nurture their licentiousness with reckless abandon. As they lay in bed they heard footsteps as they had before; however, they ignored the ramifications that their actions imposed. The footsteps grew closer and more pronounced.

Chad burst through the bedroom door. He yanked Devon from Brenna's embrace and cold-cocked him. Before Devon could recover he continued to bombard him in a fit of rage.

Brenna jumped to her feet and pounced on his back. She tried to gouge his eyes our but not before he flung her off. Her head hit the bed post and dazed her. She pleaded for Devon to escape. Chad then turned on her. She tried to fight back, but he overpowered her and battered her until she blacked out.

Sophia rushed to the hospital. News of her sister Brenna's hospitalization threw her into a panic. She hadn't been told any details. However, her niece's tone suggested a serious accident. She had no time to confer with her siblings or wait for Dave to come home from work.

When she arrived at the hospital Charlotte greeted her. They hugged each other. Then Charlotte broke down and started blubbering.

"What happened?" Sophia asked as she rubbed Charlotte's shoulders. "What room is she in? Can she have visitors?"

Charlotte continued to sniffle.

Sophia shook her. "What happened, Charlotte? Can you stop crying and talk to me?"

"First Craig and now this."

"Charlotte, can you please tell me what's going on with your mom?" Sophia was ready to go up to the information desk. "I can ask someone from the hospital, but I would rather find out from you."

"I found her lying on the floor in the living room."

Sophia gasped. "What? Is she okay?" Sophia asked.

"She was beat up. I'm assuming the guy she's been fooling around with did it. He must've dragged her from Craig's bedroom because there's blood everywhere."

"Can we see her?"

"Not right now. She's in pretty bad shape. She's in surgery."

"Wow, it's that bad," Sophia said. They sat down.

"How are you doing?" Sophia asked.

"I'm doing great otherwise. I'm having a baby."

"Oh, congratulations, Charlotte. I noticed a lump in your stomach."

"I'm getting rid of it though."

"You're putting the baby up for adoption?"

"No, I'm getting rid of it for good."

"Your mother is lying half dead and all you can think about is taking another life."

"It was her idea."

"Wow, she is just full of unpleasant surprises."

Charlotte shrugged her shoulders as they walked up to the information desk. The receptionist informed them that she had been taken to ICU.

"Can we see her?" Sophia asked.

"You can, if you're part of her family."

Sophia gasped as they entered the room. Brenna was hooked up to tubes. She hardly recognized her sister. Her left eye was swollen shut like a boxer necessitating a fight stoppage. Her lips were swollen, and her bottom lip was laced with stitches.

"Hi, Brenna," Sophia said.

All Brenna could do was moan.

"Mom, it's me, Charlotte. I'm here with Aunt Sophia."

Brenna just lay there motionless.

"Who did this to you?" Sophia asked.

Brenna could understand what she asked, however, her injuries muted her.

"Why do you have to know?" asked Charlotte.

"He needs to pay for what he did."

"I told you who did it."

"I want to hear it from her. Why would her lover do this to her anyway? He certainly wouldn't have a reason to be jealous since he's the other guy."

"All right. It was my dad. He caught them together, so he knocked her around a little bit."

"A little bit? I hate to see what a lot would look like."

"Brenna, it's me, Sophia. Are you awake?"

She tried to speak as a nurse came in. He advised them to leave while he tended to her. They decided to go grab a bite to eat.

"What's going on with you, Charlotte?"

"What do you mean?"

"Why are you getting rid of your baby?"

"I don't know who the father is, and Mom refuses to help me. I can't take care of a baby by myself."

"Why don't you put the baby up for adoption?"

"That's such a hassle. Besides, I already made arrangements."

No one said a word for the next few minutes.

"I'm going to the gift shop," Charlotte said.

Sophia decided to call family now that everything settled down. "Hi, Dave, I'm at the hospital."

"What's wrong? Are you okay?"

"Yes. It's Brenna. She's hurt pretty bad."

"What happened?"

"I'll tell you later. I just wanted you to know where I'm at."

"Okay. See you later. Thanks for lettin' me know."

"Sure. Love you."

"I love you too, honey."

"Hi, Zoe. How come you're not here?"

"Where am I supposed to be?"

"At the hospital."

"Are you okay? What happened?"

"You don't know?"

"Know what?"

"Brenna's here. She's badly beaten."

"How come no one told me?"

"I don't know. Charlotte called me."

"That figures. 'I'm always the last to know' strikes again. I should have those words written on my epitaph."

"I'm telling you now, so quit complaining. You're just feeling sorry for yourself. Are you coming or not? She's really in bad shape. She might not make it."

"I don't plan on it. She doesn't want to see me anyway."

"That's no way to be, especially as a Christian."

"Why do people keep throwing that in my face? You remember how she treated me at Uncle Jerry's funeral. She wouldn't care to see me. Besides I need to be here for Onia."

'What's going on with her?"

"She had a nervous breakdown."

"That explains why she didn't answer when I called. What happened?"

"She probably wouldn't want you to know, but I'll tell you anyway. Rachel had been giving them a hard time. She ran away and she's been missing for weeks now."

"Weeks? And I'm just now finding out?"

"I don't know why, but Onia didn't want you and Brenna to know."

"And you're complaining about not knowing what's going on? This is pretty serious. You should have told us."

"You're right, I should have."

"I guess that proves we aren't a close-knit family after all."

"We never really were. You and Brenna are distant to us in age, and you live so far away. Those factors make it hard to be close."

"That's true."

"I wouldn't shut you out of my life as if you didn't exist though. I still love and care for you as family should."

"Then come to see Brenna."

"I can't just up and leave. Besides, I told you I need to be here for Onia. I'll send her a get well card. I might have to send it anonymously though."

"Okay. I'll keep you posted on how she's doing."

"I'll keep her in my prayers too. Thanks for understanding."

"Sure. Goodbye."

"Bye."

Sophia stayed at the hospital and did everything she could to pass the time. She knew every part of the hospital by now and the day was turning dark. She hadn't seen any sign of Charlotte, so she went back to Brenna's room. "Where is she? She's gone!" Sophia rushed to the lobby.

"Where have you been?" Charlotte said. "I looked for you. Then I gave up. I thought you had left."

"Where is Brenna? Did she...?"

"No. They stabilized her. She's in a regular room now. I'll show you."

"Brenna, are you awake? How are you feeling?"

"Miserable. I feel woozy from all this medication which isn't doing me much good."

"How come?"

"I still feel pain."

"Charlotte told me Chad put you here. Is that true?"

"Yes. He caught Devon and me together."

"In bed?" Sophia asked.

"What do you think? I was with Devon when Chad walked in on us."

"Were you actually having sex at the time?" Sophia asked.

"What difference does that make?"

"I told her to use our guest house." Charlotte said. "This probably wouldn't have happened, if she had listened."

"Funny you would suggest a place that you practically live in," her mother said.

Charlotte giggled. "I could have worked you into my schedule."

"Anyway, Chad caught Devon by surprise. I told Devon to leave as I tried to scratch his eyes out. He left a little beat up. I tried to fight back, but Chad really let me have it when Devon left."

"I love the adventure. This is better than a movie," Sophia said.

"A movie is less painful," Brenna said. She winced and sighed.

"We told you to be careful. It's not the best, but maybe you should just get a divorce."

"I'm planning on it once I get enough money saved up from my job."

"What do you need to save up for? Your kids are grown. They can take care of themselves. Chad can give them the money they'll need to live on."

"Don't start with the mooching talk again. I don't have the energy to argue."

"I didn't mention a word about mooching. You don't have to be in that big house with your kids anymore. You can move out and let them stay there as long as Chad will allow them. It's his money and his house anyway. I can help you move."

"Thank you." Brenna said as she closed her eyes.

"I can tell you're tired. I'll see you tomorrow."

Brenna was released from the hospital in less than a week. Her trauma hadn't dissuaded her from her affair. However, it prompted her to more secrecy than before. She heeded Charlotte's advice to use the guest house. When it was occupied, which was more often than not, she met at Devon's.

A few weeks had passed before she talked to Sophia.

"Hey, girl, how's it going?" Sophia said.

"Much better. I can see out of both eyes again. My ribs are healed too. I have something to tell you." She said. She hesitated and swallowed hard.

"What? What is it?"

"I don't know if I can find the words to say this."

"Is it good? Quit keeping me in suspense."

"All right. I'm pregnant."

"You what? How? At your age? I mean...You know what I mean."

"Actually I don't know what you mean."

"Chad is never around. How? Oh, I get it."

"See, you're not so slow after all."

"How is Devon?"

"He's great. We're excited."

"Chad will kill you. You know that don't you? You can't stay there."

"I don't plan on it."

"Where would you go?"

"I'm moving in with Devon."

"Oh."

"You don't sound too thrilled. Aren't you happy for me?"

"Not really. You're too old, and a baby just complicates your affair. How are you going to hide the bump in your stomach from your husband?"

"I don't know yet. I could buy bigger clothes. Anyway he hardly notices me anymore."

"I think he'll notice a big goose egg in your gut."

"What do you think I should do?"

"I don't know. This is your dilemma."

"Some help you are. I thought about getting rid of it, but Devon didn't have any children."

"Isn't that hypocritical with you suggesting Charlotte get rid of hers?"

"How did you know about that? Never mind. Anyway, Charlotte doesn't have a clue who the father was. Poor little child would have to grow up without a father, and she knows nothing about being a mother."

"None of us do. You know a child isn't born with instructions. We all learn by trial and error."

"She didn't want the baby anyway."

"That's unfortunate."

"Sophia, we may never agree on much of anything."

"Well, that's something we can agree on."

"I just thought I'd let you know what's going on. I'll talk to you later."

"Did you tell Onia and Zoe?"

"No, but you can tell them if you want."

"All right. Talk to you later."

Chapter 21

Trouble in "Paradise"

"This know also, that in the last days perilous times shall come. For men shall be lovers of their own selves, covetous, boasters, proud, blasphemers, disobedient to parents, unthankful, unholy, without natural affection, trucebreakers, false accusers, incontinent, fierce, despisers of those that are good, traitors, heady, highminded, lovers of pleasures more than lovers of God; having a form of godliness, but denying the power thereof: from such turn away. For of this sort are they which creep into houses, and lead captive silly women laden with sins, led away with divers lusts."

2 Timothy 3:1-6.

Brenna lived like a nomad, roving between both homes for a while before she settled in with Devon. Much to her dismay, his home reminded her of the humble lifestyle she lived as a child. She couldn't bring her luxuries for fear that the monster she was married to would notice, so she left most of her belongings undisturbed. She kept trying to convince herself that her material sacrifices were small prices to pay for her rejuvenated appetite for Devon.

Reality set in as she tried to adjust to the disappointment of relinquishing her affluence. She felt like she was trading in a brand new Ferrari for a used Ford. Devon's single-story shack had only two bedrooms and one bath.

The neighbors were loud and engaged in parties that poured out onto their front lawn almost every weekend. Brenna tried to avoid any confrontation with the rogues despite their insolence until she came home from work to find one of their little demons urinating on Devon's lawn. She pleaded with him to talk to the parent, but he desisted. Her frustration mounted when their loud music interrupted her ability to concentrate on the news and her sleep.

"How can you stand living near these people? They're animals!" Brenna said.

"I know. It seems like this neighborhood went downhill overnight. The innocent kids morphed into wild teenagers. But I've put too much money into this place. I have to deal with it until the house is paid for. I'm just your average hard-working businessman, not a millionaire like your husband."

"He's close, but he's not quite a millionaire."

"I barely make six figures. Does that bother you?"

"Well, sort of," Brenna said. "I'm trying to adjust. It's going to take some time though. I lived in a secure, gated community. I don't know if I can withstand sharing space with rambunctious barbarians." She stood in the doorway with her hands on her hips as she turned up her nose and shook her head.

"C'mon, now. You'll do it for me, won't you? We could join them too, you know." He wrapped his arms around her waist and pressed his body against hers, rubbing his cheek against her face.

She smiled and looked up at him. "Sure. I'll do it for you."

"That's my girl," he said. He slapped and rubbed her on the bottom. "I have a jacuzzi. We could have a great time getting to know them."

"That actually sounds interesting," Brenna said, raising her eyebrows. "Let's invite them over this weekend."

"Not so fast. How about in a few weeks? Let's get more acquainted with each other first," he said. He grabbed her and carried her to one of the modest little bedrooms.

Their relationship dwindled as the days went on. Devon regretted inviting Brenna to live with him. Other than their habitual romps they didn't have much in common. He realized she was an insatiable materialist with a fetish for the media. The only respite from their differences was their intimacy and the baby that was looming.

Devon came home to a house in disarray more often than not. "Can't you clean up after yourself? I don't have a maid to pick up after you," he said.

"I'm sorry. I'm too tired when I get home."

"Too tired? I'm the one running a business."

"I know. I'll have to get used to being pregnant again. I didn't work when I had my other kids."

"Is that what you call it?"

"What? I'm not doing a good job at your business?"

"I was just kidding," he said and smiled.

Brenna cleaned up the disaster area she created in the miniscule living room before she turned on the TV.

"This is world news tonight with Stephanie Doyle. We have grim stories to share. Israel has just been bombed by surrounding countries. There isn't much left of Jerusalem but smoldering remains of buildings and carnage. Many lay dead near the Wailing Wall at the temple mound. The video footage may be disturbing for viewers."

Brenna stared at the TV with her mouth agape. She hurried to the refrigerator to grab a snack.

Devon followed her back into the living room. "Let's invite the neighbors over this weekend," he said, "I'm feeling frisky." He leaned over to kiss her. She nodded and waved him off, eyes glued to the TV. He swaggered to the kitchen to grab something to drink.

"There was a standoff between authorities and the leader of the Firstborn of Messiah's Illuminants, Jeff Hardy. Over two hundred of his followers were killed in the gunfire. Jeff Hardy was found dead with a self-inflicted gunshot wound to the head."

"Oh shoot!" Brenna yelled.

"What's wrong?" Devon said as he rushed back into the living room.

"Do you remember that cult leader who's been all over the news? He just had a bunch of people killed and then killed himself."

"Why do you watch this depressing junk?"

"It's not junk. This is how I find out what's going on in the world, even on an antiquated TV."

"Antiquated? It works, doesn't it? I need a breather and someone who accepts me for *me* without looking at the bottom line," he said as he walked out on his deck. He cracked open his can of beer.

"What are you trying to say?" She turned the TV off and followed him.

"You knew going into this relationship I didn't have money like your old man. Now that's all you do is complain about what you don't have. You sure have changed. I don't like what all your wealth has turned you into."

"I didn't mean anything by it."

"Yes you did. You always criticize my belongings, comparing them to what you had. If you want to go back to that wife-beater, go right ahead."

"Okay, okay. I'm sorry. I didn't say I don't want to be with you."

"You just don't want to be with my stuff except for my antiquated TV."

"I just want to be with you."

"How come every time I come home you're glued to my TV, watching depressing stories on the news?"

"This is what I want to watch. Now who's being critical?"

"Okay. I'm sorry."

"I'm sorry too."

They kissed and cuddled each other.

That weekend the news became Brenna's reality. Gunshots and screams awakened her in the middle of the night. She failed to realize she wasn't watching TV in her quest to investigate. Against Devon's warning and aroused by her curiosity, she rushed to the living room window only to witness someone, already laying lifeless on the ground, get shot in the head. She gasped, withdrew, and rushed back to the bedroom. Devon was crouched near the dresser with a gun in his hand like a police officer in an adventure-movie shoot-out. He yanked her down beside him.

"What were you thinking? You could have gotten killed!"

She sat speechless, slumped against the wall, eyes wide open. Her face was pale as if she had seen an apparition.

"Are you okay?" he whispered. He inspected her to make sure she wasn't bleeding. Then he slapped her lightly on the cheek.

"I -I don't think so."

"What happened? Did you see anything?"

She broke down and whimpered in his arms. "Oh, Devon, it was awful."

"Tell me! What happened?"

"I need to get out of here! They might come after me."

"*Who?*"

"I just saw...your...neighbor shoot his wife!"

"Oh, my god! Well, did he see you?"

"I'm not su-"

Bang!

Brenna squealed in horror.

"You stay here," he said.

She was fine with his request because she was too numb to move. Devon saw two bodies laying on the sidewalk when he peeked out the window. The one was still moving and appeared to be writhing in pain. He grabbed his cell phone to call 9-1-1. By the time the paramedics arrived the entire neighborhood had cluttered the street.

When the mayhem was over two lifeless bodies were carried away leaving three wailing children behind.

Devon trudged back to the bedroom, rubbing his head as he tried to fathom what just happened. Brenna was packing, and he couldn't much blame her. "I can't stay here a minute longer. This is no place to live let alone raise our child."

"Where will you go?"

"I'm going back home. Charlotte is going to have to find another place to entertain her boyfriends."

"I'm coming with you."

"That's the best thing I've heard all day."

Their continued relationship was under a lot of tension not knowing if and when Chad might show up.

Brenna grew closer to Sophia. She confided in her more often than she would have imagined. She hadn't gained enough nerve to inform Devon, Sophia being her only trustworthy source; that he was no longer going to become a father.

Chapter 22

Hard Pressed, But Not Crushed

"The Lord is nigh unto them that are of a broken heart; and saveth such as be of a contrite spirit."

Psalm 34:18

Zoe committed several traffic violations racing to the kids' house. She had overslept. Much to her dismay the children weren't ready. She hurried from her car to investigate rather than leave them. She knocked on the screen door with caution.

A robust girl in her late teens nearly tripped over a broken toy as she waddled to the door in her bare feet. She wore a t-shirt and leggings both appearing a few sizes too small. A scarf covered her head to hide rollers.

She peeked into a house that had seen better days. The screen door was tattered and it had a corner peeled away causing a tetanus threat. The doorknob wobbled as if it would fall off. From what she could see the walls and light switches were decorated with fingerprints. The smell wafting from inside reeked of Pine Sol, stale food, and urine.

"Can I help you?" she asked.

"I came to pick the kids up for church."

"Church? My mama didn't tell me anything about that."

"I usually take them every Sunday."

"Well, she not here."

Zoe was shocked. Why wasn't she called, so she knew not to come? She was reluctant, but she decided to ask where their mother was.

"If it's all the same to you she's at the hospital."

"Hospital?"

"You heard right."

"Is she okay?"

"Her little boy is there."

"Which one, if you don't mind me asking?"

"Little John-John."

"Oh no! What happened? What hospital?"

"You have a lot of nerve gettin' in my grill and askin' about our business."

"I love these kids as if they were my own."

"Uhn. He's at Children's Memorial Hospital. Where else do they take kids?"

"Thanks." Zoe said as she turned away.

She rushed back to her car and hurried to church. She knew focusing on worship would be a challenge, so she called on God's name to give her strength.

When she arrived she realized she needed God's help more than usual. She felt the need to ward off distractions from choir members who were on their cell phones during the mini rehearsal. Others were plagued with pettiness demonstrated by their disparagements.

She withdrew to a restroom before the service, longing for solitude as tears streamed down her face.

After church Reverend Thomas asked her if she was okay. When she explained what was weighing on her heart they prayed together.

Zoe wasn't fond of hospitals, but she decided to visit her sweet little bundle of inspiration. An enigma waited for her like a prowler in a dark alley as she wasn't sure what to expect; however, she knew with God's help she could handle it.

She took a deep breath as she approached the hospital entrance. When she had reached Little John-John's room she gasped. With a heavy heart she eyed the little boy who had touched her heart. She tried to keep her composure as he lay frozen. The only signs of life were the sounds of air pulsing from a respirator and a beeping monitor. His mother sat near the bed. She peered at Zoe.

"Hi, Ms. Cobbs."

Her eyes pierced through Zoe as if she had never seen her before.

Ms. Cobbs was a walking vanity chest. She wore heavy makeup, tight designer clothes, and fake hair. Her endowments and her tall stocky frame confirmed her appeal to men.

"How's he doing?"

"Not good," she finally spoke. "How did you know he was here?"

"I stopped by your house to pick up the kids for church. The young lady who answered the door told me."

"That's my oldest. She suppose to be bringing the rest of the kids. They don't know how Little John-John is doin'."

"What did the doctor say?"

"They don't know what they doin'." He had a seizure that's all. That's why I brung 'em here in the first place. Now they got him hooked up to that machine. It's nothin' new though, he's always been my sick one. He had encephalitis when he was younger. I didn't know it, so it went on for some time. It got worse, 'cuz I didn't get him treated soon enough. You might have noticed it messed up his speech."

"Yes, I have," Zoe said.

"The doctor told me he was most likely goin' to get sick with somethin' else."

As she spoke, a slender Asian man entered the room. He was clean-cut except for a mustache which enhanced his appearance.

"Hello, Ms. Cobbs, my name is Dr. Grewal," he said with a thick accent. He extended his hand.

She began to shake and sweat as she shook it.

"Your son has acquired a severe case of bacterial meningitis. When caught early there's a chance of survival, however, it usually creates long term effects. Unfortunately he has had it for several days untreated. Didn't you notice any signs of illness?"

"He complained of a headache, and he been quiet. I thought maybe he had a cold."

"A pulmonologist discussed the intubation with you. It's what's keeping him alive."

"What are his chances?"

"Very slim without respirator," he said rolling his 'r'.

Zoe wrapped her arm around Ms. Cobbs. "How long has he been here?" she asked.

"Since Tuesday."

As they were talking, a woman sauntered into the room with paperwork.

"Hi, my name is Jessica Durham. I'm the caseworker. I'm here to set up a time to discuss the next step in your son's condition. We can talk privately."

"I'll come back when you're finished discussing this," Zoe said as tears filled her eyes. She looked over at Little John-John before she drifted out to the waiting room.

Jessica motioned for Ms. Cobbs to come with her. They walked to her office.

"What do you mean about my son's condition?"

"We need to explore options for you in moving forward with him. Have a seat."

"What options?"

"We're at a crossroads with your son. There isn't much more we can do for him. We need to make plans to take him off the respirator. Do you have any other family members who need to be present?"

"Just his deadbeat father."

"Did you want to contact him to let him know?"

"I can, but I already know he won't come."

Jessica cleared her throat. "All we need to know is what day and time you want to proceed."

"Okay," Ms. Cobbs said as they walked back to the room.

The robust girl had just arrived with the kids.

"What's goin' on?" she asked.

Zoe wiped her eyes hoping they wouldn't notice as she thought about the adorable little boy who had filled her with so much joy fight for his life. "A caseworker is in the room. They're discussing what arrangements your mother should make."

"Arrangements for what?"

"They can explain it better than I can. Why don't you go in? I'll stay out here with the kids."

"Thanks."

"Can't we go in?" Tamika asked.

"It probably would be best if you didn't right now."

"Why?"

"Your mother..."

Marvin brushed past her. "You're not the boss of me."

He followed his sister and barged into the room. His mouth dropped open when he saw Little John-John.

"What are you doing in here?" His mother asked him.

He couldn't find the words to say.

"You shouldn't have come in here. I'll let you know what's going on when we're finished talking. Go back in the waiting room area."

"No!"

"Do what I told you," she said. She walked over to him.

"No! He's gon die! I wanna see him!"

"Go take him back to the waiting area, Janisha."

He tried to pull away as his sister grabbed his wrist. Ms. Cobbs smacked him on the head. He broke loose and darted from the room. Janisha chased after him.

Marvin tore past Zoe and the other kids. She called out to him. Her ignored her and kept running. His older sister wobbled after him.

All Zoe could do was observe all the chaos. She grabbed Tamika and Phillip and hugged them. Her eyes watered. She tried to swallow, but her throat was too dry.

"Now what were you saying, Jessica?" Ms. Cobbs asked.

"We can wait until you find your son. I know you have a lot on your mind."

"That's okay. I'm not worried. He can't go too far."

"Are you sure?"

"Yeah. He'll be back. He's my drama boy."

"As I was saying, we need to discuss your son's possible extubation. We could discuss it now, but I want you to have a little time to think about it and talk it over with family."

"What other choices do I have?"

"I'll be back tomorrow at one o'clock to let you know."

"Okay."

As Jessica was leaving, Janisha hustled back into the room. She nearly knocked them over. "I couldn't catch him," she said out of breath.

"He'll come back when he wants something. I didn't expect all this drama. Take the kids back home."

"But we just got here."

"I need some time to think."

"About what?"

"I have a tough decision to make. It's more serious than I thought, and I don't want the other kids to see me like this."

"C'mon, we gotta go," Janisha told the kids.

"We just got here," Phillip said.

"When can we see Little John-John?" Tamika asked.

"Not today. Mama told me to take you back home. She needs time to think."

"About what?" Phillip asked.

"I don't know. She just does. Now let's go."

"We not gon wait for Marvin?" Phillip asked.

"No. Now let's go before you get left."

"Is it okay if I go back in there?" Zoe asked.

"I don't care. You do what you want to do."

"Bye, kids. Maybe I'll see you tomorrow," Zoe said. She hugged them. Tamika hugged her so tightly she nearly choked. "I love you two."

"We love you too, Miss T," Tamika said.

Janisha yanked them away from Zoe's embrace. "Let's go!"

They looked back at her and waved as they walked away in the distance.

Zoe went back to the room. She took a deep breath before she opened the door.

"Ms. Cobbs, is Little John-John baptized?"

"Huh? Naw. What's that gonna do?"

"Is it okay if I have my pastor come to visit him and baptize him?"

"What for? Is that going to bring him back to life?"

"In a way, yes."

"How soon can he make it?"

"I'll text him and see if he can come today."

Zoe prayed as she waited for a response from her pastor. Shortly after she prayed a text message appeared. "Praise the Lord," she said as she read it. "He can make it today. He'll be here in about thirty minutes. In the meantime, we need to find Marvin."

"Just let him be. He'll show up eventually."

Pastor Thomas arrived earlier than he had said. Ms. Cobbs had notified Little John- John's dad who refused to make an appearance. He blew the incident off with disdain.

Pastor Thomas introduced himself before he grabbed an empty container from his bag. He poured water into it and stepped over to the bed. He then leaned over the boy as he poured water on his forehead three times. "I baptize you in the name of the Father, and of the Son, and of the Holy Spirit," he said after he spoke other words from scripture. "This marks you as a child of God."

"I'm goin' to see if the doctor can come in," Ms. Cobbs said. "I made my decision."

She went to the nurses' station to request to see Dr. Grewal. She waited awhile before the doctor came. They walked back into the room where Little John-John lay.

"Dr. Grewal, I want you to pull the plug."

"Are you sure?" he asked.

"Yes. I think he be alright."

Zoe's jaw dropped and her eyes widened. She glanced at Pastor Thomas.

"This preacher just performed a miracle on my son. I know he'll start breathing by hisself."

"There's a slim chance of that happening, but be prepared if it doesn't."

"You can go ahead. I'll take that chance."

"All right, I'll make arrangements. I'll let the caseworker know for tomorrow."

"Okay, thank you."

"I'm sorry, Ms. Cobbs." Dr. Grewal said as he turned away.

"He's gonna live isn't he?"

"Yes," Zoe said, "but not necessarily the way you think."

"What's that suppose to mean?"

"You heard the doctor. He might not be able to breathe on his own. But he does have life in Jesus now," Zoe said.

"I don't understand."

"It's a good thing. You can be at peace with your decision." Pastor Thomas said.

"Can you bring me here tomorrow, Miss Todvue? I'm gon need a ride."

"I'll text you to let you know if I can take off. If not I can just drop you off first thing in the morning. Do you want your kids here?"

"Naw! They can visit when he's awake."

"I didn't mean to mislead you. Keep in mind the doctor said he might not make it."

"I ain't tryin' to hear that."

"Okay," Zoe said and turned away. She felt a lump in her throat.

Zoe kept blinking to stay awake as she drove home. The stench from the hospital lingered in her nostrils.

"Marvin? You startled me. What are you doing here? You're the last person I would have expected to see."

"I have nowhere else to go."

"How did you get into the building?"

I waited for somebody to open the front door."

"What about going home?"

"I don't have a home. I'm not going back to that place."

"Well, I'd love for you to stay here, but I don't have an extra bed."

"Can I sleep on the couch?"

"I don't know if I can trust you here."

"Why?"

"Well, I've been meaning to talk to you and your mother since the last time you were here."

"A-About what?" He said. His palms began to sweat.

"I think you know," she said.

"What is you talkin' about?"

"Quit pretending like you don't know."

"How am I supposed to know? I can't read your mind."

"I had some gold jewelry sitting on my table when you came over. Now it's gone."

"Bro, I know you don't think I took it. Why would I want yo' junk?"

"Because it wasn't junk. It was real gold, and you know it."

"Don't blame me 'cuz you forgot where you put it. Maybe you need to call the Alzheimer's Hotline."

"That's not funny. You're being very disrespectful. My gold earrings and necklace were on my table before you sat on my couch and pouted."

"I didn't pout."

"All I know is my jewelry is missing and you were the last person in the room where it was. It didn't just walk off on its own."

"I didn't take your dumb jewelry."

Zoe knew proving her case was futile, so she relented. Besides, a voice inside her head told her to forgive and let it go.

"Come on in. You can stay tonight, but you'll need to find a permanent place to stay other than here."

She dragged herself into the kitchen to inspect her refrigerator. "I've had a long day. I'm going to fix something to eat and relax in the bathtub."

She reached for some leftover chicken casserole.

'Are you hungry?"

"What you got?"

"Some chicken casserole."

"I'm good."

"Suit yourself."

She warmed the food in the microwave. The aroma dissuaded the boy. "I'll have some," he said.

After she fixed their plates they ate and talked.

"Is Little John-John still alive?"

"Yes."

"Why? Why did this have to happen to him? He didn't hurt nobody."

"It's a part of life. We all will die. It's a curse of sin. Some unfortunately die sooner than others. God's got him though. Pastor Thomas came to the hospital to baptize him."

"What's that suppose to do?"

"It works faith in the heart and marks you as a child of God. The Bible says that if you believe and get baptized he will save you."

"Save you from what?"

"From death in hell with the devil and his demons and totally separated from God."

"That don't make sense."

"Think of all the bad people in your life who do really hurtful things. Those are the people you will be around forever in hell, along with the devil, demons, and lots of screaming. There's nothing good in that place, only bad."

"So, I'm used to that."

"Oh really. Then why are you here? Why aren't you at home? You said you didn't want to go back to that place. Hell is much worse than what you're dealing with at home. All the hustling you're doing can't be fun either."

"No, but I make good money."

"Life isn't always about making money, especially if you're not happy."

Marvin thought about her words.

Zoe took out her Bible and had a study on baptism with Marvin after they ate. She laid bedding on the couch for him. Then she took a nice long bath to relax.

Before she could lie down Marvin knocked on her door. "Miss T, how can people change?" he asked.

"What do you mean?"

"My mama...she with a woman now after having us."

"Really?"

"Yeah. And they suppose to be gettin' married. I'm confused."

"That's a touchy subject. But the Bible tells us it's not natural, and it's not the way he designed us."

"It don't seem right."

"It's not."

"I don't like it. They do weird things to each other. I don't like being around the buzzing noises I hear. They sound like they givin' each other a whoopin' sometimes too."

"That's why God's way is the right way. It sounds like they're coming up with ways to please each other that are not natural."

"Where does God say it's wrong?"

"You naturally can tell it's wrong, because it makes you feel uncomfortable. Besides that, God mentioned that it's wrong in quite a few places in his word since the beginning of time. It's in both the Old and New Testaments. You'll find proof in Genesis chapter one when God tells Adam and Eve to be fruitful and multiply and replenish the earth. That can't happen with two men or two women. In chapter nineteen, the story of Sodom and Gomorrah makes it clear that the men in those two cities were wrong in going after other men. Leviticus chapters eighteen and twenty, Romans chapter one, and First Corinthians chapter six let us know it is an unnatural lifestyle. Even Jesus talks about a husband leaving his mother and father, cleaving to his wife, not another man, and the two becoming one flesh in the book of Matthew."

"Let me see."

Zoe took out her Bible and showed him before he went to sleep. She called the principal to inform him that she was taking a personal day. Before she went to bed she went into her sanctuary and prayed.

"Dear Triune Sovereign of the Universe,

Thank you for using me today to share the gospel with Ms. Cobbs. Thank you for giving Little John-John the hope of eternal life with you through his baptism. Thank you, Lord, for bringing Marvin here. Lord, if you decide to take Little John-John, please give us strength and comfort to carry on without him. Please let this trying time bring Marvin and his family to you.

In Jesus's name I pray. Amen."

Two eyes had peeked through the door which was cracked open. Marvin tip-toed away and scurried to the couch as she headed towards the door.

A while later he knocked on her bedroom door again.

"Miss T?"

"What?"

"I took it."

"What?"

"I took your jewelry. I'll pay you back somehow."

"I forgive you."

"You mean you not mad at me?"

"No. I was at first. I appreciate you admitting it though. Now go to sleep."

"Goodnight," he said as he walked away smiling.

"Goodnight."

Though the couch was uncomfortable, he slept better than he had in a long time.

The following morning Zoe drove Marvin to school before she picked up his mother. She called Pastor Thomas to request his presence at the hospital.

Ms. Cobbs consulted with the caseworker and the doctor while Zoe stayed in the waiting area. When they were finished Zoe followed them back into Little John-John's room. A nurse came in shortly after. She was there to dispense medication. The doctor remained at the boy's bedside as he monitored vital signs. He had the nurse proceed with the extubation.

Pastor Thomas arrived about ten minutes later and prayed over the boy while everyone watched for signs of life. Zoe held his one hand, his mother held the other.The nurse slowly weaned Little John-John off oxygen. The little boy's chest continued to rise and fall to everyone's relief.

"He's breathing on his own. Thank you, minister, I mean reverend, whatever you call yourself, for giving him life."

"Don't thank me. It's God's will if he lives."

"If?"

"We must wait to see if he'll come out of the coma on his own," Dr. Grewal said. He had the nurse continue to cut off the oxygen supply.

"He just yawned!" Zoe said. "Isn't that a good sign?"

"Yawning is involuntary. It's just a reaction," the doctor said.

Ms. Cobbs studied her son's chest. She noticed its rise and fall becoming erratic. His breathing was raspy. She placed her hand on his arm and caressed it. His skin felt cold and appeared blotchy. He became restless and started grabbing the covers. She retracted, thinking she agitated him.

Tears clouded her vision as she watched. "Wha-what's g-going on?" she asked.

"I'm sorry, Ms. Cobbs," the doctor said.

"You keep sayin' that. Sorry for what?" She said in a high-pitched voice.

He hesitated as he noticed the monitor readings had dropped. The boy's chest rose and fell less frequently.

Zoe began to sing, "All night, all day, angels watching over me, my Lord."

Little John-John stirred as if he was trying to sing with her. A strange odor like fingernail polish remover engulfed the room. Then his body went limp as he let out a little moan. A tear streamed down the corner of one eye.

Ms. Cobbs began to wail. "He's gone! He's gone!"

The doctor checked his pulse and nodded.

Zoe's throat tightened as if someone was choking her, and she felt numb. Her eyes watered. All she could picture was a little boy with big brown eyes gazing at her with a sparkle in his eyes when she told him about Jesus. She couldn't bear to look at the cold, lifeless shell lying on the bed, so she turned away and burst into tears.

"You told me he was going to live!" Ms. Cobbs yelled.

"He is. He's living eternally now," Reverend Thomas said.

"I don't know what that means. I want my son back!"

"I'm sorry."

"Sorry is not goin' to bring him back."

Zoe left the room with her head down, tears streaming down her face.

Janisha and the rest of the family arrived at the hospital to say goodbye to Little John-John. Zoe kept to herself.

When she had collected herself, she decided to go home. The trip took longer than she had expected. Her vision blurred along the way, especially as she played songs on her CD player. She had to pull over a few times to make it home. Flashes of Little John- John's face, that twinkle in his eyes, and the cold lifeless body lying in that hospital bed kept flickering in her mind.

When she finally arrived at her apartment she plopped on her couch from exhaustion. She sat there for only a few minutes when she heard a knock.

"Marvin, where have you been? I tried to pick you up from school, but you never came out."

"I walked. I wanted time to think before I found out about my brother. What happened?"

"He didn't make it."

Marvin screeched and flung himself into her chest. She held him close to her and let him purge. Her shirt became drenched with his tears. They both trembled as she joined him. Minutes passed before they recovered.

Now he understood how much she loved them, however, he knew he couldn't stay with her. He pushed away from her and sprinted to her door. She called him, but he kept running.

Chapter 23

Struck Down, But Not Destroyed

"We are troubled on every side, yet not distressed;
we are perplexed, but not in despair;
9 Persecuted, but not forsaken; cast down, but not destroyed;"

2 Corinthians 4:8-9

"I'm not so sure how long I can do this," Zoe said as she bit into a piece of sweet potato pie.

"Do what? Eat the rest of my pie? Is it that bad?"

"No. The pie is great. I mean teach."

"Oh, come now. Don't give up already. You've only been here five years."

"I taught for fourteen."

"Hi, Mrs. Williams," one of the middle school students said as she hugged her. "How's my favorite teacher?"

"I'm fine. Aren't you going to speak to Miss Todvue?"

"No. I don't like her. She's irritating," the girl said.

She and her friends chuckled. They nodded in agreement as they walked away.

"See what I mean? I've overstayed my welcome. I should just quit. These kids and their parents are trying to get rid of me anyway."

"Don't let that steal your joy. That's nothin' but the devil gettin' into your head."

"Well, he's winning. I was just reprimanded by the principal for something some students told him."

"What did they say?"

"They said I was using foul language and making racist remarks. It's like everything I say for God's kingdom gets twisted and makes me out to be a liar. I think I know who it was too. This one student told me he was going to get me fired."

"Don't worry about that. You know how kids can be. Everyone knows you love the Lord and all the kids."

"Yeah, but it's hard coming to school every day knowing some of the kids hate you and go out of their way to show it. I feel like I'm under constant attack when I'm here."

"You are. The devil knows you're a threat. We have to stay strong. God tells us we will face persecution for doing his work."

"You saw how rude those girls were to me. I get that all the time."

"That wasn't you that was them. They were wrong," Resa said, shaking her head. "Parents don't teach their kids respect anymore."

"What's interesting is they demand your respect, but they fail to show it."

"They don't know how to show it. They only know what it's like when the feel disrespected."

"I don't know how to instill that in them."

"You're passionate, and you get too emotional. It comes across like disrespect in their eyes like you're trying too hard. It's not wrong because we all have different approaches, and God knows your heart. These kids are just ruder than ever. I'm just glad I had them when they were young and more impressionable."

"Sometimes I wish I taught the younger ones. Kids turn on you when they get older if you don't immerse yourself into their world like listen to their music or hop on the social media bandwagon."

"That makes your job tougher for sure, especially 'cuz you don't look like most of them either."

"That shouldn't matter."

"Unfortunately it does. It's hard for my people to take directives from people in the first place, let alone white folks. Correcting them makes it worse when you don't look like them."

"Should I listen to their kind of music to relate to them?"

"I would never encourage that."

"I just tell them what God would have them do."

"Sometimes it's best not to say anything. Just keep setting an example by what you do and how you live. Let God do the rest through your prayers for them."

"I suppose."

"And let me tell you, the younger ones have their share of issues too. They're exposed to so much these days...stuff that would make your straight hair curl up."

"I just don't like when they make me look like a liar. That affects my testimony."

"And who is the 'Father of Lies'?" She raised her hand towards Zoe's mouth. "You don't need to answer that. You already know."

"It wouldn't make sense for me to sing God's praises from one side of my mouth and use vulgarity out of the other. That's not genuine faith to me."

"As I mentioned, the devil knows you're a threat, so he's trying to discourage you. That's what that is."

"Am I? I feel like what I tell everybody about Jesus just bounces off them and smacks me back in the face."

"What are you talking about, Zoe?"

"I do all I can to be a witness for the kingdom, but nothing comes of it. You see how these kids treat me. Most of them treat me with contempt like I have some disease or something."

"Whatever you do, don't let them see that they get to you. They'll chew you up and spit you out."

"The ones that do like me, like Victor, says he isn't sure he believes in God because he can't see him. Can you believe kids talk like that in a school like this? That's very discouraging."

"Sure I can. Not everyone who hears God's word believes. God says many will say to me Lord, Lord, and he'll tell them he never knew them."

"It bothers me when I know people who flat out reject him, especially children. Even my own sisters shun me because I talk to them about Jesus. My younger sister listens, but she worries too much. My oldest sister hates me because I bought her son a Bible for Christmas. That was a few years ago, but she blames me for him taking his life. She claims it confused him."

"Have you prayed about any of this?"

"I pray for them all the time."

"Then let it go and give your efforts over to Jesus. You can't make them believe. Only God can work faith in their hearts, and you certainly can't believe for them. Just keep doing what the Lord wants you to do, pray for them, and let him do the rest."

"It's hard when I don't see the fruits of my labor and everybody's blaming me when things go wrong."

"Whatever you do, don't give up. Do you remember what God says in his word about our work for the Lord?"

"He says a lot of things. What are you referring to?"

"He says our labor will not be for nothing because his word will not return to him empty. What you do for God's kingdom is taking effect. You just don't see immediate results. He doesn't promise that you will. He doesn't promise that it will just be one person either. There may be other people who come along in their lives that God uses as well. These things take time."

"I guess I never gave what you're saying much thought."

"That's just it. I think you're trying too hard to make things happen with your own efforts. You're forgetting that the Sovereign of the Universe can handle it. He uses us as his instruments to plant the seed. The Holy Spirit takes over from there while we continue to pray for people and live our lives as examples."

"Thank you for your words of wisdom. You're a great friend."

"I hope you think I'm more than a friend. I'm your sister in Christ."

"Yes you are, and I appreciate you."

"You are very useful in God's kingdom. You sing his praises in choirs, you bring kids to church, and you teach in a Christian school."

"People in choir hate me and talk about me because I get solos that they want. The kids I bring to church give me a hard time about coming. That's all they want is what they can get from me, if they want to come at all, except for the littlest one. Now...he's... *Gone.*"

"What happened?"

Her voice cracked. "He died a few weeks ago and his mother is mad at me."

"What for?"

"She blames me for his death."

"How could you have control over what happened to him?"

"I told her that getting him baptized would give him new life. She took it literally and had them pull the plug after he was baptized thinking he might live physically."

"Wow, that's deep."

"I was only trying to help her out. I'm trying to be strong through all of this, but I miss him. I loved that little boy as if he was mine. His eyes sparkled whenever I talked to him about Jesus. He touched my heart...and to see him lying lifeless in that..."

"I'm sorry you had to go through that. Even though you miss him, God used you to bring him to faith. You made a difference and you'll get to see him again."

"That's true. Thank you for helping me see things from the Jesus perspective."

"Anytime, sweetie."

"Hi, Zoe." She looked up and noticed Dorothy approaching. "I haven't seen you in a while? Where have you been?"

"Oh, hi, Dorothy. I've been here. We haven't talked since my date with Brandon. You're not mad at me anymore?" Zoe said.

"I was never mad at you. I thought you were mad at me."

"Why would I be mad at you?"

"Well, now that you both have that settled," Resa said.

"My brother told me what happened on your date. You haven't talked to me since."

"That was a while ago. I spoke to you after our date, but you just ignored me."

"When?"

"Ladies, let it go."

"Anyway, my brother wanted me to ask if he could have another chance with you."

Resa cleared her throat and shook her head.

"I don't know. We have nothing in common."

"He realized he came on too strong. He wants to make it up to you."

"Well, I have to think about it."

"Can he at least call you again?"

"I guess so."

"Okay. I'll let him know," she said. Then she walked away.

"See, she's been so distant and impersonal to me lately."

"I noticed. She came over here to deliver a message and that was it. She's up to something. I can feel it in my spirit."

"Everything changed after I dated Brandon." Zoe scarfed down the rest of her pie and started on her own lunch.

"Then why would you let that barracuda back in your life?" Resa asked.

"I don't know. The Jesus in me got the best of me. I want to forgive him for what he did. Maybe he's changed and maybe Dorothy will be nice to me again."

"You shouldn't care what she thinks. Besides, she could have sat down to eat with us if she was real."

"That's true."

"Some friend. You're a better person than me."

"Tell that to these unruly kids."

"Ha, ha, ha." They both laughed.

Zoe entered her apartment after checking her mail, her usual routine. She sat down on her couch to go through it when someone knocked on her door. She raced to answer it hoping that Marvin came back. Though her place was too small she knew the streets was no place for him. She gasped when she opened the door.

"Hey, how are you doing?"

"Brandon?"

"Yes. You remembered."

"What are you doing here?" She said, running her fingers through her slightly mussed hair.

"I just happened to be in the neighborhood, so I decided to stop by."

"Unannounced?"

"These are for you, baby," he said ignoring her question. He stepped into her doorway and handed her a bouquet of flowers and a box of chocolates. "I apologize for how I treated you on our last date."

She pushed him back.

"I just wanted to apologize in person."

"I accept your apology. Now please leave."

She shoved the bouquet into his chest and tried to shut the door as he was backing out. He muscled his way in.

"I accept your apology, and thank you for the gifts."

"You're welcome," he said. He cleared his throat. "Can we go somewhere to talk?"

"We can talk here."

"I would like to take you somewhere to eat," he said as he smiled.

She hadn't eaten since lunch and fighting against his strength threw her into a realm of futility, so she agreed.

"I picked our same place."

"You made reservations? Wasn't that a bit presumptuous?"

"I wasn't sure if you would say yes. I just took a chance. I would have begged, if I had to."

"That would have been awkward."

"I would do anything to get a second chance."

"Now you sound desperate."

"I just want to make up for last time."

"That's thoughtful of you, but we don't have to go to a fancy restaurant to prove it."

"You let me be the judge of that. I want nothing but the best for you."

He escorted her to a sleek, silver BMW. "I see you have new wheels. What did you do? Rob a bank?" she said as they walked to his car.

They both chuckled.

"BMWs aren't cheap," she said.

"I came into some money doing a few extra gigs. I've been traveling with a band a lot too."

"Do you still play in church?"

"Naw. That gig didn't pay enough. Besides, you were right. I had to be upfront with my sister about going to church."

"You stopped going to church since you don't play there?"

"I didn't say that. I visit occasionally, but you don't have to go to church to believe."

"True, but God tells us to not stop meeting together to spur one another on."

"What does that mean?"

"It's a fellowship thing."

"You making that up."

"Actually it's in the book of Hebrews. It means to build each other up in the faith by praying with each other and encouraging one another."

"You can do that outside of church. Heck, we're doin' that right now."

"How many people discipline themselves to read the Bible on their own and build a relationship with the Lord? Even people who go to church regularly have a tough time doing that. Most people I know spend their free time watching TV or going out."

"Like us?"

"Yes, but I'll still make time to be with God before the day is over and I value the importance of attending a Bible-believing church."

"Well we're here. We can talk about this later."

"Or not," she said under her breath. She felt discouraged as she walked beside him. Nothing changed with him. If anything, his views seemed to have regressed.

"Would you like a drink?"

"Sure I'll have a soda."

"C'mon, have a glass of wine. One isn't goin' to hurt."

"I don't drink alcohol. I'm going to wash my hands," she said as the waiter set out dinner rolls.

"Let's have a toast - to a new beginning," he said when she came back.

Zoe sipped her soda after they clanged glasses.

"What kind of soda is this?" she asked.

"Why?"

"It tastes strange."

"Oh?" He said looking confused.

"It tastes a little bitter. I haven't tasted soda with a bitter aftertaste before."

"It's diet."

"Oh."

Their wait resembled the time span of a fast food restaurant, because the patronage was sparse.

"This looks good," Zoe said. Her vision blurred as she eyed her chicken kiev. She took a few bites and savored the buttery flavor. "Mmm," she said.

"I'm glad you enjoy it."

"I hadn't eaten since lunch. Hey, why are people staring at us?"

"I don't know. I hadn't noticed. How many black men are seen with beautiful red heads?"

She continued to ingest her culinary delight. "I suppose not too...I think I ate too fast," she said.

"Why do you say that?" he asked as he grinned.

"I'm feeling a little light-headed and drowsy."

"Maybe your fowl was foul," he said. He chuckled.

"Are you trying to be funny?" she asked, feeling dizzy and disoriented.

"I thought I was. Do you want me to take you home now?" he asked with a wry smile on his face.

"Yes, please."

Brandon called for the check.

Zoe stumbled as she stood up.

"You're not okay. Let me help you up," he said. He rushed over to her side of the table. He held her up as he walked her to his car. "I better get you home."

"Yes, quickly, please. I think I have the..." She zonked out by the time he reached her apartment. He had to carry her to the door.

"Where's your key?" he asked.

She didn't respond, so he tried to jar her awake. She moaned but couldn't answer. He searched her purse until he heard a rattle. He teetered under her weight as he shifted to one side. He used the wall to hold her up while he unlocked her door. He cradled her in his arms to carry her to her bedroom.

"Ouch!" he said as he stubbed his foot.

He laid her down gently before he turned on a lamp beside the bed. He gazed down at her in the soft light admiring and stroking her silky red hair. "You're so beautiful," he said.

She moaned.

He began to kiss her. His hands began to caress and fondle her. He peeled her clothes away as she lay there. Then he violated her defenseless body.

Zoe woke up groggy and sore. Her head was throbbing. She vaguely remembered being in Brandon's car. She wasn't sure what had happened after that. She saw blood on her sheets and realized she was half naked. Did this really happen or was this a dream?

She felt cheated. She dragged herself out of bed and stumbled to the bathroom. She showered to wash off the dried blood. Despite washing many times she could still see blood on her skin. She still felt filthy.

Why did he do this? How did this happen? Should she call the police? She had so many unanswered questions. She plodded back to her bedroom. She looked at her alarm clock. She had enough time to make it to school; however, she couldn't bear to face anyone. She changed her bedding before she called the principal to take the day off.

She collected herself and dragged herself to her battlefield, her emotions stirred. She felt like her spirit had been ripped apart. She felt angry at Brandon and at God. She knelt at the cross above the makeshift altar. Before she could find the right words to say, she slumped over the table and yowled like a lonely cat. She knocked the cross over and cried out to God. "Why, Lord? Why did you let this happen? I followed your will to wait until marriage, just to have my, my..." She couldn't bring herself to say any more.

The day had just begun to peek through the window, emanating the only ray of light for her darkened spirit.

Emptying her emotions drained her. However, her appetite waned and nausea replaced it, requiring her to rush to the bathroom to eliminate last night's dinner. When her body became too weak to wrench anymore she trudged to bed and slid under the covers.

The sun which had peeked through her window in the early morning turned into starlight before she awakened. She felt illusions of an appetite, but not enough to warrant fixing herself a bite to eat. She turned on the lamp near her bed.

Zoe, still feeling distraught and confused, toiled to her battlefield and cried out to God. "Where are you?" she pleaded. "Why did you let this happen?" she asked again. "Why can't I find peace in my spirit?" She cried herself to sleep.

Zoe woke up in a fog the next morning still lying at the altar. All she could hear was children singing words of comfort in her ears. A calm hovered over her spirit for the moment as she realized God was speaking to her.

She grabbed her Bible from her nightstand hoping to find solace. The words didn't pierce her heart as they usually did. Her emotions inhibited her from concentrating. After a few hours of staring at the ceiling and the Bible still on her lap, a peace came over her. Hunger overwhelmed her so she raided her refrigerator with voracity like a lioness consuming its prey.

She began to feel well enough to talk to God without crying.

> "Dear heavenly Father,
>
> Please instill in my spirit the ability to forgive Brandon for what he did to me.
>
> Please help me understand why you allowed my body to be taken when I was saving myself for a husband in obedience to you. Lord, you say in your word that all things work together for my good. I hope and pray you help me see the good that will come from this. Give me the strength to

find healing and to move forward. In Jesus' name
I pray. Amen."

The next day she decided to call in sick after eating breakfast and getting dressed, allowing her the weekend to recover. She decided to start fresh on Monday morning with the hope that by then she would be ready to face the world again.

Monday morning she raced into the school building with her head down, hoping no one would notice her.

"Hi, Miss Todvue, where've you been?" Victor asked.

Zoe didn't answer.

"Did you see the post about you on Snapchat?"

"No. I don't go on Snapchat."

"Somebody put your picture on the body of a pole dancer."

She gasped.

"They made fun of your eyes and called you a cock-eyed thot."

"What's a 'thot'?"

"It's a whore."

"Do you know who?"

"Now you know I couldn't tell you even if I did. That's not how I roll."

"Oh, I'm sorry. You just let people know something they would be better off not knowing to get them all worked up."

"I just thought I let you know because I like you, and I don't agree with them anyway."

"That's thoughtful of you. Now I have something to tell you."

"What?" he said as he leaned close to her.

"Thank you for letting me know." She forced herself to smile.

"You're welcome, Miss Todvue,"

"Her eyes began to water. She hurried to the bathroom to dry her eyes. Dorothy followed her and approached her with a hint of congeniality. "Hi, Zoe. Where've you been?"

There was something in her eyes and her tone that made Zoe feel uncomfortable.

"Brandon told me he tried to apologize to you, and you wouldn't forgive him. He said he brought flowers and you ripped them up. Then you threw them in his face."

Zoe's eyes widened as her mouth dropped open. "That's not what happened at all."

"Are you calling me a liar?"

"None of that happened except he showed up at my apartment when I didn't invite him."

"Some Christian you call yourself!"

"I have to get to my classroom." Zoe tried to brush past her.

Dorothy pushed her. "I guess you felt sorry for what you did, so he said you threw yourself at him to make up for it."

"That's not true! He took advantage of me!"

"Who's going to believe a lonely schoolmarm like you? You must've really been hungry for love because he said you were wild, but he enjoyed it."

Zoe's eyes widened as her mouth dropped open. "That's a lie!"

Dorothy cornered her. "He told me everything. We talk all the time. In fact we are this close," she said as she crossed her fingers. "We actually live together. He's my stepbrother with fringe benefits."

Zoe's mouth dropped open. "So you set me up. You knew what was going to happen all along."

"Pretty much. I guess you can't brag about being so holier-than-thou anymore, can you? By the way, how's your Snapchat?"

"You know about that?"

"Yep! I'm so proud of you! Now that you're in the club I wanted the world to know."

Zoe's eyes welled with tears. "How could you do this?! I thought you were my friend."

"That's what friends are for. We help each other out. I figured he was the right guy to do the job."

"You're sick. I'm going to report you."

"Go right ahead. You can't prove anything." Dorothy strolled out with a sardonic smile on her face.

After weeping for a few minutes, Zoe took a few deep breaths and fixed her face before she left the bathroom.

"Look at Miss Todvue. She looks like she's been crying," one student said as she rushed to meet Resa for lunch.

"I'll give her a reason to cry," the other student said. He threw a half eaten apple at her. It missed and smashed against a locker.

"What's the matter?" Resa asked her.

"Nothing," she said out of breath.

"C'mon, now. I know you better than that, Zoe. Something's bothering you. You're acting strange and your eyes look bloodshot."

"I said *nothing*!"

"I repeat. I know you better than that. Something isn't right. You can talk to me."

"It's just...these kids are so mean to me that's all."

"Something else is bothering you. What's wrong, Zoe?"

"One of these kids just threw something at me. Luckily it missed."

"Aren't you going to report it?"

"No."

"Why not?"

"I don't know who it was for starters."

"All right. Say, I overheard Dorothy say you went on a date with her brother again. How did it go?"

Zoe gasped. "I-I don't want to talk about it."

"Wow! That bad, huh?"

Zoe didn't respond.

"Why are you so quiet? This isn't like you. Did he hurt you?"

Zoe burst into tears.

"He did. Didn't he?" She sat down next to Zoe and put her arm around her.

"It was awful."

"What was awful?" another teacher asked.

"Here," Resa said. She handed Zoe a box of tissues. "Why don't we go into your classroom? It's available isn't it?"

"Okay."

Resa squeezed herself into one of the desks. "Did you call the police?"

"Well, I'm not sure...how...to prove it," Zoe said between sobs.

"How come?"

"I was asleep."

"Oh, one of those. What a coward among other things."

"I think he put something in my drink."

"I see. That may be hard to prove, but you have a witness."

"There was no one with us when it happened."

"I don't know why people go to bathrooms to talk in private without checking to see if someone is in any of the stalls."

"What are you trying to say, Resa?"

"Let's just say a little birdie happened to be in one of the stalls when you were talking to Dorothy this morning."

"You?"

"The one and only. You should report it even if they don't consider me a viable witness. That way he can be on record just in case he does it to someone else. Sin is stupid and gets bolder with time. And as for Ms. Dorothy, at least let the school know what she did to you on Snapchat."

"I don't want to be the cause of someone losing their job."

"What she did was out of line and unprofessional."

"What hurts even more is God allowed this to happen when I was saving myself for my husband."

"I was there when you let him get back into your life. Did you pray about your decision with a discerning spirit?"

"Well, no."

"I'm not saying what happened is your fault, because no one deserves what happened to you. What I'm trying to say is we make decisions without God then we want to put God in the mix after the repercussions. Do you understand what I'm trying to say?"

"Not really."

"You jumped into the decision to see this guy before discerning from God whether it was a good idea. Your choice to see him opened the door, not God. We aren't puppets on a string, and God doesn't always come to the rescue on decisions we make without Him. In other words, we can't blame God for decisions we make without seeking his guidance first, or expect Him to rescue us from the poor choices we make before something bad happens."

"I should have prayed on my decision to see him before I told Dorothy I would see him again?"

"Yes. Something wasn't quite right in your spirit the first time you dated him. That was a red flag."

"I was so focused on forgiving him."

"That's okay. You can forgive people and still keep them at a distance."

"You are so wise in your faith. That's why you're such a good friend. I think I know what I learned from this. I went ahead of God."

"Now the healing can begin. God will certainly lift you up and make you stronger, if you let Him."

"I feel better already. I'll report it to the police after school."

"I'll come with you, if you want. After all, I heard proof of what happened."

"I'd like that. Thank you for being such a good friend, Resa. I love you." She gave Resa a big hug.

"I love you too, Zoe. Remember, we're sisters in Christ. I'll wait for you after dismissal."

"Thank you, sister in Christ."

"You're welcome, soul sister. We're family, and we need to stick together."

They hugged each other again.

A parent scowled as she approached Zoe during dismissal. "How dare you confuse my son with your ideas."

"What do you mean?" Zoe asked as her voice quivered.

"Don't pretend with me. You know full well what I'm talking about."

"Actually I don't."

"Don't get slick-mouthed with me. I'll knock the snot outta you."

"Can we talk about this in my room?"

"No! I want everybody to know what you up to. Quit tryin' to brainwash my child!"

Zoe looked puzzled, but she dared not say anything else.

"My son is talking about Jesus too much for my likin'. Just when I thought that was bad, he's tryin' to tell me that my lifestyle is wrong."

"I'm here to tell kids about Jesus."

"My lifestyle is my business. I bring him to this school 'cuz he was bullied in public school, not for you to be shovin' Jesus down his throat."

"We're a Christian school."

"I don't care about all that. You're a certified teacher aren't you?"

"Well, yes."

"Then teach my son how to read and write, and leave it at that. You let me teach my child how to live."

"I'm sorry, Ms. Jenkins."

"You should be. If I hear any more complaints from my son, I'll have you fired!" she said before she stormed away.

Chapter 24

Powerful Petitions

"Confess your faults one to another, and pray one for another, that ye may be healed. The effectual fervent prayer of a righteous man availeth much."

James 5:16

Zoe continued to pray for Rachel's return and comfort for her family. She also prayed that Ms. Cobbs would forgive her and let her continue to take the kids to church. However, she hadn't seen Marvin since he bolted from her apartment.

She met and prayed with Pastor Thomas so often lately she thought she should take up residence in his office. She felt everything in her life was falling apart. The whole world was against her. She still struggled with what she had been through on her date with that rogue spurred on by a pretentious friendship in Dorothy.

Though she knew Little John-John was with Jesus, her heart still ached for him. She didn't understand why God was allowing all these bad things to happen to her and to her loved ones. That's all she wanted to do was live for him and be used by him to bring them to faith. She checked for scuff marks on her knees because her battlefield received more activity than ever.

Easter was a few weeks away which meant church fellowship and singing in the choir was imminent. Zoe was looking forward to the festive worship the holidays brought. She decided to call Onia to see how she was doing.

"Where have you been?" she asked.

"I've been away. You know Ryan had me committed."

"I haven't seen your family in church lately."

"I guess they haven't been going."

"Are you at least reading the Bible?"

"No. I never have."

"God's word can help get your mind off your troubles. Besides, I want you to talk to Pastor Thomas."

"Did you tell him my business?"

"Well, yeah. We've been praying for your family and for Rachel's safe return."

"I don't want busybodies knowing what happened."

"I talked to him in confidence."

"Stuff like this manages to leak out."

"So what if it does? We're here to pray for each other not judge."

"That's easy for you to say. You must've forgotten about what happened to Craig. Everybody found out. People I never met came sniffing around to offer their condolences. I felt like a celebrity being hounded by unwanted fans."

"Most people mean well. They simply want to offer prayers."

"Sure. It's the few who don't that concern me. They always stick their nose in where it doesn't belong. They offer to help, next thing you know the story somehow gets exaggerated and twisted."

"You just have to ignore them. Lord knows I sure need my church family. I feel like everyone is against me lately." Zoe hesitated. "I have something to tell you."

"What?"

"My virginity was taken away from me a few weeks ago."

"What? Do you know who?"

"Yes, and I'm in the process of pressing charges."

"Was it that dude you dated a while back?"

"Yes."

"I'm sorry this happened to you. I know how you were saving yourself for marriage."

"I don't understand, and I *was* mad at God about it for a while. That's how I know being around fellow believers and reading the Bible helps."

"I'll pass. I'm still mad at God right now. I can't believe He let this happen to Rachel and me."

"We live in a sinful world. Stuff is going to happen. God never promised Christians a perfect life. All of this craziness hurts my heart too."

"If you called to cheer me up, it's not working."

"All right. I'll keep praying."

"What's the point? You're not doing me any favors. What's done is done."

"Jesus will work it out. You'll see."

"Bye, Zoe."

"Wait!"

Click!

"Dear heavenly Father,

> Everything seems to be falling apart. Lord, you promised you would never leave me, but I don't feel your presence right now. Marvin and my niece are nowhere to be found. Now my sister Onia has turned away from you. Lord, I know you are much bigger than the struggles and the hurt that Onia and I are going through right now. Please help me to surrender and wait for your timing. I pray that your timing is soon. You promise to look out

> for children. Please help me understand what your plan is for them. I pray that part of your plan is to bring them to you. In Jesus' name I pray. Amen."

Zoe hustled to get to church when Easter finally arrived. After intense prayer for the right words to say, she convinced Ms. Cobbs to come along with her and the children.

She felt a lump in her throat while she led a song about the resurrection. Tears streamed down her face as she thought about Little John-John. She knew God's grace allowed her to prevail through her inner turmoil. However, she tried not to think about the people whom she loved who were no longer with her. Though annoying at times, she missed Marvin's spunk. She missed Rachel's verve even though many times her niece complained. What really touched her was the possibility that Craig was with Jesus.

She didn't want the service to end. The words from the sermon touched her and compelled her to anticipate singing with the angels. The comfort it brought her inspired her to think of praising the Lord as a taste of heaven. She knew God was using her to serve, and He was going to make everything work out for good.

"Your solo was amazing," Pastor Thomas said. "I could see the Spirit moving through you more than ever before as you sang."

"Great job, Zoe. Thank you for inspiring me this morning," one of the members told her. "You have such a beautiful voice. Keep using that gift."

Another member told her how much her solo brought her to tears.

Zoe left church uplifted and inspired to be able to minister to so many.

"Do you always sing like that?" Ms. Cobbs asked.

"I guess so, but I felt the Spirit of the Lord more today than usual."

"You welcome to come over for dinner if you want," Ms. Cobbs said.

"Oh, thank you. I'll take you up on the offer. I didn't cook anything."

Zoe regretted her choice to eat with Ms. Cobbs. She tried to force down something that resembled meatloaf. She bit into gristle with every bite, so she tried to be inconspicuous as she dislodged the mystery meat from her mouth. Pellets of ground beef covered her plate like spitballs.

Ms. Cobbs introduced Zoe to her partner, which was even more disheartening and awkward than eating that meatloaf. The two women ogled each other as they consumed their food-like substances. They bit off each others' forks, and divulged a persona that made their same sex encounter appear glamorous.

"Have you heard from Marvin?"

"Naw. He must be alright, 'cuz this ain't the first time he run away. He comes back when he won't somethin'. He's a survivor."

"Oh." Zoe was disturbed by Ms. Cobb's nonchalance over her missing ten year old son. "Don't you miss him?"

"Sometimes I think about him, but I have so many mouths to feed. He's probably better off where he's at."

Zoe had enough disappointment for one day. "Well I better be going," she said.

"So soon? Don't you want dessert? I made a cake."

"No thanks. We have a few days off school, but I still have schoolwork to do."

"Okay."

"Thank you for the meal."

"Would you like to take some home with you?"

"No! I mean, no, I'm fine. Thank you."

"All right. You take care. Again nice job singing."

"Thank you. You take care too."

Zoe was relieved to leave. She felt like a food prisoner trapped in a web of spiritual delusion. She stopped at one of the few open stores to buy some food. She was determined to fix herself a meal that was the farthest thing from beef she could think of to satisfy the hunger that still plagued her. She also needed to purge from the spiritual filth of Ms. Cobbs' relationship. It countered the reverence for obedience to the Lord that inspired her in church that morning.

"Hi, Miss T, how you be?"

The question puzzled her because she could only hear a voice. She peered around.

"It's me, Miss T," the voice continued before she heard some laughing.

She set her grocery bag down. She noticed a boy slumped against the wall next to her door. She stood perplexed. "Do I know you?"

"It's me - Marvin."

Zoe gasped. Marvin was hardly recognizable. His eyes were bloodshot, and he looked emaciated. He staggered toward her. He scanned the area as if someone was following him.

"You don't recognize me," he said. He sounded weepy.

"Oh my God," she said. "What happened?" She put her hand over her mouth. Her purse fell from her hand.

"What do you mean? I'm fine," he said before he slid down and fell to the floor. He started laughing again.

Confusion overwhelmed Zoe. "Lord, please help me figure out what to do." She grabbed her keys, hands trembling. After calming herself, her hands steadied enough to unlock the door. She pulled Marvin by the arm to help him get up.

"I'm hungry. You got somethin' to eat?"

"You're in luck. I just came from the grocery store."

"What ya got?" He started laughing again.

"What's wrong with you, Marvin? Why do you keep laughing? Are you on something?"

"I just had a little weed that's all."

"A little?"

Zoe caught herself before she started to preach. Her main concern at the moment was to make sure he was taken care of. Luckily she had bought a few bags of chips and some nuts for snacking. "I've got a few snacks here you can munch on while I fix dinner."

"What kinda snacks?"

"Come see for yourself. Pick what you want."

He grabbed a bag of chips and gobbled them up almost as soon as he opened the bag. He pleaded for more, but she insisted he wait until she fixed what she called real food.

"I saw your mother today. I even took her to church with the kids. Don't you miss your family?"

"I miss Tamika and Phillip. I definitely miss Little John-John."

"Don't we all."

"How are they doing?"

"They're fine. They'll be getting baptized in a few weeks."

"Oh," he said as he began to get sleepy. "Mind if I crash on your couch again?"

"You're always welcome here," she said. She grabbed a sheet from her linen closet. She folded a towel to make a pillow.

He fell asleep as soon as he lay down. She wanted what was best for him, but she knew she had to call his mother. Ms. Cobbs showed apathy when Zoe told her about her son. "I don't need his money anymore. My girlfriend helps out a lot around here. He's one less mouth to feed. I'm glad to hear he's okay."

Wow! His mother's indifference floored her. Her heart ached for Marvin. She better understood the tough front he displayed. She put a lot of love into what she cooked that afternoon. She wanted it just right for him. Things would be different between the two of them from now on. She would see to that.

Someone knocked on Zoe's door. Before she could answer, a police officer broke it down with a battering ram. What's going on? She thought. Marvin jumped off the couch and hid on one side. The officer looked around. Marvin could see him unnoticed. He spotted a closet and scurried to it on all fours. He felt safe for the moment.

The door squeaked alerting the officer to his whereabouts. The officer tiptoed to the closet and tried to open the door. Marvin pulled with all his might on the other end. He was no match for the man's strength. As the officer yanked the door open he fell to the floor. The officer drew his gun and told him he was under arrest. He whimpered like a lost puppy.

Zoe stormed into the room to find Marvin flailing on the couch. She grabbed him by the arms and shook him. He woke up gasping for air. "What's wrong?"

He looked around, eyes wide open. He sighed when he realized where he was. He buried his head in her chest, trembling and sweating. She rubbed his back and rocked him. "It's okay," she said. "I'll take care of you."

When he settled down, she said, "Why don't you come into the kitchen with me. You can help me make dessert."

"O-okay."

"I'm baking a ham. It's one of my favorite things to make on Easter." She opened the oven to show him.

He inspected it. "What are those black things on it?"

"I put cloves in it. I learned that from my mom. You don't eat them though."

"Then why do you put them in there?"

"They give the meat a kind of smoked taste," she said as she poured a pineapple juice and brown sugar mixture over the top. "This mixture is a glaze. It gives the ham a little sweetness."

"It smells good."

"I hope you taste the love in it when you eat."

"Huh?"

"That's just an expression."

"Oh. What else are we having?"

"Mashed potatoes, rolls, and spinach."

"Spinach? Um, I'm allergic to spinach."

"Nice try, French fry. That's what you kids say when you don't like something. Just try it. It'll make you stronger."

"I don't want to."

"I'll make a deal with you. You eat your spinach, and you can have an extra dessert."

"I'll think about it...Okay, deal," he said. They shook hands and smiled.

When they sat down to eat Zoe prayed over the food.

"Where have you been all this while?" she asked him between bites.

"I been doin' what I could to make it."

"Like what? Where did you stay in this cold weather?"

"During the day I go to school. I clean up in the bathroom. The cafeteria food never tasted so good. I usually go hungry on weekends. I ain't gonna lie. I snatch a bag of chips from gas stations sometimes. At night I sneak in apartment buildings to sleep."

"You are a survivor just like your mother said."

"I used to sell candy to people."

"Really? What kind of candy?"

"Nose candy."

"Is that what I think it is?"

"I don't know. What do you think it is?"

"I don't want to say because I'm concerned for you."

"It helped feed my family."

"That's no way for anyone to live, especially a ten-year-old boy. You can stay here as long as you need to."

"Thanks. You got money?"

"Why do you ask?"

"You seem rich to me." He looked around the room.

"I do alright."

"You have a lot of stuff we don't have. We don't even have a couch. We sit on folding chairs that some church gave us. Our mattress is on the floor, and it sags in the middle. I have to share it with Tamika and Phillip. Sometimes we wake up fighting because somebody bumped somebody else in the middle of the night and we get mad."

"I know how you can earn some money the honest way."

"How?"

"I could use some help around here. I'll pay you and teach you how to save. But promise me you won't go spending it on your habit."

"What habit?"

"Your drug habit."

"I don't have a drug habit. I just tried some weed, that's all."

"How often do you smoke it?"

"This was my second time. I think."

"Marvin, you don't have to be a product of your environment."

"What's that mean?"

"You can rise above your circumstances by doing better than what you see around you."

Marvin thought about it. "How much would you pay me, Miss T?"

"Five dollars a day."

"I'll think about it."

"When you decide, you can start with these dirty dishes."

He frowned.

That evening Zoe went to her battlefield, thankful for Marvin's safety. She could hear water running and dishes clanging. She smiled.

> "Dear awesome Father,
>
> Thank you for your hedge of protection over Marvin. Lord, please equip me with the right words to say to encourage him. Please use me to help turn his life around.
>
> In Jesus's name I pray. Amen."

Chapter 25

Answered Prayers

"Delight thyself also in the Lord: and he shall give thee the desires of thine heart."

Psalm 37:4

"Breaking news: Mass shootings took place at two schools today. A parent pulled out a gun and opened fire at Randolph Elementary this morning killing two teachers. Three children are in critical condition at Children's Memorial Hospital. The parent has been taken into custody.

At Pearson High School a teenage boy went on a rampage killing three people and injuring five more before turning the gun on himself."

"Mom!" Brenna heard pounding on the guest house door. She jumped. Then she peered through the curtains to see who it was.

"CJ? This better be good," she said as she opened the door. "What brings you out of your bedroom, and why are you banging on the door?"

"Come here, you gotta see this!"

"I'm watching the news. What is it?"

"Just come here, quick!"

She followed him to the house. As Brenna entered his room he motioned her over to his computer.

"Isn't that cousin Rachel?" he asked. He pointed to nude girls dancing and making obscene gestures.

Brenna's mouth dropped open. "Wow! I think that's her in the middle."

"I thought so. I didn't know I had a kinky cousin."

"Neither did I. Let me call your aunt. I wonder why she didn't tell us."

Onia had given up on Detective Warren. Though she usually regarded the news as an annoyance, she turned the TV on with the hopes of finding information on her missing daughter. As she began watching, her phone rang. She was shocked to hear from Brenna.

"CJ saw Rachel on his computer. When he showed me I knew for sure."

"What are you talking about? What was she doing on the *computer*?"

"You didn't know about this?"

"I didn't want everybody knowing, but I haven't seen Rachel in weeks. She ran away from home a while ago."

"I hate to tell you this, but she was making an obscene video."

"Are you sure it was her?"

"I'm positive. I know that blonde hair anywhere. She was in what looked like a hotel room with other girls and a few men."

"I'm glad she's alive, but I can't believe she ran away to do this."

"Umm, I don't think she chose to do this. It chose her."

"What do you mean?"

"At her age? Where have you been? Haven't you heard about porn rings? This stuff is on the rise. Somebody could have snatched her up. They could be making her perform against her will. Even if she chose to do this, it's illegal because she's not old enough to get a job, especially one like this."

"She's been so rebellious lately. I just figured she would do what she could to earn some money."

"You can't be serious. I think you should look into this. There are too many girls getting snatched up these days."

"I can't look into it right now."

"Why not?"

"Ryan had me put in the loony bin."

Brenna chuckled. "What?"

"I kept imagining I saw Rachel. I guess he had enough. He said I was scaring the other kids. It did me some good though. I feel better."

"When are you getting out?"

"I think in a few days."

"Please look into this. This is serious."

"Will we be able to get her back?"

"Maybe. The FBI can trace the website."

"How do you know about this?"

"I watch it on TV all the time."

"Okay. I'll tell Ryan. He'll get on it, if he believes me. Better yet, can you call him and let him know?"

"Sure."

"Okay. Thanks."

Ryan called Onia to inform her about his plan. He was ready to embark on the mission to find Rachel.

"When can I get out of here?" she asked.

"The doctor said you've made progress, but I think you should wait until we find Rachel."

"Ryan, if you leave me in this place I will never speak to you again!"

"Okay. Okay. At least let the FBI get a lead on her whereabouts first."

"Why?"

"I don't want you to start hallucinating again."

"I won't. I promise."

"I'll keep you posted, honey."

"You still didn't..."

Click.

Cameras were flashing, the lights were bright, and the room was as hot as a sauna.

"Great job, girls, you're lookin' good," Kyle said. "You're getting me so excited, I want a piece of you myself."

Someone knocked on the door. "Go get that, Bill," Kyle said.

Bill peered through the peephole. "It's some strange guy. Should I let him in?"

"Yes. It's just the man who wants a piece of these pies before he buys some videos."

Bill opened the door and the man barged in wearing a suit and wielding a gun. "All right everybody put your hands up!" he said.

Before Kyle and Bill could react, more FBI agents swarmed in. They handcuffed the men and had the five children file out. They were embraced and taken away safely.

"Are you Rachel?" One of the officers asked.

"Yes," a girl with dark circles under her eyes and straggly blonde hair said. Rachel stood bug-eyed trying to take everything in. She appeared undernourished and thin as a rail like she was wasting away.

"Come with me," the officer said. He wrapped a towel around her naked body. "There's someone here to see you."

"Dad!" She said as she charged over to Ryan. She hugged him so tightly that he grunted from her embrace.

"Are you okay, honey?" he asked.

All of her pent up emotions poured out like a water fountain. Her body convulsed, drawing unwanted attention. He picked her up and held her close. "You're safe now. Let's get you back home where you belong."

"Rachel, you're back!" Amber yelled. She ran to the door.

Nathan and Aaron followed behind. "What happened to you?" Nathan asked.

"You can talk to her later. Right now I want her to get cleaned up."

Ryan took her upstairs and ran some hot bathwater. Rachel lay on her bed and wept until her pillow was drenched with her tears.

Ryan yearned to spend quality time with his family. A rare day off galvanized him into taking them to eat out. "Rachel, you pick the place."

"You can pick somebody else. I don't want to."

Ryan and Onia looked at each other stunned, wondering what happened to the Rachel they knew.

An evening of rejuvenation became a nightmare. As he parked in the driveway he noticed a broken window. He rushed inside to find their home ransacked. Before the rest of the family could reach the house he told them to get back in the van.

"What's going on?" Onia asked.

"Just get back in the van! I'm calling my mom so the kids can stay with her for a while."

"Tell me what's going on!"

"I'll tell you later." He leaned into her and put his arm around her as they walked back to the van.

"Dad, why can't we go in the house?" Nathan asked.

"I'm letting you spend some time with your grandma, okay? It'll be fun."

"Yay, Grandma's!" Amber said.

The house was in shambles. Onia looked around with her mouth open in disbelief. "How dare somebody do this to us!"

"Just relax, hon." Ryan said before he called 9-1-1.

He heard wailing come from the living room. He nearly tripped as he rushed to investigate. Onia stood with her hands near her face. She yelled, "The TV, our brand new TV is gone!" Then she dropped to her knees and wailed as if she had just lost a loved one. Ryan looked at the wall where a TV had been. What was left were holes and torn plaster. He sighed before he continued to report the incident.

"Everybody is okay. That's all that matters," he told Onia who was still grieving. He knelt beside her. "I know it's a big blow, but it's gonna be okay." He wasn't sure if he said those words to convince her or himself.

"Hi, Zoe, guess what?"

"What?"

"Rachel is back!"

"Praise the Lord! I've been storming the throne for your family. How are you doing?"

"I'm okay. Our house got broken into. If it's not one thing it's another."

"I'm sorry to hear that."

"Do you remember that detective you met at the police station?"

"Yes. Why?"

"He asked about you."

"Did he find Rachel?"

"No. The FBI did."

"Good, because I don't feel like dating anyone right now."

Onia looked confused. "Why did you say that?"

"He intended to take me out for coffee when he found Rachel."

"Okay. Anyway we're going to counseling as a family. We have a long road to recovery with Rachel. She's going to need intensive counseling after all she's been through. It's going to cost a fortune, but she ran away for a reason. We need to work together as a family to find out why."

"I'm glad your family realized that. I've got good news to tell you, too. You know that boy named Marvin that I had been bringing to church? He came back like the prodigal son."

"That's great. Tell me about it sometime. I have to get going. Thanks for looking out for me."

"Anytime, sis."

"Hi, Resa, how was your weekend?" Zoe asked as she bounced into the teacher's lounge.

"Apparently not as good as yours was. My aren't you chipper on this dreary Monday."

"I'm bringing the sunshine indoors today." She sat across from Resa. She set her lunch on the table smiling from ear to ear.

"How was *your* weekend?" Resa asked, holding her fork up to Zoe's mouth like a news reporter. "I can tell you dyin' to tell me."

"I'm glad you asked. God is so amazing. My niece was found alive."

"Great news!" Resa said as she smiled.

"Do you remember the boy named Marvin I told you about? He showed up outside my apartment the other day, so I took him in. He doesn't want to go back home right now, and I don't think his mother wants him, so she's allowing me to let him stay as long as he's off the streets. That's interesting because she was the one who had him hustling on those streets."

"That's wonderful. God is good."

"Amen! Even better yet, his mother has been coming to church every now and then. She's letting the kids get baptized too."

"Awesome! See, Zoe, you making a difference."

"Slowly but surely I guess. I just get discouraged sometimes and need a friend like you to get me back on track. You lift my spirits. Did anyone ever tell you that you have the gift of encouragement?"

"Don't you think I know that by now, child?"

"I suppose you would. I've been praying for so many people lately. My answered prayers prove that anything is possible with God. Marvin and I finally built a good relationship. He used to give me nothing but attitude. He even seems to enjoy our devotions together. It's like he sees what life can be like outside of his normal. I pay him to listen anyway."

"What? Shame on you, Zoe! I can't believe you cheapening the word of God with bribery."

"It's one of his responsibilities he has to earn an allowance."

"That's ridiculous!"

"I know it's bribery, but the Holy Spirit can still plant the seed."

"Not if he's listening to God's word for the wrong reasons."

"Sure he can. Are you denying the power of the Holy Spirit?"

"No, just your method. I just mean it might backfire."

"I have to do whatever works these days."

"Touché. Let me know how it turns out."

"I will."

They finished their lunch in silence. Zoe imagined life with Marvin's whole family sitting in the church next to her, eyes glued to Pastor Thomas as they focused on his every word.

Chapter 26

Spiritual Gatekeeper

"I exhort therefore, that, first of all, supplications, prayers, intercessions, and giving of thanks, be made for all men; For this is good and acceptable in the sight of God our Saviour; Who will have all men to be saved, and to come unto the knowledge of the truth."

1 Timothy 2:1,3,4

With all the disasters and catastrophes, Zoe felt driven by a sense of urgency to witness to everyone who was willing to listen. The Holy Spirit impelled her to have the courage to satisfy the craving she had since she was little.

Despite her suspicions, Sophia became seduced by Reverend Whitaker's words and fascinated by his charisma now more than ever. He also began to look more appealing than he ever did. She refused to engage in slander about him from other church members. She became more on fire for him than she was for the Lord despite his eeriness.

She marked off the days before the cruise and persuaded Dave to lay aside his reservations. She convinced him to relinquish more money to the monetary pit bull, join a gym, and engage in shopping sprees with their new bodies, despite the financial burden the activities created. She was so proud of her accomplishments that she sent pictures of herself to Brenna who coveted her new wardrobe and seethed with envy.

Sophia sat engrossed in the reverend's TV program like a groupie watching a favorite rock star when the news broke her trance with a breaking story.

"California lay engulfed in flames as gas leaks and explosions caused a cataclysm. Cities along the San Andreas Fault sat in ruins as an earthquake measuring 9.8 on the Richter Scale caused devastating fires, killing thousands."

She found the newscast exciting and now realized why Brenna had an addiction to watching. As she became entranced by the information, her cell phone pinged. She checked her text. Zoe? What does she want? She decided to call her.

"Hi, Sophia, I'm so glad you called. I-I was wondering if you're still planning to go on that cruise."

"Of course. Why?"

"I...um...was hoping you would change your mind and go to the reunion."

"Why would I do that?" Sophia rolled her eyes and sighed. "It's pointless. I think it's a joke. I'm not going to miss this opportunity of a lifetime on a hunch."

"Well, the main reason I texted you was to plead with you to stop following that reverend. I think he's a false prophet."

"Why do people keep criticizing him? People at church have been complaining too. I don't want to hear people's opinions."

"It's not an opinion. It's research. I looked up false prophets on the internet, and his name came up. Plus the Bible describes false prophets, and he fits the description."

Sophia chuckled. "I don't believe you. What I *do* believe is you like to cause trouble in our family."

"I love you, and I just want to see you in heaven some day."

"Who are you to judge whether I'll be in heaven or not?"

"Maybe I'm not using the right approach. I pray for you all the time. I just want you to be careful. Remember the Bible tells us to test the spirits because not everyone who confesses Jesus is from God."

"All right, you made your point."

"I don't know if you've been watching the news lately, but a lot of end time prophecies are being fulfilled. Judgment Day is coming. Maybe not in our lifetime but soon enough."

"Now who's being the false prophet? From what I remember the Bible says no one knows when. Now *you're* claiming to know?"

"No I'm not. I'm just going by the signs of the end times from the Bible. A lot of what it says is happening right now."

"I watch the news. I admit a lot of bad stuff is happening, but it's nothing new."

"I see depravity smacking me in the face almost every day with the kids at school."

"What do you mean?"

"They're either being led by negative influences like bad music, bad movies, and pornography, or they're too afraid to speak up against it if they aren't."

"How do you know?"

"Not only can I tell by their spirit when they're around me, but some of the things they say and do prove it. I can't imagine what kids are like who aren't being fed God's word daily like ours."

"I think you're being judgmental."

"No I'm not. What comes from the mouth is from the heart."

"Says who?"

"The Bible says that."

"You need to live a little and get out of your sheltered world."

"What's gotten into you, Sophia? You weren't like this when you were younger."

"Things change. People change. I found out who God really is with the reverend."

"Oh really? Is God some money hungry, prosperity preaching, get rich quick schemer?"

"Is that what your lame research came up with?"

"Pretty much. I saw an interview with him. They toured his estate. He has a museum full of vintage cars. What kind of preacher makes enough money to own all of that, or *needs* it, for that matter?"

"A really good one."

"I'll keep praying the Holy Spirit will give you a change of heart."

"You do that."

Sophia sat for a while and considered what Zoe said after she had hung up. She flashed back to memories she and Dave had with Reverend Whitaker. She did notice changes in his demeanor recently. Dave certainly was suspicious. As she continued to ponder she realized how he does always want money. Maybe Zoe was right. Were she and Dave in too deep? Was it wrong to get what she wanted from this free cruise? His messages made her feel good like a breath of fresh air. She felt trapped in a whirlwind of confusion.

Zoe decided to check on her sister Onia with the hopes of better results than she had with Sophia.

"Hi, Zoe, what's up?"

"I haven't seen you in a while. I was wondering if I could come over."

"Sure. We're not going anywhere."

Zoe approached the house with apprehension. She wasn't sure how Onia would receive her during this aftermath. The Holy Spirit gave her the courage she needed.

She smiled as she walked up the porch steps. This venture reminded her of her childhood. She had pretended to be a teacher back then, telling her friends about Jesus when they played school.

Onia saw her coming and opened the door before she could knock. "Hi, Zoe, come on in."

"Hi, Onia." Zoe hugged her sister before she slid past her. Two rug rats bull-rushed her and nearly plowed her over. She gave them a group hug. She rushed over to Aaron who sat rocking on the couch and gave him a hug and a kiss. "It's great to see you all. Where's Rachel?" she asked with reservations.

"She's in her room. She stays there most of the time. She's taken up reading."

"Great, because I brought this over for her." Zoe pulled out a brand new Bible.

"Rachel! Aunt Zoe is here! She brought you something!"

Rachel's trauma lobotomized her. She became a recluse. Though she longed for her friend Ellen at times, her numbness to emotion helped her cope. Oddly enough her friend hadn't reached out to her either, compelling her to suspect that the girl she had seen during her nightmare proved what she had feared.

There were beneficial changes in the family as she recovered, however. Her family demonstrated how much they loved her, allowing her to redevelop the trust she had broken. She bonded with her siblings more than she could ever have imagined, finally realizing that she had been the catalyst for the strife.

After what seemed like a futile announcement, a shell of a girl clung to the banister as she lumbered down the stairs. Zoe heaved as she stared at a scrawny girl who looked like she hadn't slept in days, hair stringy and mussed, clothes disheveled. Zoe turned to Onia and whispered, "Has she been this way since…you know?"

Onia looked back at Zoe weary-eyed and shook her head. "She's getting better though. Counseling is helping a little, but they say it'll take years before she recovers. She most likely won't fully recover. We just have to be patient and supportive."

"I totally understand. Is she getting Christian counseling?"

"No. That's not necessary."

"I'd like to have Bible study with her, if you don't mind."

"I'm okay with it, but that's up to her."

Zoe handed Rachel the Bible. "I want you to have this."

Rachel looked at it as if it was a strange creature. Her hand trembled as she reached out to grab it.

"I'd like to read this with you sometime. Is that okay?"

Rachel nodded.

Zoe smiled and touched her on the arm. Rachel pulled away and jogged back upstairs. "When is a good time to come by? I'd like to read with her every week."

"This time works fine."

"You're welcome to join us."

"I'll let her spend time alone with you."

"Okay. See you tomorrow?"

"I don't think so. I don't understand how God could keep letting bad stuff like this happen to us."

"Onia, God gives us choices. Challenges come with our choices sometimes. When our choices don't align with his will, we have to live with the consequences. Remember what just happened to me? I went against my better judgment and warnings from a good Christian friend. Rachel made a poor choice like I did. Our choices had serious consequences. I have to admit that I was mad at God for a minute. My friend helped me realize that we have to learn from our mistakes and see the good. That's how we learn not to repeat them and learn to listen to God's way even if he takes a while to reveal what his way is. God wants us to have a close relationship with him."

"She's just a kid though," Onia said with a pained look on her face.

"Exactly. She's just a kid who thought she knew what was best for her by imposing her will on her circumstances even to the point of being disobedient and disrespectful. That's not God's plan for any child, or they wouldn't have parents. Even as adults we don't have the final say. God is over us too, which is why he's our father. We belong to him. I decided to go ahead of God in my decision to date a guy whom I knew wasn't right for me. I ignored the big, fat, red flag that waved right in front of my face from the first time I dated him."

"It's not just that. He let our house get broken into. All of our stuff that we worked so hard to get is gone."

"The Lord tells us not to get caught up into things that can be destroyed and thieves can steal. He tells us that our treasures are in heaven."

"But that was *our* stuff, not theirs. We just bought that smart TV."

"First of all, that stuff belonged to God. He entrusted it into your care. Second, all that stuff will get burned up in the fire. It will not withstand the refiner's test. Only things of God, like faith in him, peace, joy, love, and our relationship with him will matter in the end and will not get burned up -intangibles, meaningful things pertaining to God's kingdom."

"In the meantime we're not allowed to enjoy things in this world?"

"Sure. But with the good comes the bad. God tells us not to fall in love with this place. Frankly, I don't understand how people *can* love this place. So many bad things happen that make me wish the Lord would just come and take me away."

"A lot of people make poor choices, and God lets them get away with it."

Zoe sighed. "It may seem like they're getting away with things, but the Bible says, everything that's hidden will get found out."

"What's that supposed to mean?"

"We may not see their evil get exposed, but they'll be exposed on Judgment Day, if not before. We can't hide from God. Psalms says there's no hiding place. You can go further back than that to Adam and Eve in the garden."

"That was eons ago."

"God doesn't change, and he keeps his promises both good and bad. When he says he'll pour out his wrath on the wicked, he will, in his time. He doesn't just strike them down. He gives them time to repent as he did in Noah's time. That's where we believers come in to be witnesses before it's too late for them."

"Not everybody can do that. You're the only person I know who knows the Bible well enough to be a witness."

"My strength comes from the Holy Spirit whom all believers are given. He also draws us to other Christians to hold us accountable like my good friend Resa."

"All I know is, we bought a really nice TV, and someone felt entitled to it, and I lost my girl. She'll never be the same."

"She's still alive. Besides, God is a healer. If you surrender to his will you can watch him work through her recovery."

"I want my baby back now. This never should've happened to her."

"Good will come from this. God assures us in Romans eight. I hope and pray you have a change of heart and start coming to church again. I miss my sister." She hugged Onia before she left.

Zoe looked around after church, hoping her words had convinced Onia.

"Who are you looking for, Miss T?" Marvin asked.

"My sister and her family."

She left the building with her head down. She perked up when she saw Pastor Thomas in the parking lot. "Hi, Pastor, did you see Onia and her family?"

"I'm sorry, Zoe. I haven't seen them in a long time." Zoe fought back tears as she drove the kids home.

"Hi, Resa, how was your weekend?"

"I had a wonderful time. My son and his family came over for dinner. I played with the grandkids, loaded them with sweets, and sent them back home with their parents. How was yours?"

"It was okay. It could have been better. I tried to convince my one sister that she's entertaining a false prophet. I'm not sure she believed me though."

"Just remember, you can't believe for her nor be her savior. It's hard to convince someone who's been seeing someone for a long time to just turn away, even when the hypocrisy is in plain sight. Just like someone who's in love with an abusive partner. We can see things for what they are on the outside looking in, but they're in the middle of it."

"Then I went over to another sister's house. She's still mad at God over what happened to her daughter. I tried to persuade her to let go of her resentment. I hoped she would have a change of heart and I'd see her in church yesterday. She and her family didn't show up."

"Tragedies take time to heal. Maybe she'll come around."

"What happened to me was tragic, and I bounced back."

"Not right away, but sooner than most. But see, you have a strong relationship with the Lord. You're sensitive to the Holy Spirit's convictions. The average Christian isn't. We have to pray, surrender to God's timing, and let the Holy Spirit do his work."

"You're right. I'm going to miss you when you retire."

"I'll come back to visit. Besides, I'll have you over. I owe you a rain check on a catfish dinner."

They smiled and embraced.

Zoe continued to pray for everyone she could think of including her sister Brenna. She forgave her for her rudeness and aloofness. She even sent her a card for her birthday wishing her the Lord's blessings. She didn't get a response, not even a phone call to thank her.

Zoe felt the need to bring the church to the Fairweathers. She persisted in her quest to help Rachel recover. She met with her for Bible study without, much to her delight, any opposition. Summer vacation was approaching, so she intended to spend more than one weekly visit. She had noticed progress in the shattered girl as she loved her up and prayed with her. The little Fairweathers were eager to join her and Rachel too.

Onia's hostility toward the Lord festered. She was too blinded by financial worries to notice Rachel's improvement. She blamed God for everything including their money troubles brought on by paying for the counseling sessions. Ryan was too busy playing bread-winner just to keep up with the bills to bring them to church anymore.

The end of the school year brought mixed emotions to Zoe. She would miss her tete-a-tetes and prayer time with her accountability partner and friend Resa. However, summer vacation would be a respite from the attacks of students. She knew Satan used them to expose her weaknesses, but knowing the source didn't make her feel any better.

She thought maybe she tried too hard to win them over to God as Resa said which put a target on her back.

The year wasn't a total loss in satisfying her craving. She continued to edify worship and inspire people as she sang in church. God also gave her the calling to bring kids to church and build relationships with them. However, these opportunities were mere morsels in satisfying her hunger to build up God's kingdom because her attempts to convert and encourage her sisters eluded her.

When summer officially arrived Zoe decided to visit other churches. She brought the kids with the understanding that worship in a Bible-believing church was all that mattered.

One Sunday they attended a church where people were "passing out". The preacher was sweating and gasping. She looked at the kids and noticed that Phillip and Tamika looked petrified. Marvin's look reminded her of the first few times she brought him to her church. This ordeal appeared to erase months of hard work and prayer. She promised not to take them back.

The following Sunday she took them to a white-washed tomb. The building was immaculate and ornate. The stained-glass windows were picturesque. The smell of freshly cut wood permeated the sanctuary as she and the kids sat down on padded pews. However, members ostracized them as if they had a disease. She overheard a lady whisper, "Look at that white lady with those black kids." The other lady said, "I wonder where the father is. She doesn't even have a ring on her finger!" The first woman gasped. Zoe struggled to focus on worship during that service, never to return.

Zoe found her visitor's haven at a quaint little church near the edge of town. The people were warm and friendly. A soloist sang off tune, but Zoe could tell she sang from her heart because the words touched her spirit. What really impressed her was a man who couldn't speak. His impediment didn't stop him from praising the Lord in the only way he knew how, so he hummed the melody to the songs.

Tamika was roused by his efforts because she asked why he was humming.

"I guess he can't speak," Zoe answered.

She took them to that church a few more times before she returned to her church.

"Where have you been?" Pastor Thomas asked. "We missed you."

"Thank you. I just visited a few other churches."

"You're not planning on leaving us, are you?" He looked worried.

"No. I just wanted to visit other Bible-believing churches. It's good to be back though."

He smiled. "Great! Don't forget our church picnic worship is next week. Bring the kids and your appetite. Feel free to bring a dish to pass if you want."

"Thank you. I will."

The clear blue sky and warm weather, along with the worship service and fellowship at the picnic made Zoe wonder if heaven would be like what she experienced that day. Beautiful singing filled the air. The smell of grilled meat wafted into her nostrils and invited her to eat. The food stimulated people's desire to binge.

While she was noshing and socializing the kids were playing organized games. When they wanted a break from the competition they ate, played in a bounce house, or had gotten their faces painted. Everyone enjoyed each other's company so much that hardly anyone left until late afternoon.

"Did you have fun?" Zoe asked the kids when she drove them home.

"I did," Tamika said. She beamed from ear to ear. "I won some toys and lots of candy."

"We played games and won tickets. We got to turn them in for prizes," Phillip said. "Little John-John would've..."

Everyone in the car had gotten quiet. Zoe tried to ease the tension that was as thick as air on a hot and humid day.

"I know we miss him, but every day is like this for him."

"What do you mean?" Phillip asked.

"Heaven is a wonderful place filled with joy and happiness. That's where Little John-John is. He's singing, running, and playing. He's doing everything kids love, and he's able to do what he couldn't do here."

"Is that what you think, Miss T?" Marvin asked.

"It's not what I think that matters. It's what the Bible says. God will make everything new including our bodies. Little John-John is able to run and jump now."

"Wow!" Tamika said. They all smiled.

"You know what's even better than that?"

"What?" Marvin said.

"When you go there you'll get to see him again."

"I can't wait," Phillip said.

"By the way, how's your mom doing?"

"She's okay," he said. "She's been in the dumps since he died though."

"I noticed she hasn't been coming to church lately."

Marvin sighed. "I tried talkin' to her about it, but she wouldn't listen."

"Are things going better with her?"

"Not really. We never have anything. Sometimes we barely eat. And, Miss T, she married her girlfriend. I remember you showing me where the Bible says what they doin' is wrong. I tried to show my mama, but she told me to mind my own business. Why don't people wanna see what the Bible says?"

"The Bible not only comforts us, it convicts us."

"What do you mean?"

"It shows us when we do wrong. People don't want to know what they're doing is wrong because it makes them feel guilty."

"But didn't Jesus take our sins away?"

"Yes he did. We don't need to feel guilt for what we've done because he gives us a new beginning. The Bible says we're born again."

"Huh?"

"When you were baptized you were reborn. Now you belong to Jesus."

"But my mama was baptized too."

"So were my sisters. Unfortunately some people don't embrace it. They turn away and do their own thing. It's like they just go through the motions, like it's just a routine they want to be a part of to feel like they belong."

"How many sisters do you have?"

"Three."

"Do you have any brothers?"

"No. Two of my sisters live in Atlanta. You met the one who lives here."

"Do they believe in Jesus?"

"I'm not sure. We've all been baptized, but I don't know what's in their heart. The Bible says only God can see what's in people's hearts. We can only tell by what they do. My oldest sister hates me and anything that has to do with Jesus."

"Isn't hate wrong?"

"Yes, but Jesus can change hearts. I pray for her often."

"You are so nice, Miss T. I wish I could live with you."

"Me too," Tamika said.

"Me three," Phillip said. "Marvin told us how much fun he had with you."

"Thank you. I'm happy to spend time with you and bring you to church."

"We are too," Tamika said.

"You have my number. You can call me anytime."

Chapter 27

The Harvest

"Therefore the ungodly shall not stand in the judgment, nor sinners in the congregation of the righteous."
Psalm 1:5

Oblivion duped people into believing what was forthcoming was the norm. They persisted to wallow in depravity and immorality. Unbridled anger and violence raged like a wild boar, causing many to be afraid to leave their homes. Famines plagued the world, spawning the rise in missing persons as populations consumed strange meals. Pestilence overwhelmed hospitals rendering people helpless and dying. An ordinance issued worldwide created a taskforce to clean up human remains like a street sweeper cleaning up refuse. Natural disasters showed no favoritism to any part of the world.

The Staithes' lives nosedived into a new level of spiritual depravity and degeneration. None of them had regard for anyone except to feed their own sexual appetites. Brenna and Devon burned with passion for each other with endless copulations in their house of infidelity. Charlotte selected Doug as her favorite lover. Her seductions spiraled downward into lewdness which refuted the need for neighbors to view their electronic devices as pleasure portals. They instead, relished in their obscenities and encouraged them by recording what they had observed for future reference. Some even grabbed drinks as they sat on their porches to imbibe in the live perversion, cheering her and her lover on. CJ continued to indulge in his virtual relationships with women and in self-gratification. Chad began bringing women and men into his home as he indulged in lasciviousness and sodomy.

Sophia and Dave had finally lived to experience their dream trip despite hearsay about the reverend. People's accusations propelled them to foster empathy for their minister, thwarting their suspicions and creating a mystique about him that intrigued their minds.

They had lost inches with their diet and workout regimen, unfortunately, more financially than physically. Their finances were in such peril that foreclosure was awaiting their return like an uninvited guest.

Onia detected improvement in Rachel which prompted her anger and resentment for God to subside. She engaged in Bible study with Zoe and the kids, but her church attendance was sporadic. Bills from the extensive counseling for Rachel continued to worry her, compelling her to also withhold generosity when the collection plate was passed.

Ryan found his job to be more important than attending church causing it to be a bygone memory. He declined to attend Bible study with Zoe. He didn't know the Bible well enough to lead his family in Bible study, yet he was too old-fashioned to engage in any Bible study run by a woman. Besides, the newspaper became his Bible.

Now that Resa ended her career as a teacher Zoe had reached a crossroad in hers. She wasn't sure if she wanted to continue teaching in the classroom, especially middle school. She considered teaching little ones or going back to school for something totally different. Resa kept her motivated despite the contemptuousness and disrespect she faced almost daily. She prayed about her decision and decided to leave it in God's hands.

The sky looked threatening one morning as if something dreadful was about to transpire. Clouds billowed and hovered over what looked like a distant fireball coming over the horizon. Streaks of lightning permeated the darkness.

"Let us come. The time is at hand!"

An explosion ensued as the fireball in the sky came crashing down to earth. The bolts of lightning looked like arms with talon-like fingers striking everything in their path. Sirens blared like trumpets, alerting residents to the threatening skies and massive flames that engulfed the area. The noise appeared to be louder than usual, almost deafening. The tumult shocked everyone in the vicinity causing chaos and panic. Many took cover only to be consumed by the fires the lightning caused in their places of refuge.

The Fairweathers took cover in their storm shelter. An overwhelming fear came over Onia. She began sweating and felt like she was melting, yet her body was still intact. Ryan also felt hot and sweaty as if he had taken a long walk on a hot, humid day wearing a parka. They were trapped in a sauna.

"Mom, I'm scared!" Amber said. Before Onia could respond, a blinding light flickered. The kids disappeared. Onia's panic became more intense before she and Ryan also disappeared.

Brenna and Devon lay asleep after a night of sodomy. Their alarm clock screeched louder than Brenna's ears could handle, which startled her. The piercing noise coursed through her body like a shockwave. She sat up and looked around. Her heart raced, and intense fear overwhelmed her. She turned to Devon and tried to awaken him. He stirred before he turned towards her. She gasped when she saw him. Blood dripped from his eyes. He yawned and emitted a foul stench much like rotten eggs. His nostrils flared as he grunted and growled. He reached over to grab her. She shrieked.

Sophia and Dave had packed to embark on their long-expected cruise. Everyone from the church waved and wished them farewell as the ocean liner set sail. The smoke stacks billowed puffs of smoke like giant cigarettes as the ship's horn let off a horrific blast.

"I can't wait to gorge on the food," Sophia said. She smiled and studied the itinerary and planned activities. Nothing caught her eye but the mealtimes.

"I can't wait either. We virtually starved ourselves to death with our dieting and cutting back. Now it's time to binge and overindulge," Dave said. "Let me see the brochure."

"Why?" She resisted the urge to keep it to herself and handed it over.

He looked at it and smiled. "I was hoping they would have one," he said.

"Have what?"

"A weight room. I still want to work out."

"I know working out can be addictive, especially when the endorphins kick in. It's like a natural high, but we came here to have fun not do the usual."

"True."

"I'm so excited about this trip. It's going to be like dying and going to heaven."

A brawny man approached them. His head was clean shaven. "Excuse me, Mr. and Mrs. Altimoone, the reverend wants to see you."

"Tom?" Sophia said.

"Yes. Do I know you?"

"Rita told me about you," she said. She held out her hand.

He gave her hand a kiss. "Oh, yes, good old Rita. We had some good times to-" He cleared his throat. "Let me show you to Reverend Whitaker's suite."

The reverend had already gotten comfortable wearing shorts and a polo shirt. Ice cubes jingled as he brought a mixed drink to his lips.

"Hi, Reverend Whitaker," Sophia said. She looked at him as if he was a celebrity. "I didn't know you liked to drink."

He sneered at her. "There's a lot you don't know about me. Now come, sit down."

Both Dave and Sophia sat down, remembering the coldness they felt in his office.

"I want you to take the Water Walk tonight right after dinner," he said with a coldness in his tone.

They looked at each other and shrugged their shoulders. "Okay," Dave said. "What does that involve?"

"I'll let you know tonight." He sipped his drink and turned away from them.

"Mmm, this brunch is tasty," Sophia said, grinning from ear to ear.

"Isn't it though?" Dave met her grin with a smile and a wink. "Everything is so delicious. It melts in your mouth."

Sophia looked at the schedule. "Let's take in some of the fun activities before Bible study."

"Sure, why not?"

"Don't you get tired of winning?" Sophia asked.

"No."

"Well, I get tired of losing. You could let me win sometimes."

"They called me a pool shark in college. I have to live up to my reputation."

"I'm going back to the cabin," she said.

"C'mon, don't be a sore loser. I'll let you win the next game."

"Now you're trying to patronize me," she said and stomped away.

Dave followed her like a schoolboy trying to appease her.

That evening they anticipated their dinner with the reverend. They dressed in their brand new outfits. Dave wore a gray tweed, Perry Ellis, three-piece suit. Sophia wore a navy blue, lace, flare dress.

"Why did the reverend want us to dress up? I mean, I love him and all, but this is a vacation," Sophia said. "We should be relaxed."

"It'll be fine. This gave us a chance to spend our money on ourselves for a change. He gets most of it otherwise. Let's go and make an impression."

"What do you think this Water Walk is?"

"I don't know. We'll soon find out."

Reverend Whitaker waved and motioned them to his table. "Hi, you two, come on over. Have a seat." He pointed to two assigned chairs.

Sophia grabbed Dave's arm. She leaned into him. "We get to sit right next to him," she said like a fanatic as she bit her lip.

Dave's smile turned into a frown when he looked around the table. They were the only ones who stood out. He leaned over to Sophia, "Do you notice we're the only ones dressed up?"

Her mouth dropped open. She felt out of place. "I wonder why?" she asked.

"Yeah, I feel like I just showed up to my own funeral."

"You're probably wondering why you're the only ones dressed up. I wanted you to dress up for the Water Walk. It's such a special occasion. I always have my vic-, I mean volunteers dress up. Makes it extra special don't you think? You look beautiful, I might add."

Dave and Sophia looked at each other and smiled.

"Eat and drink as much as you like. There's plenty."

They gorged on a smorgasbord of cuisines until they were so stuffed they could barely sit down.

"Did everybody get enough?" the reverend asked. Everyone nodded. "Let me tell you how the Water Walk works. A platform gets placed on the side of the ship. You two will walk out on it. We'll say a prayer. Then you will walk off the edge."

"But we'll drown!" Sophia glimpsed at Dave before she looked down. She grabbed his arm. He gripped her hand and patted it with his other hand.

"I have all the confidence in the world that you won't. You have shown by your generosity that you have great faith to move mountains."

"It's not the mountains I'm worried about," Dave said under his breath.

"As I was saying." He cleared his throat. "You'll walk off the edge. Then we'll all get to see you walk on water. It'll be an amazing demonstration of faith. We'll video tape it so you can replay it anytime."

"He's really playing this up," Tom said to one of the deacons.

"Yeah, if they only knew what they were in for."

"What'll happen if we don't do it?" Dave asked.

"Well, then, we'll have to throw you overboard." He smiled as the couple looked at each other in disbelief. "I'm just kidding. It'll work out. Don't you trust me?"

"It'll work out for somebody," the one deacon leaned over and said to Tom.

Reverend Whitaker overheard him and glared at him. The man cowered and looked down at his food.

"Don't you trust me?" he asked again. He stared at the couple, eyes wide open, as if to hypnotize them.

Sophia and Dave eyed each other. "We trust you reverend. It's just that-"

"Then it's settled."

They all marched to the starboard. Deacons had already lowered a hinged door on the side about fifteen feet high. The reverend and deacons began praying to Mammon as Sophia and Dave lumbered through the opening that led to the ocean.

"What are they saying?" Sophia asked Dave. She looked at him with watery eyes as they continued moving forward.

"I have no idea. I never heard a prayer like this before." Dave grabbed her hand and held tight.

Sophia grabbed Dave's hand tightly. "I'm afraid of heights."

"I know, hon."

They closed their eyes as if they were praying when they reached the edge. They took their next step together. They fell off the edge and plummeted. As they reached the water the ship's horn tooted again like a blaring trumpet. They went under.

Zoe's craving was finally satiated. As Marvin and Rachel's godmother, she enjoyed the task of assuring their spiritual welfare. Her lasting relationship with her Bible Buddies gave her purpose as did her Bible studies with her nieces and nephews. Overall, she felt she had done a lot in the last year to bring others to Jesus. The Lord had answered her prayers.

Her dinner with Resa would be more than just catfish, fries, and coleslaw. It would be a celebration of the aforementioned realizations. She couldn't wait to bite into the meal, not only knowing how delicious Resa's treats were, but her outlook on the future would make the meal tastier than ever. She could relax and enjoy herself, knowing a heavy burden was lifted from her spirit.

The sky looked more ominous that evening than it had in the morning. A billowy cloud replaced the fireball as everything lay in ruins. It looked like it separated into fingers on the end like talons again, this time of a hawk ready to snatch its prey. As Zoe drove to the boonies where Resa and her husband lived she wondered what possessed them to live out here. However, the distance gave her the chance to listen to her favorite CD without interruption. She noticed the sky and destruction around her, but she knew she was in God's protective care.

She suddenly felt her car jolt forward. As quickly as she wondered who rear-ended her or what she ran over, her car spun and rolled into a ditch. The horn blared like a trumpet as her head hit the steering wheel.

Chapter 28

Indignation

"...and he that believeth not the Son shall not see life; but the wrath of God abideth on him."

John 3:36b

Everyone cheered as Sophia and Dave were extracted from the ocean like two rotten teeth.

"We did it! We walked on water," Sophia said. She beamed.

"Did we? Maybe we did, but I feel like I swam for miles. I worked up an appetite." Dave smiled as he escorted Sophia to the buffet.

Sophia looked around, confused. "Why is it so hot in here?"

"I don't know. I don't remember all these pipes either. The ambience sure could be better."

"Where's everybody else?" she asked when they grabbed their plates.

"I dunno. That's okay. There's more for us."

They piled on as much food as their plates could hold. They sank their teeth into the smorgasbord. At first the food tasted delicious before it turned rancid. Maggots infested their plates and crawled everywhere, invading their food and their bodies.

Sophia screamed as they swiped and swatted at them.

"We musta got a bad batch. Let's go get some more," Dave said.

"Okay." Sophia wiped her forehead. "It sure is hot in here. Maybe we should complain to the manager. This is unacceptable."

The manager glared at them with eyes that glowed like flames when they approached him. His cauliflower ears sat on his head like two catcher's mitts. His nostrils flared as he grunted at them.

"*You* tell him," Sophia said as she gripped Dave's arm. She stuttered. "I-I ch-change my mind."

"Fix another plate you fat, greedy mongrels," the creature said before Dave could open his mouth.

The two looked at each other, sweat dripping, and mouths open as the creature sneered at them. He revealed fangs and foamed at the mouth like a rabid dog.

"What *is* this?" Dave asked.

"I don't know, but he's very rude. We're never going on this cruise again."

The creature overheard them. He growled and laughed a low, guttural cackle as he said, "That's what you think."

They walked away and fixed another plate. As they sat down to eat, the food became rancid again. They gobbled up what they could stand before maggots beat them to it. They belched and worms crawled from their mouths.

They realized after a myriad of attempts that they were victims of futility. They were two caged rats stuck on a cruise ship eating garbage with worms and maggots in sweltering heat.

What the Fairweathers thought was a storm had waned, yet it left behind a hot, dark, and stuffy storm shelter. Onia left it for some fresh air. What she walked into was blazing heat like a furnace. She had walked past Ryan without noticing him. She couldn't understand why she was so hot. She had to cool off, so she went inside the house. She searched for a fan or an air conditioner, anything to cool off, to no avail. She couldn't afford to spike the electric bill anyway with only one income she thought to herself.

Where were the kids? Where was Ryan? She had so many questions, but her main one hadn't been answered. Why couldn't she free herself from the scorching heat?

She hadn't paid attention to her surroundings while she pondered what to do. Her mouth dropped open when she looked around and realized the house was completely empty. There was no furniture. Did somebody break in? "Ryan? Kids? Where are you?" she asked.

There was no answer.

Nothing could cool her off. The house was a sauna. The only place to escape the heat was outside which was more scathing than inside. She was a piece of toast in an oven.

Ryan remained in the shelter reading the newspaper. He was detached from everything around him. He hadn't noticed that Onia and the kids were gone. However, he had noticed the blistering heat. It caused his shirt to stick to the back of his chair. He peeled himself from it to open the doors. Every time he tried, a hand festered with boils would reach out and pull him back. It slammed him back down onto the chair. The hand produced a contagion that left boils all over his body. He found reading the paper more difficult as he writhed in pain. Every page read the same story anyway.

A few things had gotten his attention. He heard scratching noises and realized what the source was. Cockroaches were crawling on him, rubbing their antennae together.

He was under house arrest in a hot suffocating dungeon.

The smoke detector beeped louder than ever; however, it couldn't break CJ away from his computer trance. He sat oblivious to the smoke permeating the hallway as he stared at the images on his computer like a zombie. Flames engulfed his room causing him to sweat.

Women protruded from the screen and lunged at him. He smiled until one of them grabbed his genitalia and began to squeeze and bite. As he screamed another woman rammed her forked tongue into his mouth causing him to gag. A third woman licked him before she started slowly pecking away at his hair and flesh with her beak-like mouth. He was not completely consumed, causing the nightmare to perpetuate.

The ringing in Brandon's ears was so loud that it startled him. He woke up with a throbbing headache. Grogginess and delirium swept over him like a strong wind. He couldn't remember the weather being this hot. His clothes were soaked, and they stuck to his skin.

The previous night was a blur. He rubbed his eyes as he noticed a woman in bed beside him. How could he be so careless? He didn't usually stick around after he had his way with them. Fear came over him as he thought about getting caught. He couldn't go to prison again. He thought he had been more careful since his earlier conquests. After all, that's why he used drugs. They were his accomplice.

He slithered from the bed trying to escape. His brain was foggy as he wondered what had happened. Trying to balance himself, he knocked over a lamp. With blurred vision he teetered as he tried to pick it up without being noticed. He was too late. The woman woke up.

"Where are you going?" she asked in a commanding voice. "Get back here. We have some unfinished business." She reached out and snatched him back onto the bed. He lay there stunned, trying to make sense of everything. What was happening? He usually was the one in control.

The woman looked like Dorothy. She ran her hands down his body. She started panting and grunting. He looked up at her, eyes pleading. His eyes widened when he looked into her jaundiced eyes which glowed like a cat in the night. He turned away when the stench from her breath staggered him. Her breath smelled of rotten eggs and deteriorated into an odor of decaying flesh. Her nostrils flared.

She grabbed his chin with one of her talons and turned his head toward her. "Look at me," she said in a low drone. "You're mine, all mine."

She tore his clothes and scratched his skin. She grinned as if she was toying with him.

"No! Please stop!" he screamed. He felt like he was melting in the heat.

Her smile grew wider, showing bloody fangs. "Yes," she said. "I'm gonna eat you up!"

She sank her teeth into his flesh in the steamy room. The creature worked its way below his belt. She opened her mouth wider, and in one chomp she castrated him. He howled in agony. When she finished emasculating him, she stood over him and watched him writhe in pain. "There's more where that came from. I shall return," she said. She laughed a low menacing chortle before she left the room.

Chad arrived home drenching in sweat, alcohol on his breath. He was baffled by the overwhelming heat. He had just gotten off work, and the temperature felt hotter than he had ever remembered.

He staggered to the door. When he rang the doorbell, it blared like a horn. He burned his hand as he touched the doorknob.

Craig greeted him. His jaw dropped, and he burst into tears. As he entered, he felt no relief from the heat.

Chad hugged his son so tight his arms lost feeling. "I'm sorry for all the harm I caused you, but I was going through a lot with your mother." He wiped beads of sweat from his forehead. "How come you don't have the air on?"

Craig didn't say anything. He grabbed his father and clung on. Chad tried to pull away as Craig's grip tightened. Between his son's grip and the blistering heat, Chad felt like he was suffocating. He was electrocuted by sharp pains that pierced his back. They shot through his body as Craig's hands mutated into sharp claws. "You can let go now, Son," Chad said wincing.

Craig became unrecognizable. His eyes bulged, his ears grew larger and came to a point, and his nose grew long with flaring nostrils. The creature's claws kept their grip and blood dripped from Chad's back. Every time he tried to pull away the pain became more intense as pieces of flesh ripped away from his body.

The creature overpowered Chad. It opened its mouth. A foul odor like the smell of rotting corpses engulfed him causing him to retch. The creature sank its fangs into his neck. The pain became excruciating as the creature began to chew his flesh. He screamed in agony, but no one could hear him. When he broke away from the creature's grasp more chunks of flesh ripped from his body.

He had to get away. He rushed from the house into the blazing furnace. He ran next door, but there were no other houses, only facades. He reached the only house that looked real. He was breathless and drenched with sweat, blood dripping. He rang the doorbell. His son Craig opened the door. Chad burst into tears and greeted him with a hug.

Brenna heard footsteps as she lay in the sizzling heat. Her hair was disheveled, and her head pounded as if someone had taken a hammer to it. She couldn't get caught again. Chad would do worse than put her in the hospital. She had to hide Devon who lay next to her.

"Devon, get up! Chad's coming! I can't get caught again." She shook him. He moaned.

"Get up!" Brenna said, looking frightened. The footsteps had gotten louder, and they sounded like they were getting closer.

She shook him again. This time he turned to her. He looked at her and growled. His eyes dripped blood. His nostrils flared on a long snout, fangs protruding from his mouth. He slobbered and grunted as he grabbed her and seduced her. He began tearing her flesh.

"Chad!" she screamed. No one could hear her. She clawed back at the creature, but she was no match for him. Though he overpowered her, she managed to tear out his entrails. They screamed and grunted as they fought.

Brenna heard the footsteps again, only louder. She turned to Devon. He grunted and turned to her. Pus mixed with blood oozed from his eyes. Smoke came from his nostrils. His teeth sank into her chest. Her hair turned into snakes, biting, hissing and spitting. Through all the chaos all she could hear were footsteps getting louder as she screamed in excruciating pain hoping Chad wouldn't find her.

Charlotte couldn't believe the rude awakening she had encountered that day. She had been interrupted by a loud blast during her usual engagements. The noise, which sounded like an explosion, disrupted her intercourse with her lover.

She couldn't fathom what possessed her to decide to go to the pool when they were fine where they were, in her bedroom. "Doug," she said between kisses, "Let's go skinny dipping."

While they frolicked around in the water she noticed there were no lights on in the guest house. She convinced him to carry on with their lovemaking in their old haunt for old time's sake. She wondered why the door was already cracked open as if someone was expecting them. She shrugged her shoulders and walked in. She pinched her nose due to the stench. She screamed as she noticed a badly decomposed body hanging from the chandelier. Doug wrapped his arms around her while she trembled and buried her head into his chest.

Pain tore into her back like cat claws. She peered up at Doug who had morphed into a hideous creature. As she screamed, he stuck his forked tongue down her throat causing her to gag. The creature began groping and caressing her so hard that her flesh began tearing apart. She heaved before she broke away from him, leaving parts of her flesh and dripping blood behind.

Charlotte ran to the pool which had become a boiling cauldron. She couldn't see the house beyond the steam. She had to choose between jumping back into the pool or enduring the foul stench with her lover, turned creature, in the guest house. She chose the former.

The water burned remnants of her skin. Doug plunged in to join her. As they scampered she looked up and noticed there were no lights on in the guest house. She suggested they go in anyway. The door was open. As soon as she walked in she was overwhelmed by a foul odor. She screamed when she saw her brother's rotting corpse hanging from the chandelier. She ran into Doug's embrace. As she buried her head into his chest she trembled. He licked and kissed her. Then he opened his mouth and revealed blood-stained fangs. As he sank them into her neck, blood squirted from her jugular vein.

He gouged every part of her body as he groped and caressed her. He tore her stomach open with his talons. He gorged on the fetus inside her. He slammed his forked tongue down her throat to muffle her voice as she screamed in excruciating agony and horror.

She broke free, leaving remnants of her former self behind. She had to decide whether to jump into the cauldron or stay in the guest house with the creature.

A loud buzzer sounded, indicating the beginning of the next scene. Kyle was startled as he lay in his hotel room under bright lights that burned hotter than usual.

"Action!" the director called before he slapped the clapperboard.

A harem of girls caressed and kissed Kyle's nude body.

Each touch singed his flesh like hot flames. "It's too hot in here. Can we get some air?" he said. Every time he touched them he retracted his hands. Their flesh burned his fingers as if he had touched a hot stove.

"Cut!" the director told the assistant. The buzzer went off again to end the scene.

The buzzer rang to start the scene. "Action!" the director yelled.

The girls encircled Kyle and slapped him around. He tried to get up, but some of them pinned his arms down and tied him up. One girl grabbed his hair and ripped it out with her claw-like nails. Blood dripped from his scalp. She licked it before she began gnawing at his face and head like a rat. She gouged at his eyes. He screamed in agony.

"Shut up!" one of the girls said and started slapping him around again. She mounted him and slammed her forked tongue down his throat. The smell of rotten flesh from her breath and her sharp tongue caused him to regurgitate.

One of the girls put a pillow over his face to suffocate him. Just when he thought he would take his last breath, she would pull it away leaving him gasping for air. "This is for all the girls you tortured, you good-for-nothing loser!" She scraped her talons across his face drawing blood.

The bright lights caused the curtains to catch fire. He screamed, "Let me up!" He coughed and gagged as smoke infiltrated the room. The creatures smacked him around the more he cried in agony.

Another creature grabbed his genitals and clawed at them. She then sank her fangs into them and gnawed at them slowly, so he could feel every bite. He screamed in agony. They slapped him around and gagged him to shut him up.

Two girls caressed and licked his body before they tore his flesh open. They drooled over him causing his flesh to sting as if scorpions were attacking him. They all engaged in a bloody meal as they feasted on his flesh leaving what was left to rot. Myiasis, or an infestation of maggots, ate away at his remains, leaving a charred skeleton behind.

"Cut!" the director yelled as he slapped the clapperboard. The scene replicated with more intensity with each take leaving Kyle trapped in a porn horror movie.

Reverend Whitaker wondered if the ship had caught fire. Flames consumed him. As it burned, what seemed like wood ashes fell from the ceiling. He looked more closely and realized what he saw looked too big.

Bills were falling from the smoke-filled cabin like rain. He smiled, realizing he was finally going to have as much mammon as he wanted. He bowed down as the bills continued to fall, paying homage to his god. He rose to his feet and began reaching for them, smiling as he hungered for more. As he tried to grab them, they singed his fingers. The cauterization became more intense as he grabbed the bills until his hands began to blister. He continued to attempt to grip the money. The money scorched his hands until his hands burned down to the bone.

Flames consumed the cabin leaving a stench of burning flesh like burnt meat on a grill. As he continued to grab the money his bones became so charred until they turned brittle.

The reverend was mesmerized by the money which rendered him oblivious to the repercussions of his greed. His cries of agony didn't hinder him from continuing to try to grip the money as if some metaphysical force kept luring him in.

The money took on different forms. Sometimes it burned like paper, and other times it liquefied and oozed between his fingers like molten lava, but not before he saw the faces of his victims on it. He kept yearning and reaching to no avail as flames continued to char and scorch his flesh down to the bone.

Chapter 29

The Family Reunion

"And sent his servant at supper time to say to them that were bidden, Come; for all things are now ready."

Luke 14:17

Zoe woke up after her head hit the steering wheel. Her car wouldn't start, so she had to walk the rest of the way. She felt light on her feet like she was floating on air. Everything around her became vast with only one path leading to a beautiful pearly-gated palace. The landscape was ornate and decorated with trees filled with fruit like an orchard. The hedges were pristinely trimmed. The golden walkway was emblazoned with rocks that resembled precious stones. She squinted from the brightness as she approached the entrance.

She beamed as she eyed her surroundings. Resa had told her she didn't need to work, but she didn't tell her she was married to a millionaire. From the ambience, Zoe couldn't tell if she was dreaming. She tried to absorb everything she saw.

Her mouth dropped open when she reached the door. She tried to make sense of the enigma that stood before her, a strange man wearing a long white robe. He greeted her before her hand reached the doorbell. He glowed as he looked in a book.

"Welcome. J.C. is expecting you," the man said in a melodic voice.

Zoe's eyes opened wide. "J.C.? Who is -? How did you -?"

"Right this way." The stranger motioned for her to follow.

A lady approached her and squeezed her so tight she almost couldn't breathe.

"Resa, is that you?"

"Hi, Zoe. I'm glad you made it."

"I didn't know you and your husband were wealthy," Zoe said, wide-eyed, as she gawked at her surroundings. "This place is beautiful."

Resa chuckled. "Come join us."

Zoe noticed Resa no longer walked with a limp, and she was bright like the robed man at the entrance. They strolled to a dining hall that had no walls. The tables appeared to stretch for miles. The butler-like figure guided her to an assigned seat next to Resa.

"Come, the banquet is now ready," they heard a gentle voice boom.

The table displayed enough food for a world of people to feast on. Food Zoe had never eaten melted in her mouth like rich chocolate. She never knew olives, falafel, and a plethora of fresh fruit that burst with flavor could be so delicious. The variety of cheeses and nuts satisfied her palate.

Live music that reminded her of her CDs played in the background. She thought Resa really knew how to throw a party.

Everyone enjoyed each other's company as if they had always known each other. Zoe looked up from her feast to pass a tray. Her jaw dropped when she noticed who grabbed it. "Victor, is that you?"

"Yes, it's me, Miss Todvue." He tilted his head. "Miss Todvue, your eyes, they don't look crooked anymore."

"Oh really?" She beamed from ear to ear and her heart burned within. She wanted to give him a big hug. As she watched, the platter traveled from person to person, each with his own radiance, some brighter than others.

Zoe looked around. She hoped to see her sisters, especially Onia. Since she saw no sign of them she realized that they had hardened their hearts towards her pleas and prayers. However, she couldn't help but smile from the inside out as she continued to watch the tray get passed around. She noticed Nathan, Amber, Aaron, and...*Rachel*! She saw Tamika, Phillip, and Marvin, each with different auras. She noticed one aura shine so brightly it nearly blinded her. "Little John-John!" she said and waved. He gleamed back at her with that same twinkle in his eye she had remembered.

Her heart flipped and her mouth dropped open when she saw her mom and dad. Tears of joy filled her eyes. What amazed her more was whom they sat next to -"*Craig*?"

He smiled and gave her a wink. He mouthed the words, "Thank you, Aunt Zoe."

Zoe squinted to make sure she recognized a handsome man she had met once – "Officer Warren! It's great to see you!"

"Likewise," he said.

She turned to Resa. "Your butler mentioned J.C." Zoe said. "Those are the initials I used in my invitation to my sisters."

Resa chuckled. "He's not a butler. Who did the initials stand for?"

"Jesus Christ. I was trying to invite them to a Bible retreat in an attempt to get them to know Jesus, but it backfired."

She thought for a moment. "That's who the guy at the entrance was referring to."

"I was wondering."

After the food and fellowship the strange butler made an announcement, but not before he revealed who he was. Wings snapped open on his back like curtains in a play. A bright ringed corona appeared above his head. "Come! Let us make a joyful noise unto the Lord," he said.

Everyone arose and followed.

He led them to an enormous luminescent throne. A sea of glass was in front of it like a royal carpet. The One who sat on it looked like a consuming fire of jasper and rubies. A translucent rainbow encircled the throne.

A figure with holes in his hands, feet, and side sat next to the One who sat on the throne. His eyes were like bronze. His hair was pure white.

Everyone beamed and shone brighter than their original aura as they genuflected and laid their crowns at his feet. Then they fell on their faces. As they stood up they sang praises, and their hearts burned with adoration.

Everyone sang praises with a loud voice to the Father, Son, and Holy Spirit. Zoe stood next to the man whom she remembered could only hum. He sang out with a beautiful voice, pronouncing every word clearly. She also sang with large crowds and sang in small groups. She sang solos. She joined gospel, classical, and contemporary choirs all to glorify the One who sat on the throne and to the Lamb.

Zoe was invited to sing in a special choir for select numbers. Everyone in it sang hallelujahs to the King of Kings and Lord of Lords with the angels.

After everyone finished paying homage to the One who made everything possible and who made all things new, they spoke to one another. Everyone's aura flickered like flames as they mingled with each other. Zoe hardly recognized the wheelchair-bound lady from her church who always loved her singing because she had to look up to her. "Hi, Mrs. Baldwin!" Zoe said.

"Hello, young lady! It's great to see you!"

"You too!"

She noticed Pastor Thomas and gave him a big hug. "It's great to see you, Pastor Thomas!"

"Likewise! You sang more beautifully than ever," he said.

"Thank you." She noticed his aura was bright like hers and Resa's.

The angel rolled back a scroll to acknowledge what each person had done for the Kingdom. "Your dwelling place matches the brightness of your aura," he said. "Well done, good and faithful servants!"

"Hi, Resa, where will you be?" Zoe asked.

"I'll be in Philadelphia. My former husband is in Laodicea. I noticed there weren't very many auras dwelling there."

"I'm in Philadelphia too. We're neighbors!"

Zoe caught up with everyone she knew. Her parents were in Smyrna along with Little John-John. Tamika and Phillip were in Sardis with Nathan and the twins. Marvin was in Thyatira along with Rachel. Craig lived in Laodicea.

After the grand family reunion, everyone hugged and kissed each other before retiring to their assigned cities. Each city had dwellings unique to each person. Some dwellings were glorified shacks reserved for those whose lives were cut short before they could fully develop such as Craig's.

Everyone anticipated the wake of continued fellowship at the appointed times.

Zoe went to her mansion which was fully equipped and furnished. The words the angel had announced hung over her gated entrance – "Well done, thou good and faithful servant." Below that it read: "Thou hast been faithful over a few things, I will make thee ruler over many things: enter thou into the joy of thy lord."

THE END

CPSIA information can be obtained
at www.ICGtesting.com
Printed in the USA
LVHW040107230323
742312LV00014B/439/J

9 781489 743749